PLUM

A STEEL BONES MOTORCYCLE CLUB ROMANCE

CATE C. WELLS

Cover art and design by Clarise Tan of CT Cover Creations.
Editing by Nevada Martinez.
Proofreading by Raw Book Editing www.rawbookediting.com
Special thanks to Jean McConnell of The Word Forager, and always, Louisa.

❀ Created with Vellum

PROLOGUE
ADAM

I was ten before I learned to take a punch. Long before then, I was well-versed in how to throw one. Chin down, hands up, knees bent. Aim beyond the guy's face and punch through.

Where I grew up on Gilson Avenue—before we moved to the mansion on the bluffs—you learned early. Gilson was the worst street in the Cannery. Cannery was the worst neighborhood in Pyle, and unless you lived on the bluffs or downtown, Pyle used to be a rusted, gutted shithole. Now it's all hipsters and tech companies. I had a lot to do with that. Back when I was coming up, though, Pyle was still decimated by the collapse of domestic steel.

On Gilson, if you wanted to walk to school or get yourself some chips from the corner store with no hassle, you did what the older boys did. The ones no one fucked with. You hit first. You hit harder. And you didn't stop.

Despite the constant hunger gnawing at my belly, I was always a foot taller and thirty pounds heavier than the other kids my age, and I wasn't stupid. I put a kid on the pavement every now and again, and mostly, I had no trouble.

Not until the mansion on the bluffs.

My mother came from money, but her folks cut her off when she turned up pregnant at seventeen by a biker with a drug habit. The biker didn't hang around long after I was born, but the excommunication stuck until Mom found a way to make herself respectable again.

When I was ten, Mom managed to get herself knocked up by her boss, Thomas Gracy Wade. Thomas Wade owned a brokerage, a vintage gold cigar cutter he kept in his breast pocket, and half the men in Pyle.

He was a friendly guy.

Call me Thomas.

You've got a nice, fine grip there, son.

Hard to believe you're the same age as my Eric. You've got a good seven, eight inches on him. Smart, too, aren't you?

Mom got knocked up at a fortuitous time. The first Mrs. Thomas Gracy Wade had decided she'd had enough, and she did the rich-lady version of going to the corner store for cigarettes and never coming back. Thomas Wade needed a woman to take care of his son Eric, and my mother deftly presented herself as a solution, not a problem.

So, one late summer day, when Thomas Wade was at work, I packed our old Ford while Mom rested on the concrete stoop, hands on her huge belly with her legs crossed at her swollen ankles. Then, we drove up to the bluffs and moved ourselves into his life.

It was a different world. On Gilson Avenue, we had a one bedroom on the top floor of a four-story walk-up. My bed was a cot shoved under the eaves in the living room. There was a gap between the roof and the wall, so all kinds of shit flew in. Rain. Bees. Noise from the druggies and the working girls on the street below. I could never sleep. Still can't, to this day.

We kept my clean clothes in a laundry basket and my dirty clothes in a plastic bag, and I tripped on those damn things every morning when I got out of bed.

We did have a second bedroom, and Mom always worked, but every extra penny went to her hair stylist, her gym membership, and the secondhand store. The other bedroom was for her used Gucci and Dior and Louboutin's. We didn't have food or cable or heat except on the bitterest days, but Mom had couture. She had a plan, and it wasn't cheap. I can't fault her. It worked.

At the mansion on the bluffs—the *house*, they called it— my bedroom was twice the size of our entire apartment. My shit looked like it'd been shrunk by that laser beam in *Charlie and the Chocolate Factory*.

When we pulled up at our new home, there was a smiling man in khaki pants to direct the unpacking of the car, and when the staff—as I was told to call them—were finished, he drove the car off, and I never saw it again. Mom waddled into the house, hugely pregnant since the pre-nup negotiations had stretched on forever, and my stepfather knows how to use time as a pressure tactic. She wandered from room to room, muttering under her breath whenever she found evidence of the former Mrs. Thomas Gracy Wade. The man in khaki pants hovered at her elbow, taking notes.

I followed her for a while until I caught sight of a boy my age out back, throwing horseshoes. He was maybe two pounds shy of fat, and even though the weather was mild, he'd already sweated through a good haircut and what looked to me like a grown man's white collared shirt.

He looked overdressed and pissed off. I felt an instant sense of camaraderie.

I took off, joined the kid, and it went like it usually does between two boys, bored and unsupervised.

"You're Adam?"

"Yeah. You Eric?"

"Yeah. Don't touch my stuff."

"I don't want to touch your fucking stuff, asshole."

Silence. Scuffing shoes in the grass.

"Want to play?"

"I never played horseshoes."

"It's easy. I'll show you."

He didn't really, but I caught on anyway. It wasn't hard. You throw a horseshoe at a stake. Eric had some kind of scorekeeping system that I couldn't quite follow. It didn't seem consistent, but the sun was shining, I was outside, and I didn't have to watch my back. When Eric managed to keep his mouth shut, he wasn't the worst company.

Besides, when I was walking through the house with Mom, I'd seen the kitchen. There was a woman in a white jacket fussing around, and the smells. Jesus, the smells. In those days, I was always hungry for meat, my gut twisted for it, and unless I was dreaming, there was going to be a roast for dinner that night. A fucking *roast*.

We played a long time, Eric blabbing on and on while I fantasized about beef and potatoes, throwing horseshoe after horseshoe. And then Thomas Wade came home.

He strode across the perfectly manicured back lawn, my mom waddling at his heels, and for the first time that whole day, Eric shut up. Thomas Wade had a man's bearing, one I imitated from that day on until I carried myself the same way, my movements as economical and effortless, my face as inscrutable and vaguely agreeable.

There was nothing weak about Thomas Gracy Wade, nothing that reeked of desperation and want.

I wanted to *be* that man, and until I could, I wanted his

respect. And even though I was only ten, I'd grown up on Gilson. I knew that strength respected strength.

Thomas Wade stood, arms crossed, watching us play horseshoes, and I started to pay attention to the score.

"Ringer!" Eric crowed, skipping forward to grab his horseshoe.

It clearly wasn't. My gaze skipped to Thomas Wade. His eyes narrowed. He knew it wasn't too, but he stood silently, his lips thinned.

I dashed forward, placing myself between Eric and the stake. "It's not a ringer."

"Are you blind?" Eric's affableness was gone, his body coiled tight.

"The heel calks don't clear the stake."

"You didn't even know what a heel calk was two hours ago."

"I do now. Get a straightedge. We'll settle it."

"Are you calling me a liar?"

In essence, yes, I was. I didn't deny it. I stood between Eric and the stake, saying nothing, waiting for the obvious fury turning his face red to boil over. I wanted him to throw a punch. I was shit at horseshoes, but fighting? I never lost. And I wanted to show the man in the shiny shoes and sparkling watch, the man who hadn't once turned to look at my mother while she trotted huge and panting behind him, that I wasn't a loser.

"If the horseshoe fits." I relaxed my stance, ready.

Eric drew back and swung, but I deflected the blow—a sad, flailing mess—and drove a fist into his face. Blood spurted from his nose. He screamed in pain and fury, and I fully expected him to fall on his ass and cry, but he lunged for me, swinging wildly, missing easy shots. It was immediately clear to me that he'd never fought anyone before and that he was out of his mind.

"Adam! Stop this now!" Mom begged.

"Let them work it out, Laurel." Thomas Wade took a purposeful step back.

I had permission. It was like shooting fish in a barrel. I hung back, waiting for Eric to open his weak spots with his undisciplined swings, and then I nailed his ribs, his gut, his kidneys. He began to weave on his feet, tears streaming down his face, diluting the blood, and I glanced over at the man grimly observing us.

I still can't quite describe the look on his face. Disgust. Calculation. Indecision.

My mother worried at the hem of her maternity blouse, her gaze darting from Thomas Wade to Eric to me.

I saw an opening, and I was about to knock the kid out, when Mom shouted, "That's enough."

She flung herself forward, and I instantly froze, but Eric was too far gone. Thomas Wade had to jump in and shoulder his kid back so he didn't accidentally punch my mother. Eric was crying and babbling, his father trying to talk him down, scorn clear in his voice, and Mom got real close to my face.

"What the fuck are you doing?" she hissed.

"All right, Mom. I'm done." I was huffing and puffing, the blood pounding in my ears.

"The fuck you are. You beat his kid up, you think he's going to let us stay here? You get back in there, and you take a dive."

I was confused. My mom wasn't talking like herself. She always put on airs, never swore, always pretended she didn't know the words for the things we lived through and walked past every day.

"Go after him, and then *go down*."

She stepped out of my way, letting out a fake little cry, and she jerked her chin toward Eric. Thomas Wade had backed off, but in one glance, I could tell Eric was still out of his mind.

I didn't think. I wanted that big room. The roast. The peace and fresh air and quiet on the bluffs overlooking the river, Gilson Avenue so far away it might as well be a different world. What was a man's respect to that?

I launched myself at Eric. He swung, and I slammed my face into fist, the connection rattling my jaw, and I fell to the ground, groaning.

Eric blinked in surprise.

On my back, in the lush, even grass, I stared up at the blue sky and drew in a deep breath of fresh, clean air.

"That's enough now," Thomas Wade declared. The look on his face was clear now. Pride. Relief.

And then, to my very great surprise, Eric leaned over and offered me a hand. I took it.

"It was a ringer," he said.

"Bullshit," I replied. "Let's get a straightedge."

So, we limped together back toward the house, Eric babbling a mile a minute about the game room in the basement, ping-pong and foosball and how goose season was soon, and did I have my hunting license?

I didn't know shit about half of the things he said, but I wanted them—I wanted the kind of life where that's the kind of shit you worry about—and I knew then that I was my mother's son. I would do what I had to do to get that life. Pride is cheap. Once you've paid it, you realize it's a small price.

What does pride really matter when you're in a warm house on the bluffs, high above it all, nothing lurking around the corner? When you can put your fists down? When you have meat for dinner, and then you're never, ever hungry again?

It's a fair trade.

Anyone would make it.

1

ADAM

Eric is still an asshole, but he's my asshole.

Twenty years later, we've settled into our roles. He does what he wants. I use the chaos he creates as cover to disrupt an industry. Our dynamic has put us on the cover of tech magazines and made us Wall Street legends. We're the wunderkinds who took Thomas Wade's old-economy stock brokerage—headquartered in Godforsaken Pyle, Pennsylvania—and transformed the company into a tech juggernaut that revitalized the city.

I guess I could pay someone to babysit Eric. I could be back in my condo in the city with my tie off, watching Bloomberg with a glass of Glenfiddich.

Instead, I'm responding to emails on my phone in the corner of a dank, dimly lit champagne room in some backwater titty bar, ignoring one email in particular, trying to block out Eric as he talks dirty to a stripper. I'm on my fifth watered-down Jim Beam, my temples are throbbing, and my patience is frayed from four days straight of marathon negotiations in NYC.

With Eric, this sort of shit is a constant.

On the drive home, he got thirsty. Of course, he found the one place within a twenty-mile radius where he's most likely to get himself into trouble. This time it's a strip club on the outskirts of some shit town, an establishment called The White Van, notable only for being run by the Steel Bones Motorcycle Club. My cousin Des has dealings with the club. They're not the kind of people you fuck with.

Eric's life mission is to fuck with things he shouldn't.

"You like that, don't you, you little slut?" he asks the dancer who's sucking his dick.

The dancer mumbles. Very noncommittal.

Tonight, Eric bumbled into the ripest little spinner, purple streaks in her blonde hair, dusting of freckles across her nose. The kind of heart-shaped ass you want to take a bite out of. After an offhanded "You'll do," Eric had his face buried in her tits so fast, I doubt he'd be able to pick her out of a line up.

I can see why he's unimpressed—the girl's nowhere near hot enough for the clubs in Pyle—but there's something about her. In a room full of naked women, the first thing I noticed was her, the mean glare paired with the fake smile, the freckles that show through the caked-on makeup.

She's quite the shark, too. She's upsold Eric from a lap dance, to a jerk, and now a blow job. She's adding up the charges, no partial refund for the unfinished dance or handy. This, by the way, is how Eric managed to overpay by ten-mil when we acquired Fortnum Kenney. He bought a subsidiary, and then he didn't deduct the purchase price when he made our bid for the parent company. I still give him shit about how we paid twice for Fortnum Financial.

"Come on, baby. Take it all." Eric groans, thrusting his hips while he sits in a chair. As always, he's managed to sweat out his product, so his blond hair sticks up at all angles. "What, you don't like work?"

Work. Yeah. I force my attention back to my phone. I hesitate for a second over the email I've been avoiding, tap delete, and then open our app. The market's about to close in Hong Kong. We're testing a new product that should increase average R.O.I. by half a percent. I'm testing it with my play portfolio, along with the guys in research and development.

Eric thinks half a percent isn't worth the investment we're making, but he's never really understood scale on an intuitive level. Ten-year-old me scurried past men who'd kill for half of a percent of one million every day. You understand value when you know what people will do for it.

Which makes my misjudgment in regards to Renee even more inexplicable. I really thought she would be the perfect wife.

A bitter taste floods my mouth. I wash it out by downing my sixth bourbon.

Renee was value. Old money. Undergrad at Yale. MBA from Harvard Business. Passionate about climate change and dressage. We were golden. And then I forgot one anniversary, and she got Eric drunk and high and fucked him while I was closing a deal in Copenhagen.

When I broke off the engagement, she had the nerve to say I never loved her. Bullshit. I knew what she was worth.

Still, I knew I'd made the right call when I couldn't bring myself to give much of a shit. I've never really been the emotional type. I want what I want, but it's never been about feelings. I moved on. Eric bought me a 1951 Black Shadow, and we called it even.

Life is all good again, except the damn emails that keep popping up from a man I haven't seen in twenty-five years.

I resist the urge to check for another one, scrolling through my portfolio instead, but the numbers blur together. It's hard to focus with Eric thrusting his pelvis like he's trying to knock his dick off. Besides, the Jim Beam is really kicking in now, and my vision's going a little fuzzy. The chair's creaking, and he won't shut up.

"Swallow on me. Let me feel it."

There's a half-choking, half-gurgling sound, and my gaze flies up. I don't necessarily want to see this, but Eric left to his own devices tends to not pay attention to others. It's not that he's a bad man, but when you've been brought up to believe you're the center of everything, you don't think much about what's going on around you.

The situation across the room seems cool, though. From the grip the girl has on the base of Eric's dick, I'm fairly sure she's not suffocating to death.

She gasps and chokes again. This time I can hear it; she's playing it up. Good for her. The quicker this is over, the quicker I can head back to Pyle. Get a shower. Some sleep.

I mean to go back to my phone, and I'm going to, but I stare a moment too long, and I see it. The girl is on her knees, head bobbing, her feet tucked neatly under her ass, and her free hand is sneaking, very slowly, behind her. What's she going for?

She raises up a few inches, grabs the buckle on her sparkly white stiletto heels, and she tugs the strap loose. Then—all the time smacking and slurping—she eases the shoe off and starts rubbing the red crease marking the bridge of her small, white foot.

She moans really loud, pure pleasure, and Eric says, "That's right, bitch."

I have to cough to cover the laugh.

Eric starts panting hard, and I turn my head. We

boarded at Mountchassen together, we pledged Kappa Iota Chi together, and we lived together for a few years after grad school. I'd like to say this is the first time I've been stuck playing on my phone while Eric gets his rocks off, but it's not.

"Let me come in your mouth."

The girl grunts a muffled negative.

"Come on. I want you to swallow my cum like the dirty little whore you are."

There's a wet slurp, and then a clear, entirely unaffected voice. "Extra twenty."

"Whatever. Get back on it." The noises start again, and then Eric grunts like he's been punched in the gut.

I quickly click to make a trade and close my portfolio app. Eric's not one to linger after he finishes. In fact, he's already tucking himself into his pants.

"Card or cash, sweetie?" The stripper has him beat. She's already on her feet. When did she buckle that shoe back on?

Oh, she hasn't. She's just slipped her foot in.

Eric shakes his head. "I paid already."

"You asked me to swallow. That's twenty extra."

"I didn't say yes to that." Eric grabs his jacket.

Asshole. He always does this. Stiffs waitresses. Returns clothes he's worn. Petty shit. It's like he gets off on getting one over on people who don't have the means to complain.

I reach for my wallet, but before I can get the cash, Eric ducks out of the room. The girl's eyes meet mine. Time freezes. She's standing in the glow from a red sconce on the wall, fists balled, teeth bared. Her tits are heaving. The sight should make me hard—it does—but the feeling tightening my chest isn't lust. Not quite. It's more like when I'm at the game, and a receiver breaks free, making a wild dash for the end zone. That impulse that has you screaming *run, run, run*.

She widens her eyes. She's not pissed. Not beat down. Not beseeching.

She's righteously *furious*.

She reminds me of nothing else but a hawk who's caught sight of prey. Locked and loaded and about to tear some shit apart. She's fucking *magnificent*.

And then she's gone, racing after him, one shoe flopping loose, screeching loud enough to bring the bouncers, who are—fuck my life—patched-in brothers of the Steel Bones Motorcycle Club.

The notoriously no-longer-outlaw, but still widely feared and respected, Steel Bones MC.

I rush after, but there's no stopping what happens next.

The girl grabs for Eric's arm. He jerks, way harder than he'd ever need to. She loses her balance. She tightens her grip. He slams his elbow back, and it lands in her tiny belly, knocking the wind out of her.

She tumbles, and I lunge to catch her, but there's suddenly all these bodies around. She doesn't go down. She swipes off that unbuckled shoe and nails Eric in the side of his head.

He bellows with rage. Eric's still the type who can't take a punch. The pain pisses him off, and he expends all that rage in one, wild, unthinking swing. I launch myself in front of the girl, but a bouncer already has her by the arms, pulling her back. He's trying to protect her, swing her away, but she's fighting him, and momentum is on her side.

Another guy almost has his arms around Eric. Almost.

Eric swings, and the little fighter's hands are pinned behind her by her own guy. Eric lands an open-handed blow to her face. Her head snaps back on her thin neck.

There's four of us guys in the mix now, and for a millisecond, there's total silence.

"You *fucker*! Give me my money!"

Her shriek has the effect of a starting pistol. I go for Eric, but a seriously angry dude with a buzz cut and a SBMC vest beats me to him.

A guy yells, "Nickel, wait!" He doesn't. Nickel drags Eric through the club, whacking him into tables and chairs, using his head to fling open the front doors.

The bouncer who restrained the girl and an older, bald man called Cue follow, trailed by the wobbly dancer who's trying to walk and strap on her shoe at the same time. I bring up the rear.

A crowd forms in the parking lot, and although it's been no longer than a minute or two, Eric's done. He's weaving on his feet, and then he slams to his knees. I'm expecting Nickel to ease off, but it's like this guy's in a 'roid rage. The limper Eric goes, the harder he hits.

"Oh, shit. Get Forty," the bald man orders one of the other dancers who's come outside to gawk. "He's gonna kill him."

This is crazy.

This is *all* crazy. I'm standing in a strip club parking lot, watching my stepbrother get murdered by bikers. The guy who took the blame when Thomas found my Marlboros in the toolshed in eighth grade. Who beat Kyle Reed's ass with me as a message for Kyle's mom to back the fuck off our father. My business partner. My brother.

Shit.

I jump in, and my dumb ass forgets to take my glasses off.

I land a haymaker to the side of Nickel's head, and he

swings to face me, grinning, his teeth bloody. His face is a death mask.

I take a few shots, land them all. He doesn't even have his fists up. He's toying with me, dragging this out. Like the older kid who lets you dunk a few baskets before he schools you.

I crack my knuckles. It should be dread prickling the back of my neck, but that's not what's getting me hard, way harder than I was back in the champagne room. It's anticipation.

This is going to be *real*.

Back on Gilson Avenue, you learned how to fight the day your mom let you go outside alone. You won, or you stayed the fuck inside. At Mountchassen Prep, there were rules, unspoken, none of which had shit to do with winning. Eric's been getting me into brawls for almost twenty years, and almost always, they're unsatisfying as fuck.

But this...Nickel comes at me in a whirl of fury, blows raining down, the impact forcing me to feel.

Yes. This is real.

I beat on him, tear at him, and the guy keeps coming back harder until fear drives away the numbness I've been carrying around since I can't remember when.

I might die here.

My eyes search out a blond head with purple streaks. She's at the edge of the crowd, arms wrapped tight around her middle. The beginning of a black eye is swelling her eye shut. That gives me a shot of adrenaline enough to free myself from a headlock and bury a fist in Nickel's abs. There's a crunch, but it's not his ribs; it's my finger bones.

A shout from the sidelines distracts me, and there's a snap. This time it's my ribs. I go down, hard. I should protect my head, but I can't do anything but lie there, and then, suddenly, it all stops.

Three burly bikers have pulled Nickel off of me. A man has each of his arms, and the bald guy is hanging from his neck, choking him out. Nickel's still fighting, though.

I stumble to my feet, propping my glasses on my nose. The frame's broken. Eric's still on the ground, curled into a ball, moaning.

I take a step to help him up, but before I can, the little dancer bolts for him, shoe raised.

"He owes me twenty!"

The latest arrival, a man with a soldier's bearing who has Nickel's left arm, grabs the girl before she can reach Eric.

"For what?" the bald man asks.

The girl blinks, indignant at the question. "He wanted me to swallow. I said twenty extra. He said fine."

Eric whines, "Bullshit." If he weren't down, I'd kick him. The idiot does not know when to stop.

The bald guy must be the boss. He's frowning at her. I have the strangest urge to step between them.

"You negotiate up front?"

"He asked during." She's sweetened her tone, and she's doing her best to look innocent, but it doesn't quite work. Her eyes betray her. They're hard, calculating. Tough. Damn, she's fascinating. Everything about her. Her hair looks as soft as cotton candy, and those freckles...if you don't look too closely, she's seems like an angel. And then you catch her eye, and the fight shines from them.

She's been strutting around—and running and brawling —in nothing but a pink thong and silver sequined pasties, and it should seem sad. But the way she moves, naked and totally unconcerned—above it all—vulnerable and untouchable at the same time. She's glorious.

It's a fucking strange thought to have. I rub my head. Maybe I have a concussion.

Her boss has told her something she doesn't want to hear. She gives up the sweet act and rolls her eyes.

"Fine," she huffs. "You want me to eat the twenty along with his nasty jizz, then?"

Her words are salty, but there's a bereft note to them. She's shivering in the cold, and her eye is almost fully puffed shut. The little fighter is going to lose this round.

No one's gotten her an ice pack. Everyone's staring at Nickel as if he's the main attraction, and Nickel is eyeing me. So are his buddies. What are they waiting for? Why are we frozen in place like the world's most bizarre tableau? Bikers versus techies.

I suck down a deep breath while my brain starts working again, and it takes me a minute, but then I get it. In this moment, Eric and I are screwed, but these guys see our Maserati. They see our Brioni suits and my Breitling watch. They know that this could get complicated for them—and expensive—very quickly if I pick up my phone.

I need to end this.

I limp over to Eric and pluck his wallet from his back pocket.

"Hey," he groans.

I pull out all his cash and hand it to the girl. She snatches it without a word, turns heel, and hauls ass back to the club.

And it's so stupid, even more than getting into a fight with a biker in a parking lot, but I wish she'd looked at me. Said something. I wish I'd thought of something to say to her.

It doesn't make sense until later on the drive home, after the bald guy bans Eric for life and sends us on our way.

Much later, after I sober up at a diner and set off speeding down the pitch-black back roads to Pyle, Eric passed out in the backseat, that's when Renee came to mind. She was—is—the most beautiful woman I've ever seen in real life, hands down. The perfect body, long legs and perky tits. She's the C.O.O. for a national non-profit. She's smart, funny, connected. Her father is a partner at Portney and Clay. Her mother chairs the Arts Council.

In the five years we were together, she never wormed as deep inside me as the little stripper with purple streaks in her hair. There was something in the way she carried herself, in the determination born of desperation lurking behind her eyes, her fearlessness when she went after Eric —it reminded me of Gilson Avenue.

She reminded me of that ten-year-old boy whose dad had disappeared. The kid whose mom told him, if he didn't want a whore for a mother, he had one job. Eric Wade.

I haven't remembered that kid in a long, long time.

To be honest, I thought I'd totally sold him out.

_____

2

JO-BETH

Fuck. Clark Kent is back.

My belly flips, and my hand flutters to the little pooch above the elastic of my thong. My skin's clammy from sweating in this freezing joint, and now I've got shivers. It's weird. Clark's hot as shit, but I don't normally look at the customers that way. Especially the guys in suits.

Businessmen from Pyle are universally assholes. They tip for shit, and they smell like new car. In a bad way.

Clark scans the main floor, and then he strides over to a back booth like he owns the joint. He's got to really squeeze to get himself between the bench and the table. Dude's over six foot easy, and he's broad in the shoulders and chest. Besides the body, he's got the Superman square jaw, chin dimple, and wavy black hair. Picture the guy from *Man of Steel* with the master-of-the-universe smirk of the guy who played him in the eighties.

Oh, and of course Clark's got the glasses, the thin wire kind that cost a thousand dollars and look like they'll break if you touch 'em. Dude has money. No doubt.

Nobody's gone up to him yet. They're waiting on Cue,

wondering if he's gonna kick him out. It's only been a week or so since the guy almost beat Nickel Kobald's ass. Almost kicking Nickel's ass is like *almost* winning the Super Bowl. Like, objectively impressive, but still, everyone gets to see you lose big.

He's got a faded shiner, but he's moving like nothing's broken. I would've thought he'd have taped ribs at the least. Maybe he is made of steel.

The girls are all starin' at him like he's steak. Fine by me. I jerk my chin at Danielle, try to get her to take him. I need a distraction so I can slip off. Hot or not, ain't no way in hell I'm givin' him the two hundred bucks back.

Danielle raises her Mrs. Potato Head eyebrows and shrugs a shoulder. Well, that's a nope. Guess she ain't gonna move without Cue expressly giving the okay. After the fight, it was kind of unclear whether this guy was banned, too. Cue's still dickin' around behind the bar, so he hasn't noticed trouble walk in.

I'm on my own.

I turn my back to Clark's booth and lean into the beefy gentleman about to buy me a third apple juice, pressing my tits into his forearm. I make sure to jiggle and giggle. He ain't said nothing funny, but it don't matter none. Guys like the giggle.

"How about we take this to the way back?" I pull out all the stops. Bite my lip. Graze my nips against him. Cue keeps it sixty-seven damn degrees, so I got headlights for days.

"Ah." Beefy grins. "What's the way back?"

"The V.I.P. room. You know, the champagne room? We can be alone. You can tell me more about—" Fuck. Fuckity fuck. What was he talkin' about? His transmission? Football? "Out-of-state tuition. Sounds crazy. Who's got that kind of money?"

"Pyle State is just as good. Maybe better. And we wouldn't have to pay room and board. My ex just wants the boy to go Ivy League to screw me."

Nailed it. Tuition.

I nod, very serious. "And you'd get to keep your boy close. You don't want to know what kids get up to when they're off on their own for the first time."

I make my eyes real big, and set my hand on his thigh, close enough to his junk to feel it jerk the pleats in his khakis.

Come on, Beefy. Let's blow this popsicle stand. I spare a glance at Clark Kent from the corner of my eye. Fuck. He's staring me down. He wants that money.

Time to double down. I roll the dice.

"Why don't we go to the way back, and I'll show you exactly what kind of trouble naughty girls get into when Daddy's not around?" I make my voice breathy and nibble on the tip of my pointer finger.

Yup. Nailed it again. Beefy's a kinky one. He's pitchin' a full-blown tent now. He swallows. "Uh. Okay. Lead the way."

Will do. I grab his big ol' paw and head for the back, careful to keep my eyes away from Clark Kent's booth.

"Hold up, baby. Let me close out my tab." Beefy pats my ass awkwardly and ambles off for the tip rail to settle up.

Shit. He's left me in the middle of the tables. Maybe I should duck into the changing room. Take a piss. I don't know. This guy looks good for a hundred, one-fifty if I call him Daddy. Danielle would be more than happy to take this one off my hands. He's got easy money written all over him. Less the house's forty percent, that would be a ninety-buck piss before taxes. Fuck that.

What's he doing, anyway? Paying with change? My foot wants to tap, but that's a no-go in seven-inch platform stiletto sandals. I stop starin' at the floor and check out pervert row, and shit—Clark Kent is handing an empty shot glass to Cue, and they shake hands. Guess he's not banned. And now he's comin' for me.

Sometime while I was twiddlin' my thumbs, doin' mental math, Clark must've approached the boss. I glare at Cue, that naked-headed mole rat. He shrugs. Asshole. Guess I am all on my own. Story of my damn life.

I cross my arms, tilt my chin and stare into the middle distance, willing Beefy to stop fartin' around and come rescue me.

"Hi." Clark Kent stops right in front of me. He sounds like my ninth-grade study skills teacher, fake and way too friendly for the situation.

I crane my neck to meet his eyes.

"Do you remember me?"

"I ain't givin' you the money back." Let's get that clear from the get go.

His lips turn down ever so slightly, and his freaky electric-blue eyes darken. My pulse kicks up a notch. Never mind the overly nice tone of voice, the fancy suit, and the watch that looks like a secret decoder ring fucked an odometer. This is still a dude who can use his fists, and I ain't stupid. I ease up on the bitch face and bat my eyelashes at him a few times.

See? I'm a poor, little, helpless bunny rabbit. Let me keep the cash. Come on, rich boy. You don't need it.

"I'm not here for Eric's money."

Good.

Guess he's here to get his dick sucked like his asshole friend.

"I ain't suckin' your dick for free, neither. This ain't no pre-paid gift card deal."

"I—" He exhales, frustrated, and rolls his shoulders back. Why's he all disappointed? Is he really that pressed over a free beej? He shouldn't be. I ain't lazy or nothin', but it ain't like I'm goin' for anything besides speed and efficiency.

He takes a deep breath and starts again. "My stepbrother. He hit you."

He reaches up, cups my cheek, and lightly swipes his thumb under the bruise beneath my eye. Guess I sweated off my concealer. It cost eight freakin' bucks at the pharmacy. That's total bullshit. Had eighteen-hours written right on the bottle.

Clark takes his time messing with my face. His hand's rougher than I'd expect from a suit. There's a callus on his thumb. He's gentle, though. Not tentative, but not gropey either, if that makes sense.

"Does it hurt?"

I can't help it; I roll my eyes. My feet are crammed in seven-inch plastic shoes, my lower back aches so bad it feels like my kidneys are workin' off a month-long bender, and I've got a partially-descended wisdom tooth that's waitin' on either winning the lotto or takin' a much harder blow to the face than *Eric* dealt me to get fixed.

"I'm good," I say.

Where's Beefy? I scan the bar.

Oh, hell no. Angel and Danielle have him hemmed in at the stage bar, both purrin' in his ear. I think they bought *him* a drink.

Angel sneaks a glance over his shoulder and winks. Bitches. See if I'm trading shifts with them for the foreseeable future. I swear, when *The Bachelor's* between seasons, those sluts get up to no damn good. Drama llamas, the both of 'em.

"You sure?" His gaze is traveling lower now, resting on

my tits, and then skimming down my belly. He gets that puffed up, restless stance that men do when they like what they see and want a taste.

Damn straight he should like what he sees. He's lookin' at fifty-dollar purple highlights, an eighteen-dollar a month spray tan membership, and ten-bucks a month and two hours every other day at Future Fitness. This is as hot and tight as a bitch can look and still be broke as a joke.

"Sure, I'm sure." I cock my head back so I can get a really good look at his face. I'm thinkin' maybe this ain't what I thought it was. Maybe Clark Kent liked what he saw last time and wants a turn. A watch like he's wearin'…he might say yes if I ask for a hundred out of the gate.

"That's real sweet of you, comin' to check on me." I tug my lower lip with my teeth. "Why don't you let me take you to the way back? Show you how sweet I can be?"

For some reason, he finds this hilarious. A smile breaks across his face, all white and even teeth. My Lord. Those are car loan teeth, right there. Those are pay-off-the-mortgage teeth. I don't think they're even veneers.

"Well? Shall we?" I figure a fancy man like him, he'll like the *shall*.

"So, you're sweet, are you?"

I cock a hip and twirl a finger in my hair. Sure. Why not. I can play sweet. "Sweet as peaches."

"You beat my stepbrother with a shoe."

Yeah, I did do that. I pout my lower lip. Try real damn hard to look sorry. "I lost my temper."

"Before the—the transaction went south—you asked him to choke you with his fat cock."

I did? Does sound like somethin' I'd say to speed shit up. "So, you were snakin' then, weren't you, dirty boy?"

His face is a blank. He don't know what I mean.

"Were you watchin' me take his thick cock in my hot, wet mouth?"

He can't tear his eyes from my lips. Oh, I've got him now. He's on the hook. Now, all I have to do is reel him.

"Were you wonderin' what it felt like? I can show you. Solve the mystery. Would you like that, baby?"

"Adam."

Huh?

"My name's Adam. Adam Wade."

He's stopped perving on my body, and he's focusing on my face as if he's lookin' for something. Shit. This fucker's a squirrelly one. Almost had him, I swear.

"Nice to meet you, Adam."

"And you are?"

Not at all impressed by your fancy-ass manners, for one. But I'm also a professional.

I force as genuine a smile as I can manage. "Plum."

I offer my hand. The suits love it when I shake hands. I think it plays into their fuckin'-the-hot-chick-at-the-office fantasies.

Adam takes it and then turns his grip until we're holding hands. Right in the middle of the floor. I tug, but he doesn't let go. I'd say this is getting weird, but I've been in this game too long. Dude's not askin' me to grind my stiletto heels into his nuts; it ain't that weird.

"Plum. Where did you get that name?"

I got a line about how I'm named for my sweet, juicy ass. Got another about being ripe for the pickin'.

For some fool reason, I end up telling him the truth.

"I was callin' myself Posh, but when I came here, that name was already taken." I nod over to where Cheyenne's workin' the big bar. "My boss suggested Plum since I already had a few hoodies with a *P* done on the chests."

"I like Plum." My gaze darts up. He's not sayin' it like he's flirting. Not really. So help me, it sounds like a compliment. "It's different."

"Yeah. Can't find it on a keychain nowhere."

"I went to school with three other Adams, but no Plums."

"Not ever. Not even in your lunch bag?"

"If I had had a plum, I wouldn't have shoved it in a lunch bag."

He's smilin' real coy, as if he needs to check with someone whether it's okay that he flirts, and it dawns on me that I'm smilin' back, all goofy. He's still got my hand. He's stroking the back of it with the pad of his rough thumb.

This is a stupid conversation. I should get him in the back or cut bait.

I make my voice real breathy. "Oh, yeah? What would you have done with your plum?"

"I would have held her very carefully." He lifts his other hand and traces my jawline from my temple down my cheek. He steps closer. He's so tall, I see less of his face and more of his broad chest. He's like a campfire. His heat warms my front while my ass is gettin' chilly from the contrast.

He tilts my head back with a nudge under my chin. "You're so beautiful."

Well, that's a bit of an exaggeration. I'm a six or seven on a good day. I've got a great tush, but without a push-up, my boobs are like a buggy-eyed swamp critter lookin' in two different directions at the same time. My face is okay. I get told to smile a lot, if that tells you anything.

"Thanks." I shake my head to get back in the game. Compliments are good, but they don't pay the bills. "You want a closer look? Let's go to the back. I can dance for you. You can take a real close look at whatever you want."

"Sounds like you really want me to go to the back." He's smirking. Well, fuck him. I bet he really likes to get paid on a Friday, too.

"I want to do whatever you want to do, baby."

"Adam."

Sure. "*Adam.*" I turn it into a perfect purr. My best 1960s Catwoman impersonation. I used to love watching that show on Sunday mornings on Channel 54.

"Okay, Plum Pudding. Let's go to the back."

I have to catch myself from correcting him. He's the customer; he can call me whatever he wants. Plum Pudding's dumb as shit, though.

He leads me away by the hand. I catch Austin's eye as we go, and he follows at a distance. Although he's built like a brick shithouse, Austin's a youngster, twenty-one or twenty-two. He's also the kind of sweet that's hard to tell apart from stupid. I prefer Nickel to bird dog, but he's off tonight 'cause Story's scheduled for later.

Nickel and Story got some kind of push-pull thing going on where she thinks he hung the moon, and he's all Edward from *Twilight*.

I cannot possibly! I'm a vampire!

But he's no vampire; it's worse than that. He's a Kobald, and that's basically one-part mean-as-a-junkyard-dog to two-parts completely insane. Story's gonna catch him one of these days, and then she ain't gonna know what to do with him.

Not gonna lie. It's fun as shit to watch. Way better than *The Bachelor*.

I guess I'm a little distracted when we get to the way

back. Clark K—*Adam* hesitates and tugs my hand, eyein' the doorways hung with hippy beads.

"Card." I hold out my hand. He digs in his wallet while Austin passes me his phone with the credit card reader. "It's a hundred for a half hour, up front, extras in cash. Okay?"

He passes me a card. It's black. Don't see that every day.

I swipe it, and then I take him into the room on the left. It's the same one we were in last week with Eric the Step-brother when Adam sat in the corner and pretended to play on his phone.

Tonight, I push on his chest and plop him right in the center chair. It's ridiculous. He's so tall his knees are all folded up. He better have a long dick, or I'm gonna be grindin' on his thighs.

Austin loosens the beaded curtains and they clink together. It feels private, but there's a camera in the ceiling with 360-degree view. Steel Bones don't play with their property.

Adam glances up at the black bulb on the ceiling. I ain't particularly worried about him, but I like that he knows he's bein' watched.

I slink in a circle, take a few steps, try to find the beat. Cue's got some club music blasting back here so loud you got to shout if you aren't right up on a person. Covers up the grunts and *oh, Gods* real well.

Adam settles in, easing his knees apart and stretching them long legs out. That looks more comfortable, but he's still too much man for the chair. I better not bounce on his lap or I'm gonna break the seat.

I shake my ass. Bend over. Twerk. Check out his reaction.

He's watchin', but he ain't into it.

I learned a long time ago that I ain't a mind reader and

time is limited, so I slide on up to him, straddle his legs—
he's so solid, I can actually feel the stretch in my hip sockets
—and I lean over to whisper in his ear.

"What do you want me to do, baby?"

"Adam."

I can't stop the small huff. Fine. *Adam*. What is his deal?

Shit. Why do I care? I ain't gettin' paid to wonder.

"Adam, what would you like me to do?" I let my hair fall
around his face and raise my tits 'till he could lick 'em if he
stuck out his tongue.

For a second, it looks like he's gonna say one thing, but
then he seems to change his mind. There's a pause, a flicker
in his eye.

"Sit on my lap. Facing me."

I sink down slow, rocking as I go, careful not to squirm
too much. He busts a nut in his pants with no effort on my
part, that's at least a fifty down the drain.

"Like this?"

"Sure."

Straddling his solid thighs, my legs are spread so wide I
can't get close enough to feel what he's packin', but damn, I
can see it just fine. He's a tuck-in-the-pant-leg, not an under-
the-waistband kind of guy. His dick reaches well down
toward his knee, and there's not an inch of give in the fabric
of his pants.

I respect the beauty of nature and all, but as a business-
woman, I must say market forces just drove that fifty up to at
least seventy-five.

"What do you want to do now, Adam? You want to touch
my titties?"

His eyes flicker. "Do you want me to touch you?"

"You can do anything you want."

I'm expecting him to dive in—they usually do—but

Adam's a real surprise every time. He starts at the outside of my knees and stokes up my thighs, firm and slow, massaging as he goes.

And then, oh Lord, he gets to my hips. He digs in, his thumbs pressing hard, and then he works around until he's rubbing the small of my back, makin' small circles, pressing up my spine and then kneading the top of my ass cheeks.

It feels *so good*.

I moan. I can't help it.

These damn heels force my spine out of whack, and no matter how I stretch before my shift or build my core like Austin's always talkin' about, there's nothin' but an eight-hundred-milligram ibuprofen and a long, hot bath that'll make the ache go away.

Well, nothin' except this. Clark's got superpowered magic hands.

"Lean forward," he says.

I do until my forehead's resting on his shoulder.

He brushes a soft kiss to my temple. So weird.

"You like this?"

I moan. "Uh huh."

"It feels good?"

It'd feel better if he shut up and just kept doin' it.

"Yes, Adam. Don't stop. Oh, yeah."

He digs those magic fingers deeper, and I arch my back, putting enough space between us so that he can gaze down and meet my eyes. It's shadowy in here so you can't make out the electric-blue, but there's no hiding how intensely he's staring. Shivers race his fingers up to the nape of my neck.

Is he a serial killer or something? Is this the look before he snaps my neck and wears me home draped around his neck like a feather boa?

I tense up. Can't help it.

"What's wrong, Pudding?" He eases his strokes, still firm, but less diggy. "Did I hit a tender spot?"

"No, no. Feels good. I was just thinking, this is nice and all, but this is supposed to be for *you*."

I slide my hands down from where I'd obliviously rested them on his chest—his hard-as-fuck chest—to start fiddling with his belt buckle.

He pretty much ignores me. He slips his hands behind my knees and guides my legs up until they're sort of folded and tucked under his armpits. He can easily reach my shoes now, and he unstraps them with both hands, sending them clunking one-by-one to the floor. Immediately, he squeezes my bare feet in his huge hands, tracing firm lines up my arches with that thumb.

Oh, *sweet Lord*. That feels so, so good.

I leave off working at his belt—I can't seem to get it undone anyway—and I live for the moment.

I nuzzle my head in the crook of his neck, and doesn't he smell so *nice*. Like salon shampoo.

Nestled in his lap—cuddled really—he's so much bigger than me. He could probably tuck me in the jacket of his thousand-dollar suit. I'm guessin' at the price. I don't know anything about men's suits, but I know money when I see it.

He looks like a fancier version of the businessmen we get all the time, assholes slumming it for cheap thrills, so they can tell their buddies they partied with the Steel Bones MC. These are the type of guys who order top shelf liquor, overpay for a rub and tug, and then stiff you on the tip.

It's a nice jacket, though. Soft, not scratchy against my skin.

"This nice?" he asks.

I mumble something. My eyelids are getting heavy.

Austin better knock on the door frame soon, or I'm gonna be conked out and drooling on the customer.

"What's your real name, Plum?" His voice is low, confident, as if he'd never heard *no* in his life. I bet this is a man who gets seated in the center chair in whatever room he walks into. A dangerous man. The kind the world moves out of their way for, crushing people like me.

Tension fills my body, and he can't rub enough to make me a noodle again.

"You want to know my real name?"

"Yeah." He nips at my bottom lip. Testing, but not. He knows he can kiss me if he wants to. He paid.

"You gonna tell me your real bank account number?"

He laughs. I don't. After a few moments, he says, "Reach into my pocket. Front left."

All right, then. I pull out his brown leather wallet, and this time I notice the worn creases. It really doesn't match his fancy suit and watch and shiny wingtip shoes.

I hold it up between two fingers.

"Open it."

This feels like a trap. It probably *is* a trap. But it's also a pretty thick wallet. Doesn't quite fold all the way closed.

I flip it open. He's got a wad. I thumb through it quick. All twenties.

"Take it."

There's at least four or five hundred in there. That's the mortgage made, and it's only the tenth of the month.

This is definitely a setup.

"So, I take the cash, and then you go cry to Cue that I stole it? Is that your grand revenge plan?" There's the camera, so it's not like it'd work, but it pisses me off anyway.

I shove the wallet into his chest and try to get up, but he

has both my feet, and damn him, he hasn't stopped massaging them.

"Who's Cue?"

I huff. "Bald motherfucker? Runs the place? Pulled Nickel off you last week before he killed you."

He chuckles. Actually chuckles. "I was making a comeback."

"You were gettin' your ass handed to you."

"Yeah. Probably." His gaze turns vague, and his smile goes somehow *off*. "I was gonna lose that one, wasn't I?"

"You did lose." He's still lookin' a little down in the mouth. Don't know why I care. "Nickel feels no pain. He'll keep punchin' after he breaks his hand. You didn't have a chance."

"Are you trying to make me feel better?" The bright-white smile is back.

"I'm just sayin'. You shouldn't feel bad."

"You *are* trying to make me feel better. I knew you were soft-hearted."

"Hooker with a heart of gold. That's me." Since we're bein' friendly, I flip the wallet open again and finger through the bills. They're so crisp and new, they stick to each other. He must've stopped at the ATM. "It ain't smart to walk around with this much cash on you."

"It's not that much. Only five hundred or so."

I snort. Yeah. Only five hundred. I got my electric turned off in the middle of a heat wave over *only* eighty-four dollars and fifty-two cents. All the food in the fridge spoiled, and I had to take my cat to my girl Annie Holt's 'cause it was too hot for her inside or out. *Still* haven't gotten her back. The kids got attached.

Only five hundred, my ass.

"Go ahead. Take it." He smiles all coaxing, the way any

cartoon villain does when his nemesis is unsuspectingly walking over a trapdoor.

"I ain't fallin' for it."

He closes his eyes, as if in aggravation. "You're stubborn as hell, Plum Pudding."

"Why do you want me to take it if it ain't a setup? I ain't done shit for you."

It's strange. The question seems to confuse him. I can tell the minute he gives up tryin' to figure out what he should say.

"What's the name of the guy standing in the hall?"

"Austin?"

With no warning, Adam calls, "Austin!"

The kid comes in at a run. Austin probably thinks I've lost my mind again and started in on this guy with my shoe like I did his stepbrother the other day.

"Sir?"

"See this wallet Plum has in her hands?"

Here it comes. The net is lowered. I'm an idiot. I saw it comin', and I'm still happily sitting and waiting for it to scoop me up, all for a foot rub.

"Should I call management, sir?"

"No, no." Adam drops my feet—damn—and wraps his arms around my butt, holding me in place. "Everything's fine. I need you to hold something for Plum here."

"Yeah?"

"Hand him the money, Pudding." It makes no damn sense, but I ain't stupid. I pass the cash quicker than a blunt behind the bleachers when the teacher shows up.

"Will you hold that for her until she's done?"

"Yes, sir." Austin folds and wedges it in his back pocket. "You need anything else?"

"Only privacy, my man." Adam sounds like some action movie superspy. Shaken, not stirred. *Only privacy, my man.*

Austin ducks right out.

"Why'd you do that? You want a blow job? I ain't sayin' no, but you overpaid."

He sucks in a breath, and it takes him a long while to answer. When he does, I don't get it at all.

"I want you to tell me what you're going to spend it on."

"And then you'll tell me what it's for?"

"That's what it's for. Let's say I've decided to invest in Plum Pudding. What's my five hundred dollars going toward?"

I thought I'd heard of most kinks, but I must say, this is a new one. I don't judge, though. Not in my line of work.

"The mortgage."

"You own a house?"

Why does he seem so pleased? Oh, shit. *That's* what's going on.

He must have White Knight Syndrome. I've run into these guys. They want to rescue you from the life. Save you from yourself. There's always a catch, and the catch is *always* way worse than whoring. If a man's so desperate to save a woman, it's because he needs his women weak. If you don't turn out to be a damsel in distress, he'll make you one.

"Plum?"

Oh. What had he asked? Did I have a house? "Yeah. I do."

"Tell me about it."

I'm shaking my head before the words are out of his mouth.

"Unh, unh. You've got the wrong idea. I don't do in-house. It's here, or if you're payin', the El-Car Motel, but

Austin comes with and sits in the bathroom. And you have to wait 'til my shift ends."

"The El-Car motel?" Adam shakes his head, baffled-like. "Never mind. I'm not asking to go to your house. I want to know what my money will be going toward. Call it idle curiosity."

"I call it bullshit."

He laughs and runs a finger down the bridge of my nose.

"Did you know your nose scrunches up when you're suspicious?"

It does? Don't most people's? I shift. Adam rearranges my legs so they dangle down on either side of his hips, and I sway to work out the stiffness in my hips. I'm pressed flat against him now, and there's no mistaking the baseball bat in his pants.

Why isn't he whipping it out?

"Your house..." Adam winds his arms around me and starts in on my back again. Sheer. Fucking. Heaven. "Tell me about it. No identifying details. Is it a standalone?"

"No. A duplex."

"How are the neighbors?"

"Deaf as a stone."

"Is that good or bad?"

"Good when I have people over. Bad when *The Big Bang Theory's* on."

"What color is it?"

I don't answer. That sounds to me like one of those *identifying details*.

"Do you have a garden?"

I arch an eyebrow. "A garden?"

"You've got nothing in the yard, then?"

My yard kicks ass. It's small, but I have a decent size dogwood and a flower bed. I wish I could do more, but money's tight, and it's hard working nights and sleeping days. He don't need to hear about that, though. I grasp for something to tell him.

"I've got a birdbath."

"Yeah?" He grins like I said I've got a third tit. "A birdbath?"

"Just a cheap blue ceramic one from General Goods. With a dove perched on the edge."

"Are you sure you feel comfortable telling me the color of your birdbath?"

"It's in the back. You can't see it from the street."

"Do you get a lot of birds?"

"Some." I wait for his next busybody question, but he doesn't speak. He plays with my hair instead, combing his fingers through it and massaging my scalp. My cheeks heat, and a buzzing starts in my belly. It's the strangest sensation. So very weird, but also nice.

The silence stretches. I'm sure he's gonna stop soon. Who's got the patience for this if they ain't gettin' paid?

I really don't want him to stop, though. I should keep talking. Maybe he'll keep rubbin'. What did he ask about? Birds?

"I've seen a pair of Prothonotary warblers. Marsh wrens. And a dickcissel that must have got lost." I have no idea why I'm bragging.

"How do you know all the different kinds?"

"There's an app. For your phone."

"You're a birdwatcher, Plum?" Again, he seems bizarrely pleased. Like look at the whore, she's got a hobby, ain't it cute?

I yank my hair out of his fingers. It stings, but not much.

He hushes me. Honestly says, "Hush." He moves his hands away from my face, though.

"What's your favorite bird?"

"Tufted titmouse."

I say it to be an asshole, but when his lip quirks up and his eyes crinkle, I can't stop the giggle. With his glasses, he's kind of goofy looking when he grins.

"Titmouse?"

I giggle again—it's even funnier when he says it—and he drags me closer, resting his chin on the top of my head. There's a long moment, Adam holding me, my stupid body all boneless and hanging off him. Even though I'm in only my thong and pasties, and the AC's blowing straight down on us, I'm warm for once.

"Plum Pudding?"

"Mmmmm?"

"Go to dinner with me."

"Sure, baby." This guy is full of shit.

"I'm serious."

I sigh. I suppose the moment's over. I wriggle straight, and I try really hard to look understanding.

"I get it. You want to rescue me from all this."

I gesture around the room which is actually super-clean and decently furnished. I've definitely worked in worse.

"Maybe you feel guilty 'cause your cousin clocked me."

"Stepbrother."

Whatever. "But I'm good. I've got a man. He takes real good care of me. Like I said, I got a house. I'm putting myself through school." Total lie. You couldn't pay me to go back to school. "You don't have to feel responsible. It's all good."

I give him my best, believe-the-bullshit smile.

He sighs, and his shoulders relax. He moves his hands to cup my face. This is where he gently kisses my lips and leaves with a smile, reassured that he's a good guy and all's well with the world.

He brushes his lips across mine.

"Bullshit," he says.

Wha—?

"You don't have a boyfriend. You're not going to school. You have a house, but you're in arrears on the taxes. You owe several thousand on your Visa, and you're two months behind on your car payment. They're going to repo that, by the way. You might want to stop parking in front of your pretty yellow house."

Oh. Fuck.

He's gonna make me into a skin suit.

"Aus—!"

His hand slams over my mouth. "I want you to go to dinner with me, Jo-Beth Connolly. Saturday night."

He waits, as if I can answer with his enormous meat paw clasped over half my face. I try to sink my teeth into it, but damn, his grip is solid.

Eventually, after I mumble awhile, he figures it out and lowers his hand. Good thing my shoes are already off. If he makes one wrong move, I'm punching him in the junk and running, and I'll get away, too. I can haul ass barefoot.

"I'm not going to dinner with you, stalker."

"Twelve hundred eighty-four dollars."

Twelve—Holy hell. That's my tax bill.

"And eleven cents," I add under my breath.

"Is that a yes?"

"Why?" I know he's not going to come out and say so he can kidnap me and keep me in his basement, but hey. I'm gonna *ask*.

It takes him a long time to answer. "Because you remind me of someone I used to know. Someone I miss."

"A kickass bitch, then?"

"So kickass." That sad smile's back, but I ain't going

down that rabbit hole. This is extortion or blackmail or some such shit, and it's gonna take more than an hour in the way back to give me Stockholm Syndrome.

"I want to go someplace really, *really* nice. *Expensive* nice."

"Of course."

"And you're paying."

"Naturally."

"We meet there. And you stop spying on me."

"Done."

"How'd you find out that shit, anyway?"

"My company pays for a background check service. It's all public record."

"Public records told you I don't have an old man?"

He shakes his head. "That was a guess. You're with Steel Bones. If you had an old man, you wouldn't be in this room with me now."

"You think you know it all, don't you?"

He shrugs.

"I don't like spicy food. You know that?"

His smile flashes blinding bright again. "So an expensive restaurant with bland food. Any other requirements, Plum Pudding?"

"You know that Plum Pudding is a Strawberry Shortcake doll, right?"

He gives me a blank look.

"Little doll with a big head? Beady eyes and freckles? From the 80s?"

"You know you look like a Strawberry Shortcake doll, right?" He chuckles and sets me on my feet away from him before I can slap him upside the head.

Okay. It was a decent burn. For a weird, rich stalker.

"I'm gonna meet you at this restaurant and never be

heard from again, ain't I?" I mutter as I walk him out of the room. I feel less off-kilter when we aren't alone anymore.

"It's only dinner." He rests his hand on the small of my back to guide me up the hall.

"Cash up front."

"Okay," he says, and stops in the middle of the door to the main floor, and drops a kiss on the top of my head.

He's insane.

"Twelve hundred eighty-four dollars?"

"Twelve hundred eighty-four dollars."

I should have asked for fifteen hundred.

THAT "SEVERAL THOUSAND" I owe on my Visa is now "several thousand and forty-eight dollars plus shipping."

And I don't feel bad about it.

Much.

I break down the box, and then I unroll my new door-mat, sitting on it cross-legged to help it lay flat. It's adorable. Beige straw with bright red strawberries. It's going in front of the back door so no one fucks it up.

It's Monday, my day off. It's sunny outside, and I have a whole, glorious day in front of me to putter around the house. I told Fay-Lee I'd come by the clubhouse tonight, but until then, it's me and the birds, the vacuum, and the furni-ture polish. Heaven.

I exhale, and I lower myself flat on the floor. I'm at a slight incline 'cause of the sagging floorboards. I need to ask one of the brothers to take a look at it. It might be an easy fix. Yeah, right. I sigh and push the idea from my head. It's my day off. No worries allowed.

The straw from the doormat prickles my back through

my thin, cotton tank top, but it's not an awful feeling. I stretch my arms way over my head and flex my feet. My body doesn't ache as much as it usually does on a Monday. Maybe because of Adam's magic hands.

My cheeks heat. I think that crazy fucker asked me out on a date. If he comes through with the twelve hundred, I guess that makes me an escort.

Do I want that? I've been turning tricks here and there to make ends meet since I dropped out of school, mostly blow jobs or hand jobs. Except for a few months after I turned eighteen and got a little worried about Steel Bones kicking me out or askin' for rent, it's always been a side hustle. More like shit I do, not what I am.

God, Ma would laugh at that. She started calling me a whore when I was seven or eight, and I started hugging her boyfriend-of-the-moment whenever he brought his dinner over with him. I didn't care what she called me. Darren or Warren or whatever-his-name-was would give me half his sub, and I wouldn't go to bed with my stomach cramping. Rather be a whore than starve, any day of the week.

My body tenses, and a sour anxiousness creeps from my gut to my chest. Fuck that. It's Monday Funday. No ghosts allowed. I focus on my Kit Kat clock. She's on the kitchen wall, but I can see her framed by the pass-through. She's black with white trim, and her eyes and tail go back and forth. Her ticks echo, making the quiet seem even quieter, and my nerves calm down.

Kit Kat was a find. She's an original. I got her at a yard sale still in the box.

If this escort shit works out, and I pay off the tax bill, I can start going to yard sales again. Go back to operating on more of a cash basis. I've been putting a lot of things on the credit card. I splay my arms and legs in a starfish to flatten the corners of the doormat. I'm *not* sorry I bought it, but my stomach does cramp a little.

I hop up and grab the mat, side-stepping the floorboard that dips the most when you land on it. I head outside, knocking my hip into the back door while I shove. It opens with a scrape. I swear this house is aimin' to be the one from that nursery rhyme with the crooked man who walks a crooked mile.

Shit. Even if this escort shit pans out, I need more cash. Maybe I can pick up hours at Tasty's in Shady Grove. Or I could take Danielle up on doing one of her house calls. I've got a good six months to pay the last of the tax installments, but what if something goes wrong with the house in the meantime? Something I can't throw a carpet over?

If worse comes to worst, Steel Bones will front me, but I don't want to be beholden to them or anyone.

I shake out the mat I can't afford, and I place it carefully on the deck. Then I readjust the huge plastic pot I've got covering a torn-up board, turning the oakleaf hydrangea so you can see more buds that've bloomed.

That strawberries on the mat match the flowers exactly. Still, I shouldn't have bought it. If I were a stronger woman, I'd return it, but I'm not. Instead, I'm not gonna think about it anymore today. The tug-of-war between what I want and what I should do will tear up my stomach if I dwell on it too long.

My house is my baby. It's the first home I ever had in my whole life. Ma and I bounced from place to place until she passed: shitty apartment, friend's spare room, boyfriend's trailer. When I ran away from foster care, I crashed at the Steel Bones Clubhouse, earning my keep as a sweetbutt. A little cleaning, a little fucking, a lot of dancing. I saved up and bought my house on my twenty-third birthday.

I'd be well on my way to paying it off, except for my little addiction. It's not enough to own the house. I need the stuff, too. I *crave* the stuff. The bird bath. The wind chimes. The gingham tablecloth and braided place mats. The soft, chenille throw pillows.

I'm not stupid or out of control. I save up. I bargain hunt. I'm selective. Still. I wouldn't have fallen behind on the taxes if not for the Amish quilt and the matching shams.

My lips soften into a smile. I fucking love my quilt. I got the double wedding ring pattern.

This Adam guy could be the answer to my prayers. Cue says he drives a Maserati. He's got deep pockets.

Why is he so interested in me? I guess it could still be a revenge thing. Weird way to go about it, but crazy comes in all flavors.

Maybe he has a savior kink. Plenty of men do. Ma was aces at sniffing them out, taking them for all they were worth, which was never much. Ma knew how to hustle, even if she wasn't smart enough to be any good at it. She always fell for the users. Karma's a bitch.

I like to think I'm better than she was, but at the end of the day, the only real difference between me and her is that I've got my own place, I can spot a user a mile away, and I don't let the motherfuckers through the door.

Adam's not the kind of bad man I'm used to. He's got to be a bad, though, right? What's he gonna want for a G? What's his story?

One way to find out. I sit down on the edge of my deck, dangle my legs over, and take my phone from my bra to search him up. I'm prepared to dig a little—Adam Wade is a pretty generic name—but I hit the jackpot as soon as I hit enter. All of the first page results for Adam Wade are about the guy from the club.

There are news articles, most about business but some about *Most Eligible Bachelors* and *Top Ten Tech Disruptors in Finance*. There's a column on the right with a pic and a blurb about financial services and Chief Technology Officer and other words that don't interest me much.

I guess he's hot shit.

I click on images, and there he is in living color. Superman. The pics are all professional, or he's standing in front of a backdrop like movie stars do, wearing a sharp suit, hands in his pockets, smiling to show all his teeth, his eyes cool and blank.

In a lot of the pictures, there's a woman. She's tall, and her brown hair shines. She touches him like it's no big deal. There's a series of photos from some kind of fancy-dress ball. She's wearing a bright-red gown, and he's got on a matching red tie. They're posing in front of a red backdrop sprinkled with white diamonds.

Apparently, this ball is an annual thing. There are pictures from other years. The same party, the same backdrop, but different dates. Some wear white and have glossy, black hair, some are in red with blonde curls spilling from an updo. The women are all plastered in diamonds.

I get a sick feeling in the pit of my stomach. This ain't right. I've had men chase me around before. A few times, I had to get Nickel or Wall to run 'em off. Some men figure they're owed more time and attention than they paid for.

This man can have anything he wants. If he wants beautiful or classy or rich, he already has it on his arm.

I've lived in this world long enough. I know what I am that these other women aren't.

Disposable.

I come from a long line of disposable women. For every man Ma took for a ride, two took a bite out of her. By the time she died from the Hep C, a man was cashing her disability checks and fucking another woman in her bed—in the apartment she'd paid the rent on—while I sat by her side in hospice, resting my feet on an overstuffed duffle 'cause I knew if I left my shit in my room, it wouldn't be there when I came back.

When she died, they put me in foster care, and then that went south. I ran away and dropped out. My case worker tried to set up a new situation, but when I turned her down, she didn't do much.

On my eighteenth birthday, she showed up at the Steel Bones clubhouse, gave me a folder of papers and had me sign on the dotted line. I didn't see her again. I think she retired.

I know what men see when they watch me shake my tits. Easy pickings. A girl nobody would miss. It makes them think dark thoughts, and that gets them hard.

But that girl? That was my Ma. That ain't me. I'm not stupid.

I stand and head for the tub where I keep my gardening shit. The sky's blue, and it's not too hot, not too cold. I'm gonna weed my flower bed, and then I'm gonna lay in the yard and stare at the clouds, see if I can spot a dusky hawk or a golden eagle.

Later, I'm gonna text Cue, see which brother he can send with me on this "date" with Adam Wade. I'll ask for Wall. That gargantuan motherfucker could scare even the craziest rich perv. I don't know what this dude wants, but I'll be damned if he gets more than he pays for.

See, my Ma gave it away for free. She'd rip off whole pieces of herself for a few compliments and empty promises. I don't value myself so cheap, and I don't mind hard work.

I spent five years scrubbing biker jizz out of leather couches and never saying no, and now shit happens on my terms. If Adam Wade wants a cheap whore that no one'll miss, he picked the wrong bitch. This one's property of the Steel Bones MC, and with them, taking care of their shit is a matter of pride.

That decided, I put it out of my mind. I grab my gloves and a rubber kneeler from the utility tub. My bluebells and phlox don't really need that much weeding, but I like fussing with the flower bed, the earthy smell and the stretch in my back.

I'm trying to get the ruby-throated hummingbirds to come by this year. So far this spring, it's been nothing but squirrels all up in the birdseed. It's early days, though. I get a pay day, there's a colored glass feeder I've got my eye on, shaped like a pear, lime green with bright orange swirls. The reviews say it's guaranteed to attract hummingbirds.

I like being able to buy a sure thing.

I guess that's one thing Adam Wade and I have in common.

3

ADAM

I got another email while I was dressing for dinner. The subject line read *your father ryan Adam morrison*. All lowercase except the *A*. My finger hovers over the phone for a long minute, and then I delete it like the others.

If these are really from Ryan Adam Morrison, he's getting more persistent. He's sent a message almost every day this week. I'll admit; the first few had me rattled. Could explain why I ended up getting into a fight with a biker and inviting a stripper to dinner.

I've had some time to think, and I'm not sure what screw got loose in my head.

I guess it makes a kind of sense. Even at thirty years old, in our weak moments, don't we all still have a kid's heart? It's late at night, you've had a few drinks, you're at the end of a grueling negotiation. We want to believe it's not all shit. The father who bailed had a good reason. The hooker has a heart of gold.

In the cold light of day, you see more clearly. If the man emailing me is really my long-lost father, he wants something. Plum is like every woman who sells her ass to make rent. At the end of the day, my mom was no different, if she was a bit more particular about her clientele.

I crack my neck and lean back against the brick face of Altimeter, the only restaurant in Pyle with two Michelin stars. I should have canceled. This isn't me.

I am a man of my word, though. I stopped at the bank. I have twelve hundred dollars cash in my breast pocket and a reservation for two.

I texted Plum the time and address. She sent me her Venmo.

I think I prefer cash for a transaction like this, though. Standing here in my town, two blocks from the mid-century office building that bears my name, my temporary insanity is crystal clear. Either I'm leading on a whore, or I've become a john. Neither is consistent with the man Thomas Gracy Wade raised me to be.

I suppose I could have just sent the money. *Plum* would probably be fine with foregoing the meal, especially if I tipped. She still might not show. I drum my fingers against the brick. I don't like that thought.

I was in a strange mood that night I went back to The White Van, sleep deprived from the ArrowXchange negotiations on top of my usual insomnia, thrown by the emails purporting to be from Ryan Morrison. I'd been drinking a lot.

I've had a few days now. Juice cleanse. I'm back at the gym. With melatonin and a sleep aid, I'm getting about four hours of rest a night. Plum is getting blurrier in my mind, and I've grown curious.

There's no way she's as pretty as I thought she was. I asked Eric, and he said he couldn't tell me anything except she had purple hair, wonky tits, and she sucked like a vacuum cleaner. He asked why I wanted to know. I said I like to whack it to thoughts of him getting head, and I needed to get the details right for my spank bank.

He laughed, and we got back to business.

He's out with the ArrowXchange people tonight, slumming it at the clubs on the Riverwalk, trying to get them over their last objections. I feel a little guilty for bailing, but this kind of shit is Eric's forte. It's what he brings to the table. I won't be missed. Besides, I can always meet up with them after this fiasco.

The sun is only now going down, and the crowds on the sidewalks are thinning. I made an early reservation on purpose. I might be a man of my word, but I don't need to court unnecessary attention.

I check my phone. Plum is now officially late. No message. I prop my heel on the wall. I'll give her five minutes. I ignore how my heart is speeding up, how my nerves grate with each passing second. I'm pissed to be wasting my time. That's all.

I open Bleacher Report, and I'm forcing myself to read a piece on the post-season, so I don't see her walk up. Despite the fact I'm amped as hell, she doesn't register until she's standing right in front of me. When I look up, I get the sense she's been there a minute.

My abs clench, and my cock jerks. Shit.

She's frowning, her arms crossed tight across her chest, her hip cocked, and one foot turned out the way girls used to do in middle school. She's so short.

I go to straighten, but then I realize I'll loom over her.

On first glance, she looks pissed off, but as I stare a little longer, I see she's nervous. The scared kind of nervous. For some reason I cannot begin to fathom, this bothers me. I don't want to scare her off.

My stomach's still doing something strange, and I've got

a semi that's quickly growing into a full-blown hard on. Holy fuck. I didn't imagine it. It wasn't the sleep deprivation or the booze or the rush of the deal. What is it about this girl?

I mean, objectively, she's nothing special. She's pretty enough, and her body's tight as hell. She's showing it off in a skintight white spandex dress with bare shoulders. No one's going to miss that she's a stripper.

But she's not holding herself in the way that women do when they know they're hot. Her stance is defensive, not sultry. Her face is guarded, and her eyes are faded-blue pools of wariness and suspicion.

It makes no sense, but that expression? It makes me want to fuck her so bad. I want to turn her against this wall, shove that dress up to her waist. God, my hands itch thinking about baring that ripe ass and cupping it in my hands. Nudging her legs apart and thrusting my cock into her dripping pussy. I want to make her love it, tear her mask away, fuck it right off her, until she looks over her shoulder at me like I'm a god, and that mean, scared look melts away into neediness and greed.

"You gonna stare at me all night, or are we gonna eat?"

I kind of startle, shaking my head to clear it. What's wrong with me? I don't need to stress this. She's a whore. If I want her, it's negotiable.

"Okay. So how about while you're staring, you hand me your card."

She goes to root in her purse, I guess for her phone so she can take my card. Shit. I'm really gonna pay a prostitute on the sidewalk in front of Altimeter? I need to pull it together.

"I brought cash."

"Okay, then hand me the cash."

"Later."

She looks across the street, and for the first time, I notice the huge motherfucker on a motorcycle parked halfway down the block. His biceps are so big, he can only cross his forearms near the wrists. His legs are tree trunks. He's wearing a vest that reads SBMC, and he's got an eyebrow raised.

She glances back at me, her eyebrows raised as well, and she puts her hand out.

I take the envelope from my jacket pocket.

She snatches it and trots off across the street. It takes everything in me not to stop her, hook my arm around her middle, and haul her back against my chest.

She doesn't need to be running to this guy.

I don't want her out of my reach, which is crazy.

She hands the envelope to the big guy; they exchange a few words I can't hear because of passing traffic. Then she turns back to me, and the relief is so great, it's like a band breaks and my lungs can inflate.

"You good?" the man hollers to Plum, but he's staring me down. I hold his gaze.

She waves him off. "I'll text you."

He gives her a chin lift.

"I'll be close," he calls.

She blows him a kiss. My fists tighten. A disorienting wave of irritation rolls through me. I step forward.

"Can we eat?" she asks, grabbing my hand. It's delicate and soft. My breath catches, awareness slamming through me, priming my muscles.

She blinks at me, surprised. Did she feel that, too? I gaze down into her plain-blue eyes. The color is nothing special. I have a dozen shirts that color. Why is it so damn hard to look away?

"Come on." I guide her through the revolving door, keeping that hand covered in mine, and I calm. The hostess greets me by name, asks after my stepfather. The strange feeling passes, replaced with a slight embarrassment.

I've booked a corner table in the back, along the bank of windows overlooking the confluence of the Luckahannock and the Nocochtank. It's as private as they offer.

I eat here often. It's the best fine dining in the city. The staff are well-trained. The hostess, the waiter, the somme-lier. They all keep their faces perfectly blank as they offer Plum a chair, pour her water, and describe the evening's wine pairings.

Plum plops her huge purse on her lap, and clasps her hands on top of it. She keeps her head down. The hostess, the waiter, the sommelier. All they get from her is a tiny nod, the briefest side glance.

You could cut her uneasiness with a knife, but there's a perverted part of me that's getting off on it. She'll only look directly at me. Like I'm the one in charge. My cock is throb-bing under the linen napkin I unfolded on my lap the instant we were seated.

As soon as the wait staff walks away, she lifts her head and glares. She hasn't even picked up her menu. I ordered the charcuterie and a Moscato for her, a pinot noir for myself.

I nudge the menu toward her. "Aren't you going to look?"

"I thought you already ordered for me."

"Not the entree. Only a starter."

She picks up the menu as if it's going to bite her, stares at it a moment, squinting, her nose wrinkling. Fucking adorable. Then she huffs, flops it on her plate, and digs through her purse.

A few moments later, she pulls out a pair of cat's eye glasses. On a braided cord.

I think I'd be less surprised if she pulled out a flask or a vape.

"You wear glasses?"

She glares daggers at me over the rims.

I raise my glass. "No offense intended. I wear them myself. Obviously."

She glances back down at the menu.

She takes so long reading it, I have to wave the waiter off twice. I don't interrupt. She's too sweet to watch. She's crossed her legs, and she's dangling a shoe from her toes. Every so often, she purses her lips and huffs in frustration.

She's so intent on the menu that she doesn't seem fully aware when she reaches for her wine and downs it in three gulps.

"Do you have any questions?"

She blinks those perfectly ordinary blue eyes at me, deeply aggrieved and so damn defensive. Blood rushes to my cock.

She exhales a long-suffering sigh. "Sure."

She starts at the top of the menu, running her index finger along the text.

"Amouse-Bouche. Squab. Fois Gras Confit. Melange. Pain Perdu. Beurre Rouge."

She mispronounces everything with irritated gusto.

"And what the fuck is salmon poke and what the fuck is a raft of garden tomatoes?"

I'm about to answer when she slaps the menu on the table.

"I have another question. What is this kink? Do you get off on makin' poor bitches feel less than? Is that it? Is it like a domination thing so you can feel like a big man, all rich and shit?"

What?

"I mean, it's your money. I can be anything you want. But if the fantasy is to fuck a white trash whore in the bathroom of the fancy restaurant or whatever, you're gonna have to let me know. I don't generally feel less than, so I'm gonna have to dig deep to get into character."

It's as if she slammed me in the chest. I take a sip of wine to play for time. She glares at me, and for some reason, it's hard to meet her eyes. The tension is now mutual. And then there's my dick which only seemed to hear *fuck in the bathroom*. I'm so hard, my cock is pulsing.

Now I really don't know what to say.

I was in a weird head space? It was late. I have insomnia, and I'd been up almost forty-eight hours at that point? It was spur of the moment?

Until I saw her again, I'd fooled myself that it was a sleep-deprived bout of temporary insanity, but if I said that now, it'd be a lie. I want this woman. I'm hungry for her in a way I've never been for a woman before. It's insane. Probably unhealthy. Definitely ill-advised. Maybe it's a delayed rebound reaction to the break up with Renee. Maybe the stress of juggling Thomas Wade's expectations and Eric's mad plans is finally getting to me.

I glance out the window, and I catch my reflection. In my Zegna suit and my hundred-dollar haircut, I look like I belong. No one would think I don't.

And then there's Plum, her cheap dye job and her obvious knockoff purse. No jewelry. White pleather stripper heels. So out of place she might as well be from a different planet.

It doesn't make sense—I don't understand it myself—

but I don't want her to sit there and think I'm a piece of shit for asking her here.

I've never had trouble with women. Not at Mountchassen. Certainly not since. But goddamn, I have no idea what to do. I want her to want me back. I *need* to taste this woman. Breathe her in. Stroke that soft skin and make her moan. Pinch her tits and make her squeal. I shift and the heat of my cock on my thigh almost burns. It's stuck down my pant leg again. *Fuck.*

Thank goodness the waiter comes. "And have you decided, sir?"

While I was all up in my head, the charcuterie arrived. Plum's eating a duck rillette with a spoon.

I pause, give her space to respond. She shrugs and keeps munching on the rillette.

"I'll have the wagyu ribeye. Medium. She'll have the lobster medallions."

"And the squab," she pipes up. "I'm not walkin' out of this joint without tryin' squab."

"The squab then. Excellent." The waiter's smile is tight. I want to punch it off his face.

"And the lobster." She's eyeing me, a sparkle in those blue eyes. It sends a zing through me, that sparkle. I love it.

"Of course, madam."

"And this." She has the wine menu, and she's pointing to a two thousand bottle of champagne. Of course, there are no prices. She must have some intuitive sense, though, because she went unerringly to the champagne at the bottom of the list.

I frown, pretend to be put out. Like I guessed, pissing me off amuses her. The ghost of a smile plays at the corner of her lips.

"Sir?"

"And the champagne," I say. "That'll be all."

Her face finally breaks into a smile, maybe the first real one I've seen, and damn, but she *glows*. Her cheeks chub, and her eyes squint, and her whole body kind of quivers. I can't tear my gaze away. A primal part of me wants to reach for her, drag her onto my lap, devour those upturned lips.

The smile fades too quickly, and I'm casting around in my head for something that'll bring it back. I'm lost, though. Not surprising. All the blood that normally flows to my brain is pooling in my dick.

We sit in silence until the sommelier brings the champagne. Plum's uptight and folded—arms and legs—when he pours a sip for her approval. She deliberately stares out the window. She must be unsure of what to do. I wave him off before he can begin his spiel.

As soon as he leaves, she grabs the bottle and tops her glass off. Then she drains it, daring me to say anything with those jaded, blue eyes.

"Is it good?"

But I don't really have to ask. The look of surprise on her face tells the story, as does her moan of delight that goes straight to my cock. It's aching now, chafing against my boxers. Shit, I haven't been this hard and ready since I was sixteen. Was she serious about the bathroom?

"Yup." She pours herself another—she's not letting me anywhere near the bottle—and then she gulps down another glass. This time, the bubbles must tickle her nose because she lets loose a series of little sneezes.

"Bless you."

She looks up and blinks, like she's forgotten I'm sitting across from her.

"Yeah. Thanks." She sets her glass down on the table with a look of regret.

"Don't hold back on my account."

She blushes. Not much. Not enough that anyone else would probably notice, but I'm becoming a Plum expert.

"Don't worry. I won't." She squirms in her seat, straightening her silverware for a minute. I reach into her space for the bottle, and then I refill her glass and top off my own.

"I prefer Dom Perignon myself." I don't know what I'm saying. I just want to put her at ease and prevent myself from leaping over the table and dragging her off to the cloakroom, bending her over, and slipping that skin tight dress up over her ass and plunging in until she comes all over my cock. I pull at my collar. It's so hot in here.

"You don't have to try to impress me, Clark Kent. I already like you for your money."

"Clark Kent?"

She shifts in her seat. I don't think she meant to say that. "You know. With the glasses and the hair and all. You look like Clark Kent."

"I have so many man-of-steel jokes. None of them are appropriate for polite company."

"Don't hold back on my account," she parrots, and that grin is back. I can't help but return it, and damn, we don't feel like strangers, that this is...whatever cheap, dirty thing it is. It feels like we have a secret between us.

I think she feels it, too. A shadow of worry crosses her face before she can hide it.

"What was that?" I reach across the table and dust my fingers down her cheek. She keeps very still, but I can hear her suck in a breath.

"I don't know what you're talking about." She puts her nose in the air. Tries to look stern and unaffected.

"You feel it, too."

"Whatever you need to tell yourself."

"Touching you...it's like touching a live wire."

"That's the worst pick up line I've ever heard."

"Yeah?"

"Yeah."

"The worst?"

"It's like the lyrics from some cheesy, off-brand 80's hair metal band."

"Like Winger?"

For a second, she forgets to look hard. "Yeah. Like Winger."

"So, I'm heading for a heartbreak?"

She groans, and there's that smile again, warm and scrunched up.

As the waiter arrives with our meal, I lean back, school my face again. I'm not used to this kind of banter. Small talk, business, tech, sports. I'm used to that. I usually let Eric take the lead and interject when expected. But this feels so different. Awkward and silly and intense at the same time.

The waiter sets down our plates with a flourish, hovering longer than I'd like. I don't want anyone near us. The idea of any man noticing Plum puts me on edge. I want to take her out of here, back to my place, but the expression on her face when she sees the squab is too priceless to cut short.

She gingerly pushes the plate to the far edge of the table with her fork. She takes more interest in the lobster, but what she's really eyeing is my steak.

I take my time cutting it into bites.

"You want to try it?" I hold out my fork.

"All right." She says it like she's doing me a favor. I pass her a bite. She takes it between her lips, and my cock pulses, more blood rushing between my legs, until I'm dizzy and straining with need.

And now she's moaning with her eyes closed, head tossed back. I take the fork back and spear her another bite. I'm going to feed her the rest of this, piece by piece, and I am going to cum in my pants.

"More," she says, and I give it to her, no teasing, no hesitation. She moans as she chews, and when her eyes blink open, I see her gaze is unfocused from the champagne. Those two glasses must be hitting her.

"Come home with me." It's out of my mouth before I realize it.

Her eyes shutter instantly. "Five hundred up front. One hundred an hour."

There's a painful twisting in my chest. I feel a deep unease settle in my gut, but I'm not going to take it back. I can't. "Hand me your purse."

She raises an eyebrow, but she passes the bag to me. It must weigh twenty pounds. I take my credit card out of my wallet while I rummage.

"You have two flashlights in here." I set them on the table.

"Wrong," she says between bites of steak. She's eating right off my plate, now. Something inside me loves it. Feeding her. Satisfying her. "I have one flashlight and one diversion safe."

"Diversion safe?"

"You know. Like a fake Pringles can or a fake rock where you can hide your cash."

"You hide cash in fake rocks?"

"I hide my house key in a fake rock."

"That's not safe." My heartbeat ratchets up at the idea of Plum in her little yellow house, asleep in her bed, vulnerable, the key outside in a fake fucking rock. "You at least have a deadbolt, don't you?"

"You really think I'm gonna discuss my locks with you, stalker? You already know about my diversion flashlight. A woman's gotta have some secrets."

Her eyes aren't so blank and cold anymore. Her lip is quirking up, and she's helping herself to my potatoes now.

I finally find her phone, and it already has the credit card reader attached. The screensaver is a picture of a bird. I hold it up.

"What kind of bird is this?"

"Black-capped chickadee."

"Did you take the picture?" It's striking. The bird is clinging to a thin branch that sags under the weight, the bird and the branch both in sharp relief against a cold, gray sky.

"Yeah."

"It's good. The composition is lovely."

My words clearly make Plum uncomfortable. She visibly shrinks in on herself, tucking her elbows closer to her sides and tightening her crossed legs. She doesn't acknowledge the compliment.

"Are you going to paw through all my shit?"

"Just your phone. What's the code?"

"I'm not telling you the code to my phone." She looks at me like I'm crazy, and I feel crazy. I'm driven by an impulse I've never felt before with a woman. The only thing I can compare it to is when I discover a start-up with truly disruptive IP. Or maybe all those years ago when I smelled the roast cooking in Thomas Gracy Wade's kitchen. I want it. I want her. And so I'm treading so damn carefully, I catch myself literally holding my breath.

Forcing myself to relax, and I take my phone out of my pocket, and I slide it to her across the table. "8-4-0-0."

Her jaw drops, but then she snatches up my phone, and she has the code entered before I can blink.

She's scrolling, her brows knit over intent blue eyes. "Where's your social media?"

"I don't have social media."

She glances up for a second, nose scrunched, and then she's scrolling again. "Why do you have so many pictures of buildings?"

"I like buildings."

She blinks at me.

"I like architecture." I gesture to the view of the skyline that Altimeter is known for. She hasn't really looked at it once.

"Why?" She's back in my phone, head bent, stopping only to blindly stab one of my potatoes and slip it between her slightly parted lips. My mouth waters.

What did she ask? Why do I like buildings? I'm not really sure. No one's ever asked me before. "I don't know. Why do you like birds?"

She looks up. "That's a stupid question."

"Humor me." Her eyes are locked on mine. Another wave of arousal floods my entire body, my skin prickles, my balls throb. It's like a hit of pure ecstasy. I don't know how much longer I can sit all the way over here, not touching her, talking about fucking birds.

She lifts her pinky finger. "They look pretty." She lifts her ring finger. "They sound pretty." She adds her middle finger. "They don't cost nothin' to watch."

"Maybe that's why I like architecture."

She scoffs. "You don't give a shit how much something costs." She looks back down at my phone, and I want to grab her by the chin, force her to meet my eyes again, give me another hit.

Then her lips spear down, and she pushes back in her chair. "Who's Renee?" She holds up my phone, open to old text messages.

She's pissed. My chest tightens. My little Plum isn't as unaffected as she acts. She's jealous. This—whatever this is —she's not immune.

"My ex-fiancée."

She squints at the phone, and she must notice the date stamp. Her frown eases. "Ex? What happened?"

"She fucked my stepbrother."

"Is that what this is? Revenge or something?" Plum drops the phone to the table and sighs. "I hate to break it to you, but I don't think your stepbrother's gonna give a shit if you wet your dick in the same stripper he did."

I can't stop the growl rising in my chest, so I clear my throat to cover the sound and take a long drink of water. My muscles tense. It makes no sense, but the idea of anyone else touching Plum, the memory of her with Eric, it flips a button and sends a fighting rage coursing through my veins.

I think she notices. She gnaws at her bottom lip, her eyes shifting.

"That's not what this is," I say.

"Then what is it?" Her jaw is tight. She's daring me.

I hold up her phone and my credit card. "Code."

She swallows. "1-2-2-1."

I swipe my card, and then I put her phone back in her purse as I raise my hand to call the waiter over.

"Check. Quickly, please."

Plum sits there in silence, shifting, finally gazing out the window. She doesn't even notice the skyline. Her gaze flits back and forth, her nose stuck in the air. It takes me a minute to realize she's checking out my reflection in the glass.

Her throat bobs. She's nervous. She doesn't know what set me off. Hell, I don't, either. All I know is I'm done fucking around.

"You're coming home with me."

She stiffens and puts her cute little nose in the air. "You askin' me or you tellin' me?"

"Did you like the champagne?"

She blinks. I've thrown her off, and I love it. "Sure." She hiccups, and her fingers fly to her lips. Good timing. "Yes."

"I have an 1864 Louis Dupuis Cristal Brut at home."

She lifts a slender shoulder and sniffs. "That should mean something to me?"

"It's an $18,000 bottle of champagne."

She snorts. "You bribing me to go home with you? I told you before. Motel only. And I gotta text Wall to meet us."

"Wall?"

"Big guy? Bike?"

Fuck no. She's not bringing anyone with her. She's mine.

"Come home with me, Plum. No Wall. You can drink champagne while I eat your pussy until you scream."

"How about you eat my pussy while I put up an old-ass bottle of wine for sale on the internet?"

"What will it take for you to come home with me, baby?" I don't want her in a hotel. I want her in my bed. My sheets.

She seems to think a minute, and then she stands.

"Come over here," she says. She doesn't have to ask me twice. I go to her. She holds up her phone. "Bend." I do. "Now smile."

She takes a selfie, and then she dashes off a text.

"Am I your wallpaper now?"

She rolls her eyes. "I just sent that pic to my lawyer. I don't turn up tomorrow in the exact same condition I'm in now, she's gonna take your ass to the cleaners, and I'm gonna fuckin' retire."

"You have a lawyer?"

"Club lawyer. Harper Ruth. She's the president's sister."

I know Harper Ruth. Socially, not personally. She's dating my cousin Des. I knew she worked with Steel Bones Construction, but I didn't realize she was that connected to the club. Or that a motorcycle club provided representation for the strippers on its payroll. That's all beside the point, though.

What's sitting uneasy with me is the idea that Plum's scared to be alone with me. I'm sure she's just exercising common sense, and I can't read any fear on her face, but if she were genuinely frightened, I bet I wouldn't know. That bothers me, too. Not knowing how she really feels.

"I'm not going to hurt you." I haven't moved from her side. We're both standing next to her chair, not touching, but close.

"Good."

That's not enough for me. I cup her cheek, raise her face so she's looking up at me. "I know you're tough as nails. I know you can take me."

She snorts. "Damn straight."

"But I'm never going to do anything you don't want me to."

She moves her gaze over my shoulder. Now she's taking in the view of the skyline. She doesn't believe me.

"I'm never going to hurt you or take anything from you." I don't know why I need her to believe me. Or at least fucking acknowledge what I'm saying. My temper flares. I move my hands to her shoulders. "Will you just say something?"

She's silent for a long minute. "I don't believe you," she finally says.

She's meeting my eyes now. Fiercely stubborn, all her fight showing.

"I know." It's enough for now. It's going to have to be. "Got your purse?"

She hauls it up to her shoulder, and I gesture for her to precede me. As we leave, I'm flooded with feelings, impulses I've never had before. I want to beat in the faces of the men who notice her, and I want to cover her with my jacket, tuck her into my side.

I want to erase everything she's done, but somehow, leave her exactly like she is.

She walks proud, chin up, and her curves and dips drive me crazy, stoking the ache in my cock, but damn, she's also so *little*. She takes two steps to every one of mine. I have to force myself to slow down so I don't overtake her. I want to do things to her, dirty, filthy things, and I *need* her to want it. Want me.

For the first time in my life, I want something that money can't buy, and it's costing me five hundred dollars up front, and one hundred dollars an hour.

The irony isn't lost on me.

4

JO-BETH

Superman really wants to fuck me. I should've gone for a thousand up front, five hundred an hour. This is the big city, the big time. I should've gone big with the ask. I mean, at the restaurant, there were no prices on the menu. Can you believe it? Some people are so rich, they order off a menu with no prices on it. I think it's bullshit when you go to get crab cakes and it says "market price." Like, I'm supposed to know what the market is for fucking crabs? That's asking a lot.

I realize my brain's being stupid. I can't focus on anything. I'm pretty sure I'm making a bad choice here, but...

I can't lie and say it's because of the money. The money is...well, it's a lot, but that's not why I'm getting into this guy's car. Why I text Wall and let him know where I'm going and not to expect me anytime soon. Why my body feels so strange.

Even though it's cool outside now that the sun's been set for a while, my body's flushed. It's kind of plump and achy like right before I get my period. I can't untangle all the sensations. My belly's too full with steak and booze. My head's woolly. My nipples are hard, and I'm too aware of my pussy. My panties are a little damp, and I'm keeping my steps tight 'cause for some reason, I need the pressure. To hold myself together.

I ain't never like this. Not even when I've got a buzz on.

Adam's car smells like him, a little like pine trees and a lot like leather. There's not a speck of dirt or dust, and it's so quiet, it irritates me. I try to turn on the radio, but there are too many buttons, so I give up.

Adam flashes me a cautious smile. "What do you want to listen to?"

"Anything."

He puts on classical music.

"Country," I say. It takes him a minute, but he finds Y108.

After a few songs, I calm down some. It's something familiar. I needed that. All of this is way too weird. I should be appreciating it. I never rode in a sports car this nice before, and I ain't likely to again, but I'm too aware of the man next to me.

He's too big for the car. His elbow is in my space every time he shifts. His head nearly doesn't clear the roof. It'd look stupid if the car wasn't so obviously expensive.

It doesn't take long to get where we're going. We drive along the river, all these fancy mansions and apartment buildings to our left, and we pull up in front of the ritziest looking place, made entirely of tinted glass and steel. A young guy in a red jacket opens my door.

This is the last building before you reach Riverfront Park. I went there once on a school trip. There's an art museum smack dab in the middle, housed in a castle. It's not a real castle. It's a mansion built by one of the steel barons back in the day. The dude must have had a real small dick to need to build himself a whole castle in fucking Pyle, Pennsylvania.

The guy in the red jacket says, "Mr. Wade." He neatly catches the car keys Adam throws. It's like a scene from a movie.

There's another man who opens the front door for us, and then another man behind a desk at the end of a huge foyer. There are real lemon trees in marble planters along the walls, and some kind of glass mobile hanging from the high ceiling.

Adam grabs my hand and leads me to an elevator separate from the rest. There's a man just standing along the wall, wearing the same red jacket. This guy has a walkie talkie and a gun in a holster, though.

That's three men guarding an empty foyer and some elevators. I wonder how much they get paid to stand there and say "Mr. Wade" and act like they don't see me. The guy behind the desk even gets to sit.

The man by the elevator swipes a card and presses the up button. I guess there are more demands to the job than I figured at first.

Adam still has my hand. It's so huge, it completely covers mine. It's warm, and this place is chilly. I don't mind it.

None of the men in red jackets seem fazed at "Mr. Wade" bringing a whore home. Probably I ain't special, and he does this all the time. There's no way they miss what I am. I saw the pictures of his dates on the internet—their hair, their clothes. I ain't nothin' in comparison. Shit, you can almost smell the plastic in my dress. Shows off my ass like nobody's business, though.

There's a ding, and the elevator doors close. Part of me braces, expecting Adam to pounce as soon as the eyes are off of us. I ain't blind. I noticed the hard-on he's been sporting this whole night.

He don't make a move, though. He keeps holding my hand, and he watches the floor numbers light up. This is a new elevator, but it's made to look like one of those old-fashioned ones. It's got thick red carpet, and there's real wood paneling.

We get off at the top. The tenth floor. There's a short hallway, framed painting of circles and squares hanging in it, with one door at the end. Adam leads me there. He opens the door, and my brain shorts again.

"Make yourself at home," he says. Yeah, right. There's no fucking way. The place is opposite of homey.

It's like the deck of a spaceship from a sci fi show. There are no walls. It's all window. Facing forward, you can see the river. The Riverwalk is lit by streetlamps, so you can make out the water even though there's no moon tonight. To the left, you can see the lights running along the drive to the art museum, and the art museum itself is lit bright as day.

I don't like it. It feels too exposed, too high. Like I should be prepared for a bird attack.

Adam drops my hand, takes out his wallet and keys, drops them in a bowl on a hall table, and heads off to the kitchen. This is what they call "open concept" on the home improvement shows. It's really, really open. And everything is only one color. No patterns. No prints.

The L-shaped sofa is brown leather. No pillows. No throws. There's a funnel thing that goes clear to the ceiling with glass at the base—a fireplace, I think—and it's black. There are more paintings of shapes on an interior wall, and they're all reddish orange.

Shit, every appliance in the kitchen is stainless steel, so

it's wall-to-wall gray. He doesn't have any magnets on his fridge or appliances on his counters. *Nothin'*.

That's where he is now. Rummaging in his fridge. Weird. How's he still hungry? We just had dinner. I did eat most of his steak, come to think of it, though.

I don't know what to do with myself in this space. There's nowhere to hang my purse. This has to be the most uncomfortable house I ever been in, and I bunked with Ma on some hippy's closed-in porch for a whole summer one time. There was no electric, and the compost was right next to the house.

"Is there a bathroom?" I ask. I don't really have to go. I just need a minute to get my bearings.

He's getting bowls from a cabinet. "Back that way. First door on the right." He waves to a doorway in the interior wall.

There's a hall, dimly lit with wall sconces, and I go exploring. One door is open. It's a bedroom, and the far wall is all window. I don't care if it's tinted, I'd never sleep a wink in a room like that, feelin' like someone was watching me.

I wander past the bathroom door. The end of the hall opens on another big room. I'm curious, and Adam's still clanging around in the kitchen, so I peek in. Holy shit. This must be his bedroom. The walls are glass on two sides, and there's a bed...must be a California King. It's made perfect, with a white cover and white pillows, perfectly placed. Does he have a maid? He's gotta have a maid.

There are circular stairs that lead up to a loft with a desk. It's only a slab of wood on what looks like steel sawhorses, but it's massive. And there's shelves and shelves of books up there. He's even got one of those ladders so he can reach the books up high. He's so tall, the ladder's got to be just for show, but still. Damn.

I creep along the wall to check out the doors along the right wall. They're both open, so all I have to do is reach in and flip the light. One is a closet filled with what must be a hundred suits. Two hundred. And twice as many pairs of shoes. The farthest door is a bathroom. He's got a jacuzzi tub and a shower. Separate. And the shower has two shower heads.

All this fancy shit, and nothing to look at but orange squares and triangles on the wall. I shake my head.

"You get lost?"

I nearly jump out of my skin. Adam's standing in the doorway. He fills it up, and he's backlit, so I can't make out his expression. My heart beats faster.

"Nope. Just casing the joint."

"You planning on robbing me?" His voice don't sound like he's joking. It's deep. Gravelly. Not what I'd describe as friendly. Shit. There's no way out of here except past him down the hallway.

I try to keep it light. "Nah. I ain't into paintings of orange circles."

He laughs. Now he don't sound mad. Maybe I'm not reading shit right. I am kind of out of my element.

"My interior designer assured me the paintings improved the flow of the rooms," he says.

"You paid someone to decorate this place? Well, fuck. How exactly do you get that job?"

"I think you have to know people."

"I heard that's the way of things." I casually saunter to the bed. Just in case he does think I was trying to steal his shit, I know a way to distract him. I sit, slowly crossing my legs, making sure to accidentally flash him my panties.

It's hard to make out, but I think he groans.

"Come to the kitchen with me." He holds out a hand.

Okay. I guess he's a slow mover. Wouldn't have figured that based on the wood he's been sporting all evening, but different strokes for different folks as my grandma used to say.

I go to him, take his hand, and like before, it feels...I don't know how to describe it. His hand's big, mine's little, and his grip is firm, but careful, too. Like he ain't pullin' me nowhere or showing me he's in charge. This ain't that I belong to him. It's more he wants me *with* him.

I don't know. That's a lot to get from the way a dude holds your hand, but he ain't my usual customer. It's perturbing, and my brain's running crazy.

He leads me back to the kitchen, and I set my purse on the island since there's nowhere else. There's a bottle of wine sitting in an ice bucket on the counter. I guess that's the infamous $18,000 bottle. There are also two glass bowls, the kind on pedestals, and two long spoons sitting on a counter. Looks like chocolate pudding.

"Would you like a glass?" He's got a corkscrew in his hand. My heart about leaps into my throat. This is just like the time Danielle had her keys inches from the paint job on Bucky's Wide Glide. I mean, fuck Bucky, he's an asshole, but you don't mess up something that expensive unless you got no other options.

"No!" I raise my hands like *put the corkscrew down easy.* Adam's lips twitch.

"I forgot. You want to sell it on the internet."

Shit, I wasn't serious. When he says it like that, it don't sound right. I get kind of uncomfortable—more uncomfortable—and Adam finally drops it. Puts the corkscrew in a drawer, and picks up the two spoons.

"Do you like mousse?"

"I like chocolate pudding."

"Yeah?"

"Sure."

Now that the champagne is safe, I'm noticing Adam more. He's really intent on me. He's staring at my lips, and every so often, his gaze drags down my front, lingering on my tits. It makes me squirm. I swear I don't know what he's waitin' for. He paid.

"Come here." He picks up the bowls and spoons and walks me over to a huge leather armchair. It's the kind with the bronze nail heads, like something Sherlock Holmes would sit in.

"Sit," he orders.

I perch on the edge. The leather is buttery soft but cold against my palms.

He sinks to his knees in front of me.

"What are you doing?" Why do I sound freaked out? I clear my throat.

"Dessert," he says. Okay. I guess he's into eating a woman out. Fine by me. Less work.

He sets one bowl and spoon next to him on the floor, and he hands me the other.

"Your feet hurt?" They do, but I don't have a chance to say so before he's sliding my heels off and putting them to the side. I wiggle my toes and sigh. I can't help it. It's the best minute of the day, ain't it, when the bra and shoes come off?

He digs his fingers into my arches, and rubs his thumbs over the red lines left by my shoes. Even my feet are small compared to his hands. This is a big man kneeling at my feet.

Somewhere along the way he lost his jacket and tie. He's unbuttoned the top of his crisp, white shirt. Chest hair peeks out, black like the hair on his head. I'm not big into chest hair, but it looks smooth. I kind of want to pet it.

"Sit back."

It's a really deep chair. I scoot back, and now the leather is cold on the back of my thighs, and my legs are sticking straight out. I draw my knees to my chest, gripping the mousse in one hand and the spoon in another. My dress has creeped up so it's bunched mid-hip. I must look a sight.

Adam sits back, too, legs bent, super casual, watching me closely. He takes a bite of his mousse.

"Aren't you going to try it? I didn't make it. My stepfather's chef did."

"Your stepfather's chef makes you food?"

He grins. "Whenever she makes something she knows I like, she sends me some. She's always appreciated my appetite."

Huh. Must be nice.

"Try it."

I take a bite, and I can't tear my eyes away from his. He follows the spoon. He's so focused on it, that I can't help myself. I take my time, lick the back and then the front, real slow.

It's like I cranked a knob all the way. The hungry look on his face intensifies by a hundred, his blue eyes casting off sparks behind his glasses, his throat bobbing. There's a weird fluttering in my belly. Why isn't he grabbing me?

"Do that again," he growls. It's an order, not a request.

I do. I watch him while I swallow. He doesn't seem to know what to look at: my mouth, my tits, my legs. He keeps coming back to my eyes, like he's checking for something. My skin heats, tingles dancing along my exposed skin.

I don't hate this.

I experiment. I scoop up a big, heaping bite, and I shove it all into my mouth, slipping the spoon out with a pop.

He moans. It's almost a growl.

"Please do that again." He's leaning forward now, bracing his forearms on his knees.

I take an even bigger spoonful, and for the first time, I notice the taste. It's creamy. Sweet and light and foamy. Not as dense as pudding.

"Do you like it?"

I blink. Huh. I'd closed my eyes. Hadn't even realized it.

"Yeah. It's good."

He smiles, really pleased.

"Is this your kink? You like to watch women eat?"

His smile disappears real quick. Shit. I don't know why I said that. I ain't an amateur. I got no business shaming the client.

This one irritates me, though. He ain't even touching me, but he's bossing me all the same. And my stupid body seems to be forgetting we're on the clock.

"I like to watch *you* eat."

"Why?"

He lifts a shoulder. "I like to watch you walk. I like to watch your face when you see something that blows your mind. I like to watch you when you try to read me."

I don't know what to say. "You ain't blown my mind yet, my friend." I clutch my knees tighter.

"I will. When you let me."

"You don't gotta ask. You paid." I kick myself as soon as the words are out of my mouth. You sell the fantasy; you don't fucking poke holes in it.

I glance at him out of the corner of my eye, but he don't seem fazed.

"Plum?"

"Yeah."

"I'm going to take my shirt off."

"Suit yourself." Fuck! I am off my game. "I'd like that," I

try again, using my sultry voice. It comes out as a squeak, though. I shove another spoonful of mousse in my mouth just to cover up my awkwardness.

He's already hung his shirt onto the arm of the sofa. He's back to sitting knees bent, but he's leaning back on his hands so I can see everything. And the man is *jacked*. A six-pack. That V dipping down into the waistband of his really fancy black pants. A sprinkling of black hair trailing down his belly, disappearing at his belt buckle.

He's got the popped veins in his arms like Wall, and Wall goes to one of those gyms where you pay them to throw tractor tires.

I suck my gut in, even though he can't see it the way I'm sitting.

"Are you full?" he asks. His voice has an edge to it.

Oh. He must want me to keep going with the mousse. I take another bite, and really swirl my tongue around the spoon. It is good. The chocolate isn't bitter at all. I hate dark chocolate. Doesn't seem right to me, chocolate that ain't sweet.

Adam's breath is getting quicker. All those muscles are standing out in stark relief. He's tense, ready.

"What do you want me to do, baby?" Maybe I can move this along. Part of me wants to get this over. The mousse is good, and the chair's comfortable now that I've warmed it to body temperature, but I feel strange. Exposed. And these flashes of heat keep rolling through me. Sweat has broken out behind my knees.

"I want you to relax."

"Not possible." Again. It's out of my mouth before I think better of it.

"I know what you mean."

He does?

"I'm so scared you'll change your mind."

"I—" What is he talking about?

"I'm afraid you're going to hide even further behind that mask, or maybe figure out you can just go and take everything I want with you."

"You paid." I ain't gonna rip off the dude with the penthouse that overlooks Riverfront Park.

"Not for what I want."

"What do you want?"

"For you to want this. As much as I do."

I shove a spoonful of mousse in my mouth just to buy time. I don't know what to say. My brain is screaming *bullshit*, but my belly's all flipping and fizzing, in a good way, I think. And between my legs, I'm swollen. My panties are soaking. If my tits weren't hidden behind my knees, he'd see my nipples are hard.

I don't like this. I don't know what to do with this.

"Do you feel it, too?" His eyes search mine. The words form in my head. *Yeah, baby. I feel it, too. I want you so bad it hurts. Make me feel better, baby. Please.*

I've got the words, but they don't come out of my mouth.

Instead, I say, "I don't understand what's going on." My voice is breathy. Almost a whine.

"Do you trust me?"

I blink. Shake my head, left to right. No. I don't. I'd be a fool to.

He turns his head, stares at something out the windows. His jaw is tight. It looks like he's thinking.

Then his eyes are back on me, burning blue, the glare on his glasses doing nothing to hide the intensity.

"*Will* you trust me?"

Do you? *Will* you? My brain can't tease out much of a

difference, but it's fuzzy from the sugar, and my body's going haywire, which is a hell of a distraction.

Adam's eyes on me...it's causin' a reaction. The heat and prickles have been joined by an aching and a need to move. This dress is too tight across my tits, and my legs want to stretch. I want to sprawl, and I want him to watch.

I'm never like this. I like sex as much as the next girl, and I ain't never made work unpleasant that didn't need to be. Still. Most of the time I need to rev myself up. Picture a movie star and touch myself. Most dude's like to watch, so it's a win-win.

In this chair, though, I can't think of anyone else but the man lounging in front of me. I'm above him, but it don't feel as if he's beneath me. Not at all. It's like I've got a tamed lion at my feet.

"Trust me to touch you." His body's coiled even tighter. I guess I was takin' a long time to answer.

It should be nothing to say yes. That's what I'm here for. It don't come easy, though. Matter of fact, I can't bring myself to say nothin', so I look back at him and will him to read my mind.

In a split second, he's on me, his hands cradling my face, and he takes my mouth. It ain't a kiss; it's everything. He's somehow wedged his broad body between my knees, and I'm open to him, but I can't even process that because he's eating at my mouth, hungry and demanding, and even though my brain can't keep up, my tongue knows what to do, twining with his, lapping at him, just as eager. More eager.

Then he's pressing his forehead to mine, brushing light kisses across my cheeks, and he's gasping for air, shaking in my arms. Or am I the one who's shaking?

He nibbles at my lips, a soft tug, and then he's braced

above me, looking down, his glasses crooked, a dumb smile on his face.

I wriggle to sit upright. Somehow, I've slid down and now my neck's bent almost ninety degrees with my shoulders stuck between the cushion and the back of the chair. My heart's galloping, and his weight lifts—I think to let me up—but instead, he slides down between my legs, and he's slipping off my panties.

"You come with me," he says, and he grabs my hips and pulls me down to the floor after him. He's kneeling, sitting back on his heels, and I'm straddling him, my dress bunched at my waist, no panties—they're dangling from his hand—and my pussy lips are spread open. He's hard against my clit, but he's still wearin' his pants, so there's also rough fabric rasping against my folds and his belt buckle nipping at my belly, but that ain't stoppin' me.

I grind down, 'cause it feels so crazy good, and he's urging me on, arm wrapped around my back, the other hand touching me everywhere, tangling in my hair, then stroking my cheek, then cupping my ass. He's making these noises, greedy noises, and I pull my head back 'cause I want to see, but he don't like that.

He hauls me closer, kisses me deeper, and I feel a dampness on my cheek. I can smell my pussy. He's got my panties, and he's pressing them to my cheek.

"You're wet for me, baby. You're soaking my pants."

It's like he's trying to persuade me that I'm into this. Or himself. He reaches between us and strokes his fingers through my folds, gathering cream, and then he drops the panties to the floor and paints my lips with his fingers. "You want this."

His lips brush mine when he talks, and his face is so

close, our noses nestle. I'm wrapped around him, and he's all over me, and it feels so...tangled.

"It don't matter if I do or I don't." Oh, fuck. What is wrong with my mouth tonight?

He stiffens in my arms, but he doesn't let go, not an inch. "What you want matters to me. More than anything else."

This is crazy talk, but damn, they're such *pretty* words. I know it's a fantasy, but it makes me high, this lion of a man with his glasses all askew, holding me, exploring me, treating me like I got the keys to the kingdom.

All I have to do to make this real is pretend that it is.

I know better—every minute of my life has taught me better—but I dare anyone to be this tempted and say no.

I don't even have to say anything. Instead, I lean back, and I kiss him, devour him like he tried to devour me, but he ain't as hungry as I am. He ain't gone as long as I have without.

I plunge my fingers in his hair, wrap myself so tight around him that when he stands, he don't even need to hold me up.

He stumbles for the bedroom, but I can't wait. He's bracing me now with his forearm under my ass, so I can rock my pussy against his hard cock—I can feel the heat through his pants, and I've soaked the fabric near to dripping. He's biting my neck, and I've got my fingernails in his back.

When he drops me to the bed, he comes with me, tearing at my dress, and then when he only manages to pull half of it above my right tit, he goes to work on his belt, which he can't seem to manage either.

I'm laughing, and then he's laughing, and I undo his belt for him, and he shucks his pants while I wriggle out of my dress and bra.

And then I see his cock, and I ain't laughing no more. Clark Kent is packing *steel*. I ain't lyin' when I say I never saw a bigger one. He's palming it, but other than that, he's payin' it no mind. I can't tear my eyes away. You don't see this every day. Good thing I'm really wet. Maybe I should use some lube anyway.

Adam seems totally oblivious to the fact he's built like a goddamn beast. He's feasting his eyes on my bare tits, every so often flicking his gaze to my face. Checking.

What's he checking for?

The moment from the living room has kind of broken, and we're back to wary, in our separate corners, so to speak. I'm thinkin' again, and that ain't good.

Adam goes to his night stand, pulls out a strip of condoms.

I guess we're gettin' down to business.

He props a knee on the side of the bed, rips the packet with his teeth, and rolls it on. Then he straddles my hips, and his rubber covered cock rests between my pussy lips. I spread my knees as far as they'll go and tilt my hips as much as I can. This ain't gonna go in easy the first time.

I'm as ready as I can be.

He tickles his fingers down my belly. My hands instinctively fly down to push him away, and I can't help it. I squeal.

"What was that for?"

He's grinning down at me, pleased as punch.

"I like the way you squeal. You sound like someone stepped on a squeaky toy."

"Are you makin' fun of me?"

"I would never make fun of the way you squeal like a very small piglet at the state fair."

"I'll make you squeal like a piglet." I dig my fingers into

his ribs—I have to do a half-crunch to do it—but his face
don't crack.

"I'm not ticklish. I have no human weaknesses." And he
puts his hands on his hips like Superman and lifts his chin.
He's ridiculous. He's swole as hell, model perfect, naked
except for a condom and completely goofy.

I draw my legs back and rest the bottoms of my feet on
his hard chest.

He raises an eyebrow.

I slide one foot up until it hits his face and then I keep
going, smooshing his face to the side.

"Revenge?" he mumbles.

"Cry uncle."

"Cry uncle." He says it like he's remembering something.
"You mean surrender."

"Yeah. Surrender."

And just like that, the mood changes again. He bends
over me, stroking up my arms until he meets my hands,
twining his fingers in mine, resting them on the pillow
above my head.

"I surrender." He takes my mouth again, and then dips
down to kiss my neck, my shoulder, his hands leaving mine
to heft a breast, stroke my ribs, cup my ass and then lift my
thigh to bare my pussy. His hot tongue swipes across my
nipple the instant he begins to wedge his huge cock
inside me.

This is happening. I adjust my hips, try to open up. He's
panting. Sweating.

He suckles my tit, and there's a draw between his mouth
and my clit, a pulsing that has me squirming not to accom-
modate him, but to draw him deeper. I want more.

I raise my hips, and he groans.

"Please, baby. Let me do this my way. I don't want to hurt you."

He's only an inch or two inside me, and it's not enough. I whine. Sneak my hand between us to find my clit. He slips deeper. A few more inches. He's not all the way in yet, but I'm stretched to the limit. I run my fingers where he's splitting me apart, and I'm taut. Burning. I want to see.

I shove his shoulder, and he raises himself on his arms, no fuss. I miss his hot mouth on my nipple, but the cold air feels good, too. I do a crunch and stare down. He follows my gaze.

"You're going to take all of me, baby, aren't you?" It's bossy, commanding, but I don't miss the note of desperation. He needs this.

"Yes. Yes." He grabs my hips and thrusts in to the hilt. I shriek. He's filling me, stretching me, covering me totally, and he's so big, and then he's moving, stroking, and he's kissing me again, everywhere, lapping at my nipples, running his hands over every inch of me.

I sob, a low, continuous moan. It feels so good. He's hitting a spot that makes me jerk and buck, seeking more.

"Harder." Now I'm bossy, but he does what I say, wrapping his strong arms around me, holding me to him as he jackhammers me into the mattress. I can't move. I can't reach my clit, but I don't have to. His pelvic bone is hitting me just right, and I come so quick I hardly knew it was coming.

My pussy clenches on his cock, and I shake, hot and cold all at once, and it takes me ten times as long as the orgasm to generate a useful thought.

He's still going.

He's got his eyes closed, and he's fucking me, so intent and serious. He's slowed down, and he's braced himself up on his arms again. He's sweating, and I realize, so am I. We're slip-sliding together, and every so often he kisses my lips or sucks my throbbing nipples.

Inside my belly, there's a coiling, a bearing down. It feels so good. I want more. I want to tell him that but my mouth is dry and my brain won't make words.

He eases his hands behind my knees and pushes them toward my chest, and the angle changes, and now he's nailing that spot, the coil furling tighter and tighter, hotter and hotter, and I need him to do something. I don't know what, but I have to cum. I have to, or I'll die. I'm gasping for air, and he keeps going, murmuring in my ear...I don't even know what.

"Adam," I gasp.

"Yeah, baby. Say my name." He kisses me, dusts kisses across my forehead, drops one on my nose.

"Adam." It's a demand. Almost a sob.

"Okay, baby." Then he flicks my clit with his thumb and drives into me. My breath flies out, and I explode, pulsing around his cock, waves of pure bliss rolling from deep inside me all down my arms and legs. I scream. It's heaven, and I'm spasming, and I don't want it to ever end.

He shouts, his back arching. I can't feel his cum because of the condom, but I can feel him pulse against my walls.

He drags in a deep breath, and he kisses my chest, right between my tits. I'm sweaty. He's *really* sweaty.

"Are you okay?" He pushes the hair from my face. I nod. "Stay here."

He slides out, and I immediately feel empty and sore. I draw my knees together and pull them to my belly. He strokes my thigh. "I'll be right back."

He goes to the bathroom, and I hear a flush. Then he heads for the kitchen.

Is that my cue to leave? Shit.

My body is totally boneless. I don't feel capable of speech. And fuck, Wall probably went home. I'm going to have to catch a ride share. I'm going to have to wait for a ride share in that lobby with three men in red coats pretending they don't know I just got my brains fucked out.

My hair has got to be out of control. Maybe Adam won't mind if I take a shower before I go.

There's a hollow ache in my chest. I don't want to go.

I force myself to sit up. I just need a minute to pull myself together. I'm fine.

And then Adam's back, pressing a cold glass into my hand. "Drink."

Ice water. I down most of it in three swallows. I was so fucking thirsty.

"Spread these." Adam's pushing my knees apart, and then he slips an ice-cold wash cloth between my legs and applies pressure.

I bat at his wrist. It's too cold.

"No. Let me. You're gonna be sore."

He's so much bigger and stronger, there's no use in pushing him away. I let him ice pack my pussy, and I don't fuss when he maneuvers me so we're spooning. I'm facing the windows, so I can see all the city lights, and above the orange halo, a handful of stars, way high up. It should be beautiful. It makes me cold.

I roll so that I'm facing Adam. This is better. I'm surrounded by his scent and heat. He strokes the small of my back, and then he lifts my leg and slings it over his hip. The wash cloth falls loose, and I feel him harden against my chilled skin.

He runs him thumb over my lower lip. "Are you still thirsty?"

I nod. I feel like I ran a marathon.

"Here." He holds up the glass. I sip, and it dribbles down my chin and onto his hand. He laps the drops, and then finds my mouth. His kisses are calmer now, but somehow, no less hungry. Only slower.

His hot, hard cock nudges me. There's no condom now. I can feel his pre cum drip on my clit. Suddenly, even though I'm exhausted and raw, I'm ready again. Every inch of my body is swollen or aching—my tits, my pussy lips, my hip sockets, for some reason my biceps—but I also *crave* more.

"Baby," he's whispering in my ear while his big hands stoke the fire. "I'm clean. Let me cum inside you."

He prods at my tender opening, and aren't I God's own idiot, 'cause for a minute, staring at his beautiful face, his square jaw and his hooded, punch-drunk eyes, I actually consider it.

I want to feel all that silky hardness bare, dragging along my channel. I want him to cum fast because he can't help himself, he wants me so much. I want his cum dripping from my pussy, making me messy, ruining the sheets.

I want this to be real, but it's not. I tense, jerk away from his touch, suddenly mad that he asked. I'm pissed that he made me remember that none of this is real.

"Oh, baby. Hush. Never mind." He grabs a condom, rolls it on, and again, he doesn't slide right inside me. He spends a long, long time smoothing his hands over my shoulders and back, kissing my fingertips, swooping down to lick the divot of my ankle, then nibbling up the inside of my leg to lave at my pussy, twirling his tongue around my clit until I beg him to fuck me.

He doesn't make me ask twice. He strokes slow and steady until I explode all over his cock, trembling and making no sense when I try to ask for more water, or mercy, or both.

The sun's coming up when I finally pass out, wrapped in his arms, every inch of me tender, his lips against my temple and his hand pressed against my heart.

～

I WAKE UP ALONE, naked, and freezing my ass off. Someone's in the kitchen. I think it's Adam for a second, until I hear a man's snore from behind the desk in his loft.

I sit up, and my body freakin' *creaks*. If I crane my neck, I can make out Adam sleeping in his desk chair. He's got a pair of sweat pants on, and his head's tilted straight back. He looks so uncomfortable.

He must've been really uncool with the paid help falling asleep in his bed. Heavy was like that. Once he was done, he didn't want to be rude, but he also wanted you gone.

I rub my chest. The aches are everywhere. I need an aspirin from my purse, and I need to get the hell out of here. It's so bright; I have no idea how anyone can sleep, let alone upright in a chair.

Maybe he went to check his work email and passed out. That was some high intensity fucking. Even for as fit as he is, that had to have been a workout.

Maybe I should go wake him up. Let him know someone's in his kitchen. He could be gettin' burgled.

I sigh and swing my legs over the side of the bed, kicking out the kinks. Who am I kidding? I ain't never gone to a client's place before, and I definitely ain't never been so stupid as to fall asleep, but I know the drill. He gets off; I get gone. If he wanted me to stay, he'd have said.

He said enough touchy-feely shit last night. If he'd

wanted me to, he could have said, "Stay. Be here when I wake up?"

My stomach rolls. Shit. Am I hung over? Not from two glasses of wine.

What am I even thinking about? I got stuff to do. I work tonight, and I got a load of laundry in the dryer and the washer.

And *fuck*. I also got no ride back to Petty's Mill. Wall said he'd be at his buddy's gym late, but after closing time, I was on my own.

I clip on my bra and yank my dress over my head. I can feel that my hair's a hot mess. It's kind of tugging too much on one side.

My shoes and panties are in the other room. I glance up at Adam, consider waking him. But what would I say? Thanks?

I'm frozen there a minute, staring at the bed. My eyeliner smudged his white pillow cases, and the sheets reek of sex. Even so, the bedding is blinding white, and even rumpled, it's clear they're expensive. They ripple; they don't wrinkle. I've probably ruined them.

Goosebumps break out all over my arms and thighs. It's so damn cold in here. I tug down my white Lycra dress. I need to go.

I walk out, and I couldn't be stealthy if I cared to be. I'm almost limping. My pussy's sore, my hamstrings are tight and aching, and with each step, some joint cracks.

I make my way to the main room, and Adam ain't gettin' robbed. I was right. He does have a maid.

She's a short, older woman in stretchy black pants and a maroon collared shirt that reads *Riverfront Home Services*. She's glaring at my shoes next to the easy chair, her nose turned up like she smells shit, and my white lace panties are pinched in her fingertips.

"Thanks," I chirp and grab 'em. I step into them at the same time I slide on a heel. The maid folds her arms and watches me.

"Mr. Wade is home?" She's checking to make sure I ain't up to no good. I could be pissed, but she's gotta know my type, so I don't take offense. I ain't never been a thief. Shoplifted a bit back in the day, but who didn't? Still, if I were her, I'd give me the hairy eyeball, too.

"In the back. Sleeping."

She blinks. This seems to surprise her.

"He's not usually here this late." She gnaws on her cheek. Nervous.

"That right?" I'm going for my purse, and wouldn't you know it, the ice bucket's still on the counter. With the $18,000 bottle in it.

I wonder if champagne's like beer where it skunks if it gets cold then warm again. I grab the bottle. The maid narrows her eyes.

"I need cab fare. How am I expected to get home?" It's a diversionary tactic, but it's also the truth. It's probably a hundred-fifty bucks to get a driver to take me back to Petty's Mill. Wall's holding my cash, and I don't have any available credit. Not after the doormat.

"I—You could—" The maid's casting around the apartment, looking for some solution to my problem. For some reason, the maid's averse to waking up her boss.

"I'm just gonna take some cash from his wallet." I fish it out of the bowl on the hall table. "Just tell him that Plum took—" I take out three bills. Shit. "Sixty bucks."

How does this guy live here with a maid and he's only

got three twenties to his name? My day just got way more difficult.

The maid's really giving me the stink eye now. I can't be bothered to care. My stomach has started to hurt. This does feel like a hangover, except the thought of bacon and eggs makes me want to puke.

"Right. You have a good one." I kind of raise the $18,000 bottle to her, and then I tuck it in my purse on my way out the door. She ain't gonna say nothing about the champagne now. She's worrying over the sixty bucks in her head.

This is a real coup, but I don't feel right.

Maybe I'm getting sick? I wrap my arms around my middle while I wait for the elevator. I wish I'd brought a jacket. This dress feels too tight which is weird 'cause usually Lycra stretches.

My eyes prickle.

There's a noise behind me, and I whirl around, my heart leaping and then crashing. It's only the maid turning the deadbolt. The elevator beeps, and the doors slide open. I step on. Check my phone. I'm at six percent 'cause my dumb ass didn't plug it in.

When I get to the lobby, I walk real slow. There's a woman behind the desk now in a red jacket. She glances up, and then she looks through me. The doorman smirks at me too wide and way too long.

There's no ding of the elevator. No running footsteps.

Of course. This ain't a movie. I'm being stupid. This is real life. I am what I am, and what I am now is in need of coffee, wifi, and a ride home, in that order.

I walk a few blocks until I find a coffee shop, and I treat myself to a mocha while I charge my phone. Sixty bucks ain't gettin' me all the way back to Petty's Mill, so I may as well dip into my funds for caffeine.

The farther I get from that penthouse, the clearer I can think. I call Cue, and after he bitches me out on principle, he says hold tight, and he'll call me back in ten. He rings back in five. A prospect from Smoke and Steel, the MC's support club up in Shady Gap, is gonna come get me and drop me at their clubhouse. Grinder's there helpin' to plan a poker run, so he'll ride me home once he's done. There goes the whole day, and I don't see me getting a shower before work, but part of me don't mind.

I can still smell Adam on my skin. The spices in his cologne. His sweat. It's faint. Almost gone. But as I gingerly perch my ass on the wooden chair of the coffee shop, muscles aching, chilled despite picking a seat by a vent, the scent's the only thing that doesn't suck.

And the $18,000 bottle of champagne zipped in my purse.

This prospect better not ride like no maniac. He breaks my bottle, I'm gonna break his fucking nose.

5

ADAM

S he robbed me.

I wake up from the deepest sleep I've had in months—maybe years—and Plum's gone, along with the money from my wallet and the bottle of Louis Dupuis. At least my maid had the good manners to leave a note.

Mr. Wade—

Your guest took money from your wallet for cab fare. She said it was okay.

I should have been at work hours ago. I need to take a shower, wash the sex off, get my head on straight, but I can't stop pacing from room to room. I'm so fucking pissed, I want to put my fist through a wall.

I want to go after her, drag her back here and fuck her again until she won't even think about sneaking off. Lock her up. Redden her ass until she cries, until she's sorry she walked away like that was nothing.

Even I realize these urges are insane. Last night was nothing. A lapse in judgement.

Except for the missing money and champagne, there's

hardly evidence she was here. The dishes are washed and put away. There's only the rumpled bedding that smells like her, musky with a faint trace of fruity bodywash. The smell reminds me of her skin, how she felt against me, soft at first and then sticky later, her plump tits and her firm, jiggly ass.

My dick throbs, and that pisses me off, that she's not here to ride me, take my cock as she screams and mewls until her eyes roll back in her head. I wasn't imagining that. You can't fake that kind of response.

I collapse on the bed, raise the sheets to my nose and take my cock in hand. I'm hard, so hard thinking about how her tight pussy pulsed, gripping me, how her blue eyes blurred after she came, how she clung to me, molded to me so perfectly.

She loved it. I know she did. I felt her walls squeezing my cock, and afterwards, she tucked her chin in the crook of my neck and pasted herself to me. She must have loved it.

Fuck. My balls ache, but I can't get in the head space to rub one out.

She couldn't have loved it that much. She bailed as soon as she could, helping herself to one hell of a generous tip. My first time with a whore, at least she wasn't a cheap one.

My fists clench, and tension tightens my shoulders.

I know she hated my place. She didn't even pretend to like it. Literally everyone who visits can't get over the skyline. It's the best view in Pyle. That's how the management company markets the penthouse. She turned up her nose at everything. Except me. She couldn't get enough of me.

Yeah. Right.

I know she's a whore. It's her job to spin a fantasy. She does her job; she goes home. I get it, but I can't shake this irritation. Makes me think crazy shit. She was supposed to be here when I woke up. I didn't say the night was over.

I should call the cops. Have her arrested. Make her beg me with those plump lips to drop the charges.

Fuck that. I should hunt her down, spank that bouncy, heart-shaped ass until it's bright red, and she knows who she belongs to. That she doesn't get to leave until I say so. She's mine.

I've never been so gone, so out of my mind, as I was last night. Nothing has ever felt so good. Not just the sex. Everything. How could she not feel the same thing? How could I be such a cliché asshole?

I can't think about this anymore. I've got a dozen voice-mails on my phone, ten times as many emails, and the acquisition of ArrowXchange isn't going to settle itself because I decided to insert my head up my ass. Fuck.

I get in the shower, twist the temperature to scalding, and when I've scrubbed her off my skin, I turn the knob to cold. It takes a while, but my dick eventually goes soft. I dress, and every time a memory pops up—her tongue licking the dessert spoon clean, her whimpering and shoving her tit deeper in my mouth as I suckled her—I force it away while my adrenaline amps up another notch.

It was fun. A good time. I can do it again if I want. Five hundred down. A hundred an hour.

Why'd she go before I woke up? She could have been raking it in while I slept.

Shit, I know where she lives. I should take that key from her fake rock, climb into her bed, tie her down and tease her pussy 'til she cries.

Now I'm even more pissed off 'cause I've got all these thoughts that aren't me. I'm not the kind of man who gets distracted by women. Certainly not by ones paid hourly.

I check my messages, and while it's mostly my assistant reminding me to check various emails, there's also Eric bitching about having to sit in on a research and development meeting for me. And then there's a voicemail from my mother. She wants to meet for a late lunch.

I don't need this today.

After listening to the last message—Eric warning me I better be in the office by noon so he doesn't have to cover the meeting with the ArrowXchange risk management guys —I change my mind about lunch with Mom. Pissing Eric off will at least cheer me up a little bit.

Besides, if I put Mrs. Thomas Wade off, she'll start calling, and it's harder to get her off the phone than to wrap up a lunch. I text her assistant to set it up, and then I spend some time going through my inbox. My eyes keep straying to the bed, and each time, a surge of irritation cramps my muscles. I don't know who I'm so angry with.

Plum?

Myself?

I'm in a truly foul mood when I arrive for lunch at La Fortuna. Mom is a creature of habit. She likes three restaurants downtown, and she can't be persuaded that any others could possibly do a decent Caesar salad. At least La Fortuna is close to work.

I dread what'll be waiting for me back at the office. I never take time off. I'll definitely need to stay late tonight. Not seeing my bed or the easy chair, not constantly springing a hard on at the memories and then instantly fighting off rage all over again...yeah, working late doesn't sound so bad. I don't know why I can't muster up my usual dedication.

Mom's already seated when I arrive. She stands and offers me her cheek to kiss. She's the perfect society matron at this point. The young woman who schlepped our dirty clothes to the coin laundry on Gilson Avenue is long gone.

"Adam." She arranges herself in her chair, back straight. Imperious. "You look perturbed."

"Mom." I sit, ignoring the observation. I know she won't pry. She never does. "You look lovely as always."

"I ordered for you. I figured you'd want to get back to work as soon as possible."

"The filet?"

"Of course."

I'm a creature of habit, too.

Mom chatters as we wait for our drinks. She's in the early stages of planning the Hearts and Diamonds Gala. She's thinking about going with a different flower vendor this year. The dog had to go to the vet. He's fine. Marjorie dropped chemistry but she doesn't need it to graduate. She's fine.

I nod occasionally, and I wait for it. These lunches are always about the same thing.

"And how is Eric?" she finally asks after her salad arrives.

"Eric's fine."

"Thomas says he's been going out with clients. A lot of late nights."

"That's Eric's job."

Mom sniffs. "Thomas says at the board meeting last week, Eric stumbled in late. Disheveled. Maybe you should shuffle around responsibilities. I'm sure there are VPs who could wine and dine the clients."

"Eric's good at his job." And he sure as shit wouldn't stop doing it because I told him to.

"Thomas is concerned."

"Did he speak to Eric?" That might explain why Eric's

been pushing the limits lately. He's never responded well to Thomas riding his ass.

"Your stepfather spoke to me. And I'm speaking to you."

"I'm not Eric's keeper."

"Aren't you?" Mom narrows her eyes.

I see we're getting down to brass tacks. She exhales, taking a moment to slowly swirl her spoon in her glass of iced tea. "Thomas has been talking about taking a more active role in the company again. Lending his expertise to mergers and acquisitions. Spending some quality time with his sons, wooing the clients. *Getting his hands dirty.*"

It's clear that Mom's quoting Thomas Wade, word-for-word. Her bored, haughty veneer has been replaced with a look I remember from back in the day. Calculating. Cunning. A tinge desperate.

She lowers her voice. "I'm sure you want him back on executive row almost as much as I want him at hotel bars and strip clubs."

Goddamn. This day keeps getting better.

"I owe Thomas everything. It's his company." This is my standard line, and as far as it goes, it's true. My stepfather inherited the company from his father, and it was a respectable institution in Pyle. A big fish in a small pond.

After I saved the company when it hit the skids during the last recession, Thomas retired from daily operations, and Eric and I have built Wade-Allyn into one of Fortune's twenty-five most important private companies. We have offices all over the world, from Wall Street to LaSalle, The City to Marunouchi.

We're still headquartered in Pyle because Thomas is chairman of the board, and he has strong ideas about honoring your roots.

Whenever we're in New York, Eric and I spend some

time checking out real estate, daydreaming about a spinoff venture free from the old economy bullshit Wade-Allyn has written into its DNA. For now, though, this is Thomas Wade's company. He owns a 51% stake. And he's our father.

I do owe him everything. And even though he doesn't fully understand where we're taking the company, he's given us the keys to the kingdom. More or less.

The reminder adds fuel to my sour mood. Eric and I can do whatever we want, but not until Thomas votes aye. He never votes nay, but the ayes take longer and longer as time goes on. ArrowXchange will probably be overtaken by its competition before we get the deal past the board. It's so much of a given that I have Eric schmoozing the competition's C.E.O. on his off time.

I'm so lost in my thoughts that I don't notice Mom's face, not until she speaks. Her voice is low, but she's spitting out the words.

"You owe *me* everything. Do you think this is a joke? That I'd bring this up at all if it wasn't serious? Maura Dorsett's husband just left her for a twenty-five-year-old *hostess*. Maura's quit the Hearts and Diamonds planning committee. She's going to St. Bart's for the winter so she doesn't have to watch some gold digger sit at her table at the Christmas Auction."

"Thomas isn't going to leave you for a hostess." He likes his home life easy.

"I did not get us this far to lose it all." She's serious. She's twisting her wedding ring.

"You're not going to lose it all."

"Of course, I wouldn't lose it all. Only my dignity. My position."

"You're worrying about something that's never going to happen."

Mom thins her lips. "I did not put in all these *years* of work to stand by as Thomas Wade becomes a regular at Faro under the guise of bringing his errant son to heel."

"You've heard of Faro's?" It *is* Pyle's premiere gentleman's club, but it's the kind of place that doesn't advertise. Not like the billboards for The White Van all along Route 29. My neck heats. I ignore it.

And then my classy mother, the woman who will only cross her legs at the ankles and nags Marjorie about wearing pajamas in front of the staff, says, "I know *everything*. I know Eric fucks whores and snorts coke. And he fucked Renee, and I've said it before, but he did you a favor. She was unbalanced. I know your father gets a massage with a happy ending from the Ginger Spa every Tuesday which is why I am going to wait until tomorrow evening when he's nice and relaxed to ask for a fifty thousand dollar increase to the Hearts and Diamonds budget."

Holy hell. Mom is never this frank. I don't know how to respond. "If the fifty thousand is for the new flower vendor, you're getting ripped off."

"It's not, and you know I don't get ripped off. And I don't leave things to chance. Get Eric in line. Call your father. Take him golfing. Invite him along on one of your trips to Palo Alto or Cupertino or wherever. Bore him into giving up this idea about *getting his hands dirty*."

"You're overreacting."

"You're forgetting," she bites out. "I pulled us up from *nothing*."

"Was it really so dramatic?"

"When you have a child, you won't ask me that anymore." It's almost a throwaway line.

We both know that neither Marjorie nor I was the reason my mother sunk her claws in Thomas Wade. I almost ignore the comment, but my brain throws up an image, a mashup of the past and the present.

Plum, round belly making her look like Humpty Dumpty, sitting on a concrete stoop in front of a rundown tenement on Gilson Avenue.

It socks me in the gut. I want it, Plum belonging to me in some irrevocable and undeniable way, needing me, and the idea terrifies me, and it seems right and impossible. It's dizzying.

I need to wrap this up, calm my ass down, and get back to work. Besides, I'm arguing out of habit more than anything else. I'm not going to turn my mother down. We've been partners in crime too long.

"Eric is Eric. He's not on some downward spiral. I'll get him to shower and shave before board meetings. It'll be fine."

"It better be."

"You worry too much."

"Not worrying is a luxury I can't afford." My mother raises her hand, beckoning the waiter.

It's while we're waiting for the check that it pops out of my mouth. I wasn't even thinking about it. Not really. But it's been living in the back of my head for weeks now. A drawer in my mind that keeps sliding open.

The email from *your father ryan Adam morrison.*

"I think my father has been trying to contact me."

Mom has her phone out, scrolling. "Well, call him back."

"Not Thomas. Ryan Morrison. He emailed me."

She freezes, and then very slowly, she looks up, carefully placing her phone on the table. I swear, she looks like the T-Rex in *Jurassic Park*. Cold-eyed. Predatorial.

"Did you talk to him?"

"I didn't reply."

"What did he say?"

"Something about reading my name in the paper. He asked me if I wanted to get a beer."

"And you didn't reply."

"No."

I know he was a junkie who left us broke, that we were nearly homeless because he took the car, which caused my mother to lose her job. I know he was the reason my mother's family cut her off. That and some vague memories of a man in a baseball cap and a gap-toothed grin is all I've got. And a dozen or so emails that read more or less the same.

"That man is trash." Mom sniffs.

"So I gather."

"He wants something from you. Money."

"Possibly."

"*Definitely.*"

"I don't plan on responding."

She pauses, purses her lips. It looks like she's going to say something, and then she thinks better of it. "I'm surprised he's on email."

"You are?"

She gets a faraway look in her eye. "He was always very clever with numbers. Like you are. He was awful with reading and writing, though. Dyslexic, probably."

It's the first thing besides his crimes against us that she's ever shared. The disclosure lets me dare pry. I never have before.

"Why *did* you give it all up for him?"

Mom's raises her eyebrows, but to my surprise, she answers. "You don't remember Grandma and Grandpa Anders very well, do you?"

I don't. Once Mom married Thomas Wade and gave birth to Marjorie, the Anders took her calls again, but by that point, I was at Mountchassen. I saw my grandparents a few times on holidays, but Eric and I would bail as soon as we scarfed down the meal.

"They weren't very...demonstrative. I was an only child. Summers were boring. Ryan Morrison worked for the company renovating the stables. So cliché." Mom's face darkens under her thick, flawless makeup. "He had a motorcycle. I was young and stupid. I had no idea what really mattered in life."

"You fell in love." It's hard to imagine Mom swept off her feet. I've never known her not to know exactly what she's doing.

"I miscalculated." For a second, there's a flash of pain in my mother's cold blue eyes. Then, she gives herself a shake and dabs the corner of her mouth with her napkin. "Anyway, you should steer clear. I can't imagine what good could come from Ryan Morrison."

Neither can I, but still. There's a part of me that wants to know, and it's unsettling, because it isn't the desire of the man with the corner office on the top floor. It's the desperate longing of a cold, hungry boy throwing punches in a vacant lot.

I shake it off, but it's another layer, another distraction eating at me.

I pay the bill, escort Mom to her waiting car, and then I walk to the Wade-Allyn building. There's a chill in the air, and a brisk breeze coming off the river. The morning's hot anger finally ebbs into something detached and hard, leaving a stale, bitter taste in my mouth.

Lunch with my mother put some things in perspective.

Plum did me a favor. An eighteen-thousand-dollar bottle of wine and some petty cash is, after all, much cheaper than a lifetime of symphony boxes and tables at the Christmas

Auction. And wondering—hell, probably *knowing* that the woman beside you in bed sees you as a meal ticket, not a man.

It was a memorable night. She scratched an itch I didn't know I had, and then she stole from me and reminded me what she was.

I learned a lesson I shouldn't have needed. I can wallow in the humiliation, or I can do what I always do.

I nod to doorman as he greets me. "Mr. Wade."

My head is clear again. Well, clear enough. It's time to get back to work.

AT SIX O'CLOCK, I throw in the towel before I end up throwing my monitor. I'm struggling to make easy calls, and I keep asking questions and not listening to the answers. My team's getting frustrated. I disconnect from the video conference with instructions that they go home.

I pour myself a bourbon and stare at my screen.

I should be working on ArrowXchange.

I decided last night was a one-off. I dodged a bullet.

Fuck it.

I navigate to the background check service we use, and I pull up Plum's report. There's more missing than there. She has no social media. No high school diploma. There's a short criminal record that I scroll past without reading. I know, or I can guess, and I don't want to know.

There are two addresses listed for her, the Steel Bones MC clubhouse, and then her house. Her mother, though. There were pages of addresses, sometimes long gaps between domiciles. A half dozen addresses were Gilson Avenue.

The mother, Lorna, died from complications related to hepatitis when Plum was fifteen. No father on the birth certificate. No grandparents, other relatives. The mother had a rap sheet ten times as long as Plum's. Soliciting, assault, possession, panhandling, breaking and entering.

I read it all, but there's nothing to explain why this woman is under my skin.

We have less than nothing in common.

I'm restless, though, and I've got this awful day-after-Christmas feeling, as if everything good is over. I'm almost grateful when Eric interrupts, bounding into my office without knocking per usual.

"Brother! Where the fuck were you earlier?" He sprawls into the chair across from my desk, scrolling and tapping, grinning at his phone.

"Lunch with Mom." I minimize the report on Plum and spin to face him.

"That sucks." He finishes whatever he's posting and looks up. "What's she worried about now?"

I sip my bourbon, consider my words. "Apparently, Thomas has been talking about taking a more active role in the company again."

"The fuck you say." Eric's eyes flash. "What's he gonna do? He doesn't even know the business model anymore."

I have to play this carefully. "Mom thinks he wants to spend time with you."

"Bullshit. Don't act like you don't know the man. He thinks we're too far off the chain. He needs to tug the leash. Show us who's boss."

"He's majority shareholder. He is the boss." That's the difference between Eric and me. Eric always assumed that what belongs to Thomas Wade belongs to him, and that his hard work is his own. I've always understood how much I owe my stepfather, that I work for him.

It doesn't sit easy, never has, but it's a trade I made a long time ago with my eyes wide open. I play my part, and I get access to resources most people can only ever dream of.

Poor Eric doesn't realize it's a contractual relationship. He still thinks it's a family.

"That's why we need to stop fucking around. Cut ties."

"And lose the IP."

"And create our *own* IP. Don't you want to do something without having to put Dad's name on it?" Eric's leaning forward, earnest, his cheeks flushed from whatever's in the flask or baggie he keeps in his jacket pocket.

He's oblivious to the irony. I do this, and I'll be putting a different Wade's name on my ideas. I can't pull the VC money without Eric's connections. He's the public face of Wade-Allyn, and no one would risk the kind of startup cash we need on one-half of the dynamic duo.

"Thomas gave me his name. It seems like a fair trade."

"Man, that's the past." Eric's standing now, pacing. "And you know this isn't some heart-warming story of fatherly love. He *owns* you. How are you cool with that, man?"

My grip on my bourbon tightens. "Yeah? Who owns you, Eric?"

"At least I *want* to leave. Make something that's *ours*." I can see his passion, and once upon a time, I felt it, too.

Lately, though, it's all felt hollow. Trading one set of strings for another. I love the work, but the work comes with the bullshit, and at the end of the day, the work keeps me alive, nothing more. To be honest, nothing in my life has made me feel as alive as this last week, and how fucked up is that?

"I don't know." I wave a hand. "The grass isn't always greener."

Eric's face flushes bright red. "Are you backing out?"

I don't know. I can't seem to care about any of this. "We've been talking about this for years. Since when do you have a timeline?"

"Is this about Renee?"

I sigh, and set my glass down with a clink. "It's not about Renee."

"It was one time, man. I was drunk. If I could take it back, I would." Eric's wearing the "sincere" expression that I've seen him use a hundred times, to get out of detentions at Mountchassen, speeding tickets, fights with girlfriends, every time we were called on the carpet by Thomas Wade.

I should feel betrayed—I should have felt betrayed when I found out that he fucked my fiancée—but I don't. I'm mildly embarrassed for him and disgusted by myself.

How is it that I'm stumbling through this life, so much so that I was totally prepared to marry a woman I didn't actually give a shit about, and the most alive I've felt in years is with a stripper named Plum?

"It's not about Renee. I swear. It's—I have some shit going on right now. Can we focus on the present?"

"If Dad gets involved again in the day-to-day, I'm going to lose it."

"Agreed." Thomas would rather gouge his eyes out than sit through a project management meeting, but shit runs downhill. He puts the staff on edge, and all of a sudden, I've got software engineers worried about dress codes instead of coding.

"So, what do we do?"

"Mom seems to think it's about spending time with you. It's probably about feeling useful. Can't you invite him on some golf outings? Take him to the convention in San Diego?"

"Fuck." Eric sinks into the chair, listless. "Can't you?"

I don't bother answering. I'm tech. He's sales and marketing. "And maybe pop some breath mints. Mom said he's worried about your drinking."

"I'm going to need a shit ton of breath mints if you expect me to buddy up with the old man."

"Feel free to expense them."

As if I reminded him, Eric pulls out his flask and takes a swig. "So, what's this shit that you've got going on?"

A picture of Plum, hugging her arms close as she glares at me on the sidewalk in front of Altimeter, flashes in my mind. I cast around for something else, anything else.

"I've been getting emails from a man who says he's my father."

"No shit? You write back?"

"No."

"What does he want?"

I shrug. "He says he wants to ask me something."

"Money?"

"Mom seems to think so."

"You should write him back. Find out." Eric leans forward, his elbows on his knees. "That would drive me nuts. Not knowing. How many emails has he sent?"

"I don't know. A handful."

"Don't you want to know?"

"Know what?"

"Shit. Where he's been all these years? Why he left?"

"There's a good reason that a man leaves his kid?"

A shadow falls across Eric's face, and I wince. "I don't know. My mother...you know I can't remember her smiling once? She cried a lot. Locked in the bathroom. The way I see it, she saw her chance, and she took it. The older I get...the less I fault her."

We sit in silence a moment. Thomas Wade is a powerful man, a dedicated family man. But you know where you stand with him, and it's in direct proportion to how well you conform to that ideal he holds himself to. I used to admire his principle. Now, it exhausts me.

"You should reach out. Find out what he wants. Get your head straight. If we see our chance, we need to be ready." Eric slaps my shoulder.

I nod.

"I can't do it without you, brother."

His words are a weight, another tether tying me to this desk, this building, this town. It chafes, and after he leaves, and I'm left staring at a DMV photo of Jo-Beth Connolly's scowling face, I can't take it anymore.

I pull up Ryan Morrison's email, shoot him a reply, and I wait for some relief, some break in this unbearable tension. Nothing. I'm drawn back to the photo, and a manic energy drives me to stand, throw on my jacket, and head down to the garage.

As soon as I'm on the road, my heart starts thudding in my chest, and adrenaline roars down my veins.

Fuck Wade-Allyn.

Fuck what everyone wants and what I'm supposed to do.

And fuck that little thief who's crawled into my brain like it's nothing, who's lit me up so I can't help but see I've been a zombie staggering from place to place for too damn long.

She doesn't get to walk away like it was nothing. She doesn't get to decide. I do.

And I'm going to own that ass of hers, take what I want until I can think again and the ground is even again under my feet. If it takes a couple thousand, so be it. If money can't buy love, it sure as shit can buy Jo-Beth Connolly. The thought tears up my guts, and I use it to push away all the shit until I'm clear-headed and roaring down the highway, high on speed and what counts in my life as freedom.

6

JO-BETH

The good news is it's been over twenty-four hours, and if Adam was gonna have me arrested, he'd probably have done it by now. It's not like I been hiding. I worked last night, and I'm at work now.

I searched for the champagne on the internet, and he wasn't shitting me. $18,000. So now I've got it on a shelf in my basement, hidden behind some paint cans. I figure that's close to a wine cellar. I don't know what to do with it. I can't sell it. That's grand theft. I got this vague idea that I could tell the cops I thought he meant to give it to me. That might hold up if I look really sorry and give the bottle back.

The bad news is my brain's gone stupid. I keep thinking about the other night. Not about the fucking. Well, not only about the fucking. I think about dumb shit. Like how Adam kept his glasses on during sex. He was sleeping in them, too, up in his desk chair. He's gonna break 'em doing that.

And when he was on his knees, on the floor at my feet. The way he looked up at me. Like he was lucky or something.

I hate that man's apartment, though. He had absolutely

nothing to make it feel like a home. The only thing on his bedside table was a lamp. No lotion, no catalogs, no charger. Nothin'. Who's got absolutely nothing on their bedside table? Not even a tissue box?

Except for the loft with all the books, it felt like a hotel room. Maybe he don't really live there. Maybe it's his place to crash and take hookers.

I frown. Danielle catches my eye from across the bar and flashes me a fake grin, drawing a big smiley face with her fingers. I was bitching about my tips being off earlier, and she said it's 'cause I look like I'm sucking lemons. More so than usual.

She's probably right. I'm cranky today. It's been pissing me off when customers cop a feel. Usually, it's water off a duck's back. I need to get my head in the game. Eight hours last night and three hours tonight, and I ain't been able to scrounge up one lap dance. Given, it's been slow, but I can't pay my bills on tips from the floor show.

It don't help that I'm fixated on my phone. I keep excusing myself to the bathroom so I can check for messages. I'm an idiot. I know Adam ain't gonna text me. After the stunt I pulled, I'm truly surprised he didn't call the cops. Him letting it go is the best-case scenario.

And what am I thinking? He's gonna be all *wyd*? Still, I keep checking. And every time there's no message, my stomach sinks. Which is stupid.

You can't miss someone you only met three times.

And it's dangerously foolish to convince yourself that you've caught feelings for a customer. That's how you end up giving it away for free and losing your job along with your mind.

"If you gonna flat out wear your bitch face, I'm gonna send you home," Cue rasps in my ear and slaps my ass. I startle and wobble dangerously on my heels. Shit. He snuck up on me.

I follow Danielle's suggestion and plaster on my fakest smile. "Better, boss?"

"How's that even scarier than your other face?"

"Look like I'm up to somethin'?"

"Looks like you're *on* something. Like meth." Cue cackles at his own joke. I grind my teeth and smile wider. "Go work the booths. And quit pretending to take a piss so you can check your phone. You keep it up, I'm gonna dock your pay."

"Hey. Maybe I got female problems. Did you think about that?"

"*I* got female problems. Go make me some money." Before I can answer, he's on his way toward his office, his phone in his hand, scrolling. Jackass.

I sigh and hobble off to the booths. I'm wearin' my pink rhinestone leg straps tonight in an attempt to boost my tips —it usually works—but that means I have to wear my pink rhinestone stilettos, and they're unstable as fuck. I got to put all my weight on the balls of my feet and tiptoe around like I've got Barbie doll feet.

I'm frowning again by the time I reach the first booth. It's a group of business men. For some reason, their suits make me sad. They're talking shop. One of them waves me off with a "Maybe later."

The next booth is more my type. Bikers. Not Steel Bones, just recreational riders, but they're friendly. I'm chatting, perched in some guy's lap, finally getting somewhere, when someone grabs my upper arm and hauls me to my feet.

I yank and spin, ready to pop the motherfucker, but as soon as I see the black hair and glasses, all the wind goes out of my sails.

He's here.

Suddenly, I feel naked. I realize that's ridiculous. Still, I fold my arms across my tits. "What?"

"Hey. He botherin' you?" The biker I was with half-rises from his seat. I wave him off.

"He's a friend."

"A friend?" Adam arches an eyebrow. Yeah. Point taken. He sure as shit don't look friendly. He's wired, and his blue eyes are hard. Mean. His black suit's rumpled like he slept in it.

"Listen—" My gaze skitters around the room, searching for what, I don't know. Something to say besides, "You're here."

Adam tilts his head like *I'm waiting.*

Shit. I got nothing. Besides, my mouth is bone dry. My heart's fluttering. I know it's probably the fear of getting busted, but there's this lifting, bubbling sensation in my belly, too. Like happiness. Don't make sense.

I'll just stand here. He's gonna tell me what he wants eventually.

"You owe me." His voice is almost a growl, and it's got a nasty edge. Oh.

Taking the bottle was stupid. Stupid, stupid, stupid.

"I'm sorry." I try to look contrite, but I've got no control over my face. I'm gawking at him, eating him up with my eyes. I didn't think I'd see him again. I gobble up every detail. The dark smudges under his eyes. His poorly tucked shirt.

His jaw is tight, and his shoulders are squared in fighting stance.

"You know what?" he says. "I think this is now a pre-paid gift card kind of deal."

Huh? I vaguely remember saying that to him when he came back the first time. So, this is about the bottle, and he's gonna be a predictable ass. The happy feeling sort of fizzles flat.

"I'll give it back. I ain't sold it yet."

He seems surprised for a second, and then he shakes his head. "I want a lap dance."

"Um. Okay."

He steps forward, closing the space between us. He bends close to my ear. "And then you're going to suck my dick. And ride my cock. And then I'm going to fuck your ass."

My heart trips, and I forget to keep my weight on my toes. I lurch. He reaches out and steadies me. I shake his hand off. It's a reflex, but he reads it like I'm being a bitch. He snarls. Actually snarls.

He's so pissed, it's coming off him in waves. From the tautness of the muscles in his neck and his jaw, he's barely containing himself. He wants to wring my neck. My blood starts racing in my veins, and I'm flushing from what he said, but I ain't new at this game. I don't really know him. I need to be careful.

"Now," he growls.

"Let me get Austin."

"No. No Austin. No credit card. No cash. You owe me. Let's go."

He takes me by the elbow and hustles me to the back. His fingers dig into my skin. Now that he's close, I can smell bourbon. He's had a glass or two. How long was he here before he came over?

Cue and Forty are talkin' to some customers by the stage. They clock what's happening, and they don't seem concerned.

Austin's at the door. There's a prospect bar backing

tonight, and Nickel's somewhere around. If I holler, they'll come running.

Maybe I should call for Cue. But then maybe Adam will tell Cue that I ripped him off. Cue don't tolerate his girls running game on the customers, and he'd see it that way. As I'm dithering, Adam's ushering me to the way back.

When we're almost there, Danielle catches my eye. She raises her eyebrows. I glance up at Adam. I know when a man is dangerously angry. I was raised up around junkies, criminals, and bikers. People who don't give a fuck. Adam don't seem dangerous to me. Honestly, the closer I look, the more miserable he seems. Tormented.

Is this his pride talking?

What if he's holding on to me so tight 'cause he missed me, too? I can't believe it, but the thought warms my belly and gives me courage.

"Stop, would you. It hurts." I yank my arm forward.

He looks kind of stupefied, and he lets me go.

I give Danielle a little shake of the head. Shit. I hope I don't live to regret this.

"Which one?" Adam's face is hard again when we reach the back, all business.

Nickel's propped on a stool, bird-dogging. "You good?" he grunts. He don't even seem to recognize Adam from the other night, or he don't care. Nickel's got his own shit going on.

Adam don't know that, so he tenses even more.

"I'm fine," I say. "Here." I hustle Adam into a corner room, a different one from the last time. This one has fake velvet benches built into the wall. There's a small disco ball hanging from the ceiling.

Adam takes his jacket off, unbuttons his collar, and sits back, all cocky business man, leg crossed at the knee, arm draped along the back of the bench. His phone dangles from his hand.

"What's going on?" I stand in front of him, arms folded.

"This is a strip club. You're a stripper," he says. "Dance."

His face is brewing up a storm. Come to think of it, I ain't never seen a man this intense who wasn't about to blow. Shivers race down my spine. Maybe I am being stupid here. Seeing what I want to see. Strike that. I'm definitely being stupid.

"Are you waiting for something?" He cocks his head. Asshole.

"Listen. I get that you're mad." I aim for a reasonable, calming tone of voice, but God didn't make me that way. I sound snotty. I own that.

"Yeah? You ever get robbed while you slept?"

I suck in a deep breath. That stung, more than it should, but it ain't untrue. My stomach drops, but I don't let it show. I need to smooth this over. I don't need to be bringing trouble to work.

And if I'm being honest, his shitty attitude is getting to me. Makes me itchy. Unsteady. Kind of like when I do something that pisses Heavy or Cue off. Like I'm mad, but I also don't like that I'm makin' him mad, either.

"I told you I can get the bottle. I don't even really know why I took it." That's the truth. It felt like I was squaring something up, getting even somehow, but that don't really make sense. I just did it.

"I'm not interested in why you took it. You made yourself clear. You're the pro. I'm the customer. This is business. So here we are. You're on the clock, Plum. I'm paid up. Dance."

Why is he so intent on rubbing my face in this shit? He damn well knows where he met me.

"That's right. So, *customer*, you gonna tell me what you're lookin' for?"

"I trust you know your job."

Oh, this guy. He's got a mean streak a mile wide. And I thought the stepbrother was the piece of work. I'm swiftly caring less and less that I pissed this guy off.

"Why don't you tell me what you like?" I smile real fake.

"What I like?" he laughs. It's an ugly sound. "Show me your tits."

I exhale slowly. Oh, yeah. Adam Wade's doing me a real favor right now. I almost got my head twisted, but ain't no way I'm pressed over *this* guy.

I get that his ego took a hit when I snatched his fancy wine, and he's gotta come hard like every other man on the planet when a woman gets one over on him. But he thinks he can come in here and push me around, like I'm breakable or something? Like he even knows the words that would faze me?

Man thinks way too much of himself.

I untie my top, let it drop. Then I shimmy my shoulders and cock a hip. My nipples instantly harden. That's why Cue keeps it cold. And to keep the sweat stank down. I cup my tits and lift them up. "You like this?"

"You like showing me?" His voice drops lower.

"I love it, baby." I'm gonna start thinking about my Amazon wish list in about thirty seconds. "What do you want now? You want me to shake these titties for you?"

"I want you to stop talking and dance."

What is this guy's problem? He wants a pound of flesh? I told him I'd give him his fucking bottle back.

"What's the issue?" he asks when I don't start dancing right that instant. "You're a working girl, right? Work."

He's so different tonight. A spoiled little shit. I'd never

have gone anywhere with this asshole. Well, I'd never have gone home with him. I should walk out the door now. Go get that bottle and crack it over his entitled fucking head.

"All right. If you're not going to dance, why don't you get on your knees and come suck my cock." He reaches for his buckle.

It's like a string that was holding me together snaps. Fuck. This.

I don't really know what I'm saying until I say it.

"I'm never going to do anything you don't want me to," I drop my voice, mimic his bullshit from the other night. "Remember that?"

At first, he doesn't respond, but I can tell when he remembers. His expression changes. Some of that smug asshole gets wiped off his face.

"I'm never going to hurt you. I'm never gonna take anything from you." I spit his words back at him. All his bullshit lines. I can hardly believe I remember. I don't usually pay attention to that kind of crap.

His face kind of goes wary. He blinks like he's waking up.

"You want me to dance? Sure. Whatever, asshole. Just as long as we're both clear that I'm a *pro*, and you're a lying sack of shit with issues for goddamn *miles*."

I'm righteously pissed, so I don't wait to find a beat. I squat, stick out my ass, and I'm so riled up, I forget to keep my weight on my toes. As soon as I step on my right foot, the heel cracks, and my whole foot bends sideways at the ankle. An agonizing pain shoots up my leg, and I scream as I pitch forward, slamming onto my knees.

"Whoa!" Adam leaps to his feet. He almost catches me, but not quite, and I crumble like a rag doll. He follows me down to the floor.

Oh fuck, it hurts. I'm pushing him away while I struggle to sit on my ass, get my foot out from under me.

He's in the fucking way. "Move!" I slap at him.

We're all tangled up, and then we're not. We're both breathing heavy, staring at each other. His glasses are askew.

"Are you okay?" he asks.

"No. My ankle's all fucked up!"

He kneels, examining my leg. "What happened?"

"I twisted it, dumbass."

"It hurts?"

"Of course, it hurts."

He kind of rolls his eyes at me, and then he maneuvers me to sitting against the bench, his hands roaming up and down my leg. All the while, he makes this low-throated hushing sound like I'm a wounded animal. The pain's receding until only the twisted part throbs.

He props my foot in his lap, easing off my heels. He presses gently on my ankle until I whimper.

"Ouch! Quit it!" He stops applying pressure instantly, and he strokes my calf, shaking his head.

His gaze searches mine, and he seems...changed. He's not mad anymore, at least that's something. He's cradling my foot, and then his gaze searches the room. I don't know what he thinks he'll find. There's nothing in here except velvet benches and a funky moth ball odor.

"Where is the first aid kit?"

"I dunno. In the locker room, maybe. Help me up. I need an ice pack."

"It's swelling. Fuck, Plum. Sit still. It might be broken. Hold on." He's got his phone, and he's scrolling. He won't drop my foot, and it'd hurt too bad to yank it away, so I leave it in his lap.

"How about I give you a rain check on the lap dance and

revenge fuck or whatever. How's next week for you?" I shove at him with my good foot, but he won't budge.

"Stop." He glares at me and sets down the phone with a sigh of exasperation. Guess he couldn't find what he was looking for.

"Why don't you just go?"

"Plum." His jaw tightens. "I'm sorry."

"You didn't do anything. I was the one that wore the shoes." Hold on. He *was* being a complete jerk. "I take that back. You should be sorry. Asshole."

He doesn't answer, just keeps on stroking my calf, stopping well clear of my ankle. It's a weird feeling. The pain's too much for it to feel good, but his touch is doing something to my stomach all the same.

After a few moments of silence, he glances up from under his thick, black lashes, his blue eyes burning. "I don't know what I'm doing," he says, clear and direct and raw.

"I can tell."

"I've never done anything like this before. I've never been this way. I *am* sorry."

The way he sounds—like a police officer testifying in court. The apology doesn't take anything away from him. He's still in charge. Arrogant.

But he isn't mad anymore. And he's here. With me. I thought I'd never see him again, but he's right here, stroking my calf, saying sorry. Which he *should*.

I got my own shit going on at the moment, but I can tell. He's never done anything like this before. This man is off-kilter. And I made him that way. Knowing that...it's a heady feeling.

He's kneeling, my foot in his lap, and he's still staring me down. I stare back, and a warm, fizzing sensation swirls in my belly again, somehow dialing down the volume on the screaming ache in my ankle.

He's here, and I thought I'd never see him again, and when I believed that, I was *sad*. I have no fucking business being sad over a man. I know better. He's not for me. Maybe someday I'll shack up with one of the brothers or a plumber or something, but this guy's got a Wikipedia entry, for fuck's sake.

He can't be for real, and I cannot possibly be this stupid.

And good lord, when those warm fizzes disappear, my ankle *hurts*! I burst into tears, and he loses it.

"No. Stop. Don't cry. It's going to be fine." There's an edge of panic to his voice. "What's going on? Does something else hurt?"

"You were a *dick*." I'm sniffling. "Why are you so mad about that bottle? I told you I'd give it back."

He exhales and leans back. "Oh, Plum. I'm not mad about the bottle. I'm mad that I've lost my goddamn mind. And I was pissed that you left."

"Then you should have asked me to stay."

"I—" He catches himself. "Yes. I should have asked you to stay."

"I can't read minds." Now, I'm being a brat. It makes my ankle feel a little better.

"If you could read my mind, you'd run."

I half-snort, half-sniffle. "No, I wouldn't. Not on this ankle."

That gets a ghost of a chuckle from Adam. Lightens the mood at least. I don't think either of us are comfortable talking about this type of shit. I'm more than ready when he changes the subject.

"Listen, you need to see someone. I have a concierge doctor. I thought I had his number, but I don't. I can get it from the office. He'll meet us at my place. Do you think you can stand the drive back to Pyle?"

I wipe my cheeks with the back of my hand. I got distracted and the tears stopped. "I ain't going to your place."

"Your ankle needs to be seen."

"I ain't driving all the way to Pyle, and I ain't going to your place. I can go to the urgent care."

We're arguing about that when the beaded curtain implodes, and Cue and Forty barrel into the room. Day late and a dollar short. I guess they finally noticed the camera feed.

"Plum. What happened?" Forty looms above us, and Adam stiffens. His face goes stone cold, and the "sorry, baby" softness disappears. He's the man from that first night again, in charge, born ready to throw down. He rises to his feet.

"She'll be fine."

"She don't look fine," Cue observes.

"She twisted her ankle. I'm taking her to be seen."

"At the urgent care," I add.

"He hurt you?" Forty searches my face.

"Just my feelings." It's a joke. But it's not.

"I've got this. I'll take care of her." Adam's chest to chest with Forty now, and you can see just how fit and tall Adam is for a banker or computer guy or whatever it is he does.

He towers over Cue, and I bet he benches as much as Forty, and Forty is ex-military. The glasses and the fancy suit make him look like a pussy, but he ain't intimidated, and he ain't backing down, even though Forty's flexing.

"She's property of Steel Bones," Forty says. I warm a little, like I always do when one of the brothers says it. I earned that protection, and it's worth a lot to a woman like me.

Adam, though. He don't have the same reaction. His lip snarls, and his eyes flash. He does manage to keep his voice even. "She needs medical attention. I'm taking her to see a doctor."

They size each other up, silent, each waiting for the other to blink. I glance around to see if there's a piece of furniture I can use to haul my ass up. Fuckin' male bullshit.

Forty sniffs. Adam's left eye twitches. Then it's over.

"Return her in the same condition, or we'll fucking kill you, shove you into the trunk of that Maserati, and drive it into the Luckahannock." Forty waits a second for emphasis, and then he tromps back out the door.

"Call me when you know what's wrong," Cue says to me. "I'll clock you out." A true helper, that one.

"Can you get her clothes? And a bag of ice?" Adam asks Cue who's still loitering by the door.

"I'll send one of the girls," Cue lingers, waiting for God knows.

"She's fine," Adam says, real serious.

Then they exchange a look, and I can't quite peg it, but Cue nods and finally leaves.

When we're alone again, Adam bends over, scoops me up, and sets me on the bench. He shrugs off his jacket and wraps it around my shoulders.

A few minutes later, Danielle shows up with my duffle bag and the ice. Adam's been spending the time gently removing my leg straps, easing down the garter belts and then working them off without jostling my foot. It's harder than you'd think it'd be.

My ankle's definitely sprained, at the very least. It's already bruising, and when I go to pull my yoga pants on, I can't put any pressure on the foot. Not that Adam lets me. He holds me up with one muscular arm around my waist.

Oh, fuck. How long am I gonna be out of work? I cannot afford this.

I wriggle out of Adam's arms, leaning against the bench to pull on my purple tank top and hoodie. It's his damn fault. He had to go and make me mad.

And now that I'm thinking about my paycheck, I'm mad all over again.

"You ready?" Adam's got my bag slung over his shoulder. I reach for it.

"I changed my mind. Call Cue. He can take me."

Adam takes a step back, and I can't go after him. I'm too wary of putting weight on my ankle.

"I'm going to take care of you," he says.

"Heard that before." I hold my hand out, palm up. "Gimme my bag." He doesn't.

"I'm going to make this right."

I snort. "Nah. You're gonna say a bunch of sweet shit, then get weird and mean, and frankly, I got troubles now. I don't have the time for the drama."

I aim for matter of fact, but I can't keep the hint of hurt from my voice. He probably won't notice, though. I'm pretty good at hiding what I really feel. You have to be in my line of work.

Adam exhales, a touch aggravated, and takes a step toward the door. I ease myself down to sit on the bench.

He waits. I put my nose in the air.

He glares. I turn my head.

His shoulders fall, and he comes back over, easing down to the bench next to me, very careful not to jostle me.

He takes a few seconds before he speaks. "I know I'm not handling this well. At all."

"I don't know what you're talkin' about."

"You're going to make me say it?"

"Say what?"

He chuckles, glances up to the ceiling. "Of course, you're going to make me say it. I'm talking about the fact that you make me crazy. I haven't slept since I woke up and you weren't there. I haven't been able to go a minute without thinking about you. How is it you don't feel this, too?" He sounds equal parts mystified and aggravated.

We're both facing the door, side by side, not looking at each other. I'm trembling. I'd like to blame the temperature, but it's his words cutting through me, wringing me out.

I do feel it.

I'm sure it's a trap, I know it's stupid, and there's no doubt it'll end in heartbreak with me somehow worse off than I already am, but Lord help me, I feel it.

He walks into a room, and all of a sudden, everything's in high definition. Colors. Smells. Sounds are crisper. And my heart don't ever beat right when he's close by.

It's crazy, but it also feels like a glass of ice water after a fever breaks. Pure and perfect and everything you need.

"You feel it, too." He says it so confidently.

I slide my hand over slowly until the side of my palm presses against the side of his. Then I curl my pinkie over his.

"Hard to feel much besides the broken ankle," I grumble.

"Okay, then. Let's go to the urgent care, Jo-Beth." He leans over, kissing me softly on the temple. Then he stands and lifts me in his arms. I wind my arms around his neck. He nuzzles the top of my head. Something inside my chest spills over like a waterfall.

"Don't call me Jo-Beth."

"Why not?"

"Steel Bones calls me Jo-Beth."

"I'm not calling you Plum. This is not a business relationship anymore."

"It ain't?"

"Nope. We're dating. How about I call you Josie?"

"I got two perfectly fine names. Don't need another."

"Jo-Beth it is, then. How far is this urgent care?"

He keeps up the banter as he eases me into his Maserati,
propping my foot on my duffle bag and settling the bag of
ice just so on my ankle. I give him directions to the 24-hour
urgent care on Gracy Avenue. He turns on the country
station, and shoots me a tentative smile.

"How bad is it?"

"Hurts like a bitch."

"I'm sorry. I was—"

I wait, but he doesn't finish the thought. Too bad for
him, I ain't one to drop shit.

"You were what?"

"Out of line, for one."

I nod. He was. "And for second?"

"For second?" He smiles, but it's soft, not mocking.
"Don't you ever get mad when you're disappointed?"

I think about it. "Nah. I get tired and kind of *fuck it all*."

"I get furious."

"Feel like you should always get what you want, eh?"

"Maybe." He glances in the rearview, and then slides me
a glance out of the corner of his eye.

"You still pissed?"

"No. I have what I want."

Then we're pulling into the parking lot, and there's a lot
of fussing as he carries me inside and gets me registered. He
seems surprised I have insurance, but Steel Bones is no
chickenshit operation. They take care of their people.

He insists on covering the co-pay, which is fine by me.

The place is busy, so we settle in for a wait. He takes up the whole armrest, and after a minute, he grabs my hand. He winds his fingers through mine and strokes me with his thumb.

My ankle throbs, but his touch is still nice. Distracting. I lean my head on his shoulder. It feels weirdly natural. Peaceful, even with all the coughing and the TV blaring.

"You shouldn't have left." He's staring straight ahead. It takes a second for me to realize that he's talkin' to me.

I kind of shrug. "I'm sorry I took your shit. I really don't know why I did it."

"I didn't care about that. Was it not—" He cracks his jaw and glares at the TV hanging on the opposite wall. "Was it not good for you?"

My breath catches, and my cheeks heat. I can't answer that. "You were sleeping at your desk. I thought, you know, time's up. I ain't never slept over before."

He finally glances down at me. "You've never slept in a— in a client's bed before?"

"I ain't never slept in any man's bed before." He blinks. He don't believe me. "What? I like my place. And before, when I lived at the clubhouse—well, you know. If you passed out in a brother's bed, you were down for another round whenever he woke up, and I ain't working when I don't have to, you know?"

His face tightens. He don't like the turn of this conversation. Oh well, buddy. I don't hide what I am. Bad enough the way people act like women who do my kind of work don't exist, unless it's time to get their rocks off. I ain't doin' no one the favor of pretending I ain't what I am.

The way I see it, if I got to deal with your face judgin' me, you're gonna have to deal with the fact I got no shame. Maybe if I'd had better choices, I'd have chosen differently.

But I didn't, and I ain't beatin' myself up 'cause life gave me lemons.

Adam chews on what I've said awhile, pretending he's watching the TV, and then when there's a commercial break, he clears his throat.

"I don't want you working anymore." He lays it out like a demand, real tough. Real sure of himself.

I bust out laughing. "When in the last hour did you become the boss of me?"

He raises an eyebrow. "That's the way it's going to be, Jo-Beth."

"You're nuts," I tell him, but he's got to know that already. "Hand me that magazine."

Of course, he ignores me. "You're not dancing on that ankle. And you're not...doing the other stuff."

"People always do what you tell them to?"

"Over five thousand people in twelve offices in eight countries. Yes. Always." He's proud of that, and I'll admit, it's impressive. However.

"I don't work for you no more. We're dating. This is a—how do you say it? This is an *egalitarian* relationship."

"Egalitarian?" You can hear his surprise that I know a word like that.

I grin. "I guess you never met Heavy Ruth. He's the president of Steel Bones. Man's like a word-a-day calendar. Proletariat. Iconoclast. Halcyon."

"Yeah?" He's smiling. It tickles him, me saying big words, and I don't mind. He's cute when he grins. Boyish.

"Most of his words ain't useful for shit, but egalitarian comes in handy."

"Yeah? When?"

"For hassling Cue about the schedule, for one. Also,

when explaining to the man I'm dating that he don't get to decide shit unilaterally."

"Is that another one of Heavy's words?"

"Huh? No. Probably got that one from the news."

He's eyein' me now, speculation in his eyes.

"What?"

"Jo-Beth, you're not a dumb woman, are you?"

"I dropped out at the end of tenth grade."

"Why?"

Oh, no. I ain't gettin' into my hard luck story, not when my ankle's busted, and I can't get comfortable 'cause these damn chairs are the kind that look upholstered but are really hard plastic with fabric glued on.

"You can't pay no water bill with high school credit."

For a minute, I think he's gonna press, but he don't. He's got a one-track mind. "If money's the issue, you don't have to worry about that anymore."

I snort. "Money's always the issue. And you ain't the boss of me, so you better drop it, or that's it. We're not dating no more."

His face is set to keep arguing—all stern and lord-of-all-he-surveys—but he must see something in mine that convinces him to ease up. "You'd end it, then? Just like that? You're a cold woman, Jo-Beth."

"I am." I snuggle my head into the crook of his neck. "I'd miss you, though."

"You would?"

"I did." And then quick, 'cause I can't believe that came out of my mouth, I say, "Hand me that magazine now, won't you?"

His eyes light up, crazy blue, and I can tell he wants to press, but he don't. "This one?" He holds up a copy of *Popular Mechanics*.

"What do I look like? Your dad? The one with the pump-kins and flowers on the cover."

He hands me a copy of *Home Life*. It's from this month. Sweet. I settle back in the plastic chair.

My ankle really does hurt, a hot throbbing, but it's strange. I'm more relaxed in this waiting room than I have been in a long while. Adam seems to chill, too, spreading out in his chair, stretching his legs and resting his arm around my shoulder, occasionally rearranging my ice pack.

When I have to pee, he helps me over to the bathroom and lowers me down on the toilet. I ain't as shy as some— my job won't allow it—but it's still a little embarrassing. After, he props me up, my back to his chest, so I can balance to wash my hands. I can't resist. I give my ass a wiggle. He's hard and pokin' me in no time.

It relieves my mind. All this feeling shit is disquieting. With sex, I'm on firmer ground.

"You better stop that." Adam's hands skate down my arms, and he nuzzles and nips at my shoulder. His breathing picks up. It's soothing, knowing I got his number.

I giggle, and I stop the wiggling. "You better take me back out then."

He huffs, but he does, and we get called back a few minutes later. They stick us in a cubby for what feels like forever, waiting on the doctor. I'm on the gurney, and Adam's in a chair next to me. His face got real serious when we were taken back. It didn't seem like he was impressed by the set up. He gets right on his phone and starts typing.

"Whatcha doing?" I peer down. His fingers fly.

"First thing tomorrow, I'm having Dr. Das see you. He can drive down here."

"You can get a doctor to drive all the way from Pyle to Petty's Mill?"

"Of course."

"Being rich is a foreign land, ain't it?"

Adam grins up at me, the corners of his eyes crinkling. "That's kind of poetic."

"I have my moments."

Then the doctor comes in, and Adam stands. The man examines my ankle while Adam looms, grim-faced. You can tell he feels guilty, the way his mouth turns down at the corners. Part of me doesn't like him feeling bad, but the smart part of me that's made it this far in life keeps her mouth shut. A little guilt can soften a hard heart, and it never hurt no one.

The doctor orders an x-ray, which is more waiting, and then we spend some more time in the cubby. Adam gets comfortable, hanging his jacket from his chair. His phone buzzes, and he checks it.

I've turned to my side on the gurney; I can never stand laying flat on my back. The pain in my ankle is a dull ache now. The doctor gave me a fresh ice pack, the gel kind. The waiting is giving me time to worry.

Maybe it ain't as bad as it seemed; the doctor will say rest it a few days, and I'll be back to work by the weekend. Maybe.

To distract myself, I nudge Adam. "What are you doin' down there?"

He blinks, and then he smiles. "I got a notification that a stock I've had my eye on hit my price point."

"Oh, yeah?"

"Yeah."

"I guess you're a busy guy, eh? With being a billionaire and all."

"I'm not a billionaire."

"No? A millionaire then?" Millions. Billion. Is there

really a difference?

He takes the question seriously. "Well, it's one thing if we're talking net worth, another if we're talking liquidity ratio...I guess it depends on how you count."

"I count the usual way. You have a billion dollars in your bank account?"

He kind of half-smiles, but he doesn't answer.

"I don't see how we can be dating if we can't talk about money, Adam." I'm teasing, but I'm also not. "Well?"

"Across several accounts, and counting my real estate investments and shares in private companies—none of that liquid, mind you—I'm worth maybe fifty million. Give or take."

"I knew it! A half-a-billionaire!" I crow, even while it makes me kind of sad. I don't want to look too closely at that uneasiness, don't want to mess up the quiet vibe in our private, little bubble behind the blue fabric screens at the urgent care.

"Is that going to be a problem?" He's intent on me again, the phone forgotten in his lap.

"Oh, yeah. Most definitely." I stifle a sigh. I guess we are gonna go down that road. How can we not? Only well-fed children who've never been cold think that money don't matter.

"I can't tell if you're joking."

"Of course, I ain't joking. You know it's a problem. It already is."

His eyes darken, and he turns to face me full on. "I don't see a problem."

"'Course you don't. You're the rich one. *Money is no object,* right?"

His expression gets vague. "Money is always an object.

And it's all relative. If you need more than you have, you're broke."

I snort. "What do you need that you don't have?"

This throws him, and he shifts in his chair, breaking eye contact. "You still haven't told me why my money is a problem." He's changing the subject, but I let him.

"Have you never watched a soap opera?" Fay-Lee, a former sweetbutt who's Dizzy's old lady now, is obsessed with soaps. We get together sometimes to watch hours on the DVR.

"Can't say that I have."

"Well, you'd know, if you did. Your family is gonna think I'm a gold digger, and they'll turn you against me. Or they'll set up an elaborate scheme and make it seem like I cheated on you, and you'll believe them over me, and it'll break my heart."

"I'd never fall for it." Adam's eyes are twinkling, and it pisses me off.

"Or you'd take me to a fancy dinner and get ashamed of my bad table manners."

"I've already taken you to a fancy dinner. You ordered two entrees and then ate off my plate."

"See?"

"I wasn't ashamed. I was hard as a rock."

"That's 'cause slumming it is your kink or something."

There's a silence, and I don't want to know what it means, so I check out my nails, pick at the cuticles. I don't want to be right, but I probably am.

After a long time, Adam exhales, and when he speaks, his words are careful, deliberate.

"When my mother met my stepfather, we were living on spaghetti made with water from an electric kettle and bread from the day-old rack. My stepfather owned a brokerage."

I remember cooking on a hot plate and shopping off the damaged and dented rack at the grocery store. Ma never met a rich guy who'd take us away from it all, though.

"How'd they meet?"

"She was a secretary."

I nod. "I've read that in a few books." It sounds like the romance novels that Deb passes around the clubhouse when she's done.

"She wasn't *his* secretary. She was *a* secretary. She worked in the purchasing department or something like that. She stalked him. Slipped on the elevator at the last minute. Hid in the parking garage. That kind of thing."

"So, she stalked him." I wink at him. "Kind of like I did when I kept showing up at your work—Oh. No. That was you. Not me."

"The genes are strong."

"So, our babies are doomed to be little creepers?" I'm joking, but damn, as soon as it's out of my mouth—Adam don't find it funny. His jaw firms, and something flashes behind his bright blue eyes.

"Joking," I say, trying to lighten the mood again, but his attention is all on me, and it's a powerful thing, all that focus and intensity pinning you down, an unknown storm raging behind his eyes.

"Do you want that, Jo-Beth? A baby?"

Well, fuck. I don't know. I always thought I didn't. One woman like me alone with no family ain't strong enough to protect a little one. But I don't want to say *no* now, in this moment. I don't know why, but I don't.

"I thought we were talking about how your parents met?"

"Are you not going to answer my question?"

"Ain't you gonna answer mine?"

After a beat when he seems to wrestle with something dark, he lets his lips slide into a casual smile, and he relaxes back into his chair. He don't look relaxed, though. It's like he's shoved on that confident, detached mask he's got, but he was in a hurry, so he hasn't got it on quite right.

"All right, Jo-Beth," he says. "I'll tell you anything. My parents? Well, my mother got knocked up by a loser when she was barely eighteen. She struggled—we struggled—and then she met my stepfather, and now she lunches and organizes soirees like she never had to make ends meet once in her life. You think this is crazy, you and me, but I don't. I've seen it work."

"So your mom and stepdad are gonna welcome me with open arms? And that stepbrother?"

His gaze drops to his lap. Yeah. That's what I thought.

"They'll know what I am. Ain't no hiding it."

"It's not their business."

"I don't even know why we're talkin' about this. We just met. I don't even know if I like you." I struggle up to sitting. I can't be all hopeless and lying down at the same time. Adam rises to his feet to help me, and then he stays close, standing at my side, stroking his big hands down my shoulders.

"You like me." His lips brush against my temple, his breath hot against my skin. My pulse kicks up a notch.

"You like me more." I can't help it. I raise my face, eyes closed, searching blindly for his lips.

He kisses me, long and slow and gentle. "Maybe. It doesn't bother me if it doesn't bother you."

"I'm scared," I whisper against his rough cheek.

He leans his forehead against mine. "I'm fucking terrified."

And then a throat clears, the doctor enters, and Adam leaps back like we got busted by the police in the back seat of his car. Turns out, I have a severe sprain. I need to wear an ankle support, and I'm supposed to stay off my feet for four to eight weeks. He says a whole bunch of other things, but after "four to eight weeks," I hear nothing.

I can't *not work* for a month or two. The bank don't *not* send the mortgage bill if you send them a doctor's note.

Maybe Cue will hook me up with some desk work at one of the other Steel Bones businesses. Deb is always stressed out. I'm sure she could use some help with the paperwork. I don't know computers, but I'm not useless.

Fuck.

I look up, and I realize the doctor and Adam are both staring at me.

"Yes?"

"He asked you if you have any questions."

Shit. I have no idea what he was saying. I look to Adam.

"I got it. Thank you." Adam shakes the man's hand, and he leaves.

A nurse comes in with an ankle brace and crutches, miraculously quick this time. They get me set up, and then I'm hobbling out on Adam's arm. My mind is whirling, and the stress and pain and general craziness is getting to me. I'm hungry, too, and I don't do too well hungry.

Adam puts me carefully in the car, and then gets into the driver's seat. I expect him to turn the key, but instead, he waits.

I deflate like a balloon, and lay my head against the window. "I don't know what I'm gonna do."

"You're going to remind me of the address of the little yellow house so I don't have to look it up. And when we get there, you're going to elevate your ankle and take a painkiller. I'll make dinner. And then we're going to bed, and I'm going to fuck you very, very carefully."

I must be truly gone, 'cause his words make me forget everything and focus on his body, his shoulders brushing mine, his solid thigh pressing into my knee. My pussy tingles.

I sigh. "Okay." I can't solve tomorrow's problems tonight. I might as well lose myself in the fantasy man squiring me around town in a freakin' Maserati.

I yawn and press the button that warms the seat.

"You don't have to worry about anything anymore. Not about money. Not about anything," Adam swears, gruff and serious. He grabs my hand to his lips. I trace his bottom lip with my thumb. His lips are so soft, especially compared with his scratchy, stubbly cheeks.

"Your mom," I ask. "She doesn't worry about money or anything anymore?"

Adam's silence is its own answer.

"How about you let me have my worries. I'll let you share them, maybe."

"Yeah?" His lip quirks at this. "You'd do that?"

"I'd let you have half. How about that?"

"You're a generous woman, Jo-Beth Connolly."

"When a woman has so much, it's easy to give."

"There's my poet." Adam moves his eyes to the road, and we pull onto Gracy Avenue, smilin' at each other. He finds the country station, and I rest my hand on his thigh when he shifts, enjoying the play of muscles. He's so strong, so sure of himself.

Which is why it's so odd I feel the way I do. Fierce. Protective. Like I need to pull him back from the edge and warn him that he's being too reckless, too easy with his feelings. It's dangerous, the kind of want I see in his eyes. I'm kind of worried he's losing it.

If I were a different woman, if I were my mother—hell, if

I were almost any other woman at The White Van, I'd be counting his money right now. As it is, instead of figuring out what I'm gonna do with a sprained ankle, I'm worrying over a grown man, wondering who's looking out for him, especially since he seems to be a functional lunatic, if that's a thing.

I guess I've lost it, too, 'cause it seems like I'm gonna let a man in my house. It's been a strange few days.

7

ADAM

Besides feeling like the world's largest asshole, I feel like the world's largest person.

Jo-Beth's house is perfectly sized for her, but I have to duck every time I enter a room. When I go upstairs to take a piss, my shoulders brush the walls.

I don't think she was exaggerating about never having a man in her house. Her sofa has two seats, not three. There's one toothbrush in the bathroom and one chair at the small table in her kitchen. There's another chair, but it's pushed against a wall and stacked with catalogues and magazines.

I knew she was overthinking letting me in, so I didn't give her time to back out. As soon as we pulled up in front of the house, I picked her up, ignored her fussing, and barged in with her in my arms. I saw the rock where she keeps her spare key. That's coming inside tonight.

I sat her on the sofa, propped her foot on an ottoman, and then I left her to piss and poke around her kitchen to see what I can pull together. I could hear her stomach grumbling in the car, and she needs to eat to take one of the pain meds.

She hasn't complained once since the club, but there's strain around her eyes. Every time I notice it, I get more pissed at myself. I'm keeping it calm, though. She needs a break from the drama. We both do.

She's unsettled, following my every move, tense and fidgeting with the hem of her hoodie. "What are you looking for?" she calls.

She has a pass-through between her living room and kitchen, so I can keep an eye on her. I'm in and out of her sight, though, and she's craning her neck to keep track of me.

"Something to make for dinner."

"I ain't been shopping lately."

From the looks of her staples, she hasn't been grocery shopping in a while. She has some peanut butter, ramen, spaghetti, potatoes in a box, and cans of soup, corn, and tuna. There's no meat in the freezer. No fresh vegetables. She does have green bananas in a fruit bowl, so she has been grocery shopping. This is what she bought. Damn, but it reminds me of the Gilson Avenue days. My chest tightens.

"How about a peanut butter and banana sandwich?" It's been awhile, but Cook used to make that for me when I came begging for a snack before dinner.

"That's gross."

"What would you like then?" I don't see any pasta sauce. I suppose I could flavor the noodles with butter.

"A peanut butter sandwich is fine. *With* a banana."

I chuckle under my breath, and make us sandwiches. I pour us both glasses of milk, and I take it to her in the living room, but she's already up, unsteady on one leg.

"Whoa. Where do you think you're going?"

"We're not eating in here."

"We're not?"

She looks at me like my mother did when I mixed up the salad fork.

"Mice. No food except in the kitchen." She points to the other room.

"You have mice?"

"I do not. And I ain't gonna, either."

This place is rough around the edges. Jo-Beth's obviously house proud, but all the scrubbing and decorating can't hide how the living room floor gives in the middle, how the appliances are from the nineties and the fixtures are from the fifties.

This whole subdivision was probably housing thrown up for workers during the war when steel was flowing out of the blast furnace at Petty's Mill. The planners surely didn't build it to last eighty years.

Still, I like it. I love it.

I'm not sure if Jo-Beth's ever let me see the real her. Maybe when she was curled into me, naked, struggling to get her breath back, but that could be my ego talking.

Here in her house, though, the real Jo-Beth is on display everywhere. There are books. Heavy, coffee table books, arranged like decorations and stacked in pride of place on the mantle. *The Conquistadors and the Rise of the West. The History of Spice. Deep Space: Images and Imagination.*

"You read?" I glance at her collection.

"No, I just stack 'em. Like Jenga." She rolls her eyes at me. I guess I had that coming.

The books are all odd shapes, oversized. They go with the rest of the place. Nothing matches, and Jo-Beth has *a lot* of useless stuff, but her house isn't cluttered. It's decorated.

Like in her kitchen. She has two guest towels hanging perfectly folded—ironed, I believe—from the oven bar. One is delicate, a crisp yellow cotton with lemons and limes embroidered in swirls. The other is thick terry with a pug in a sombrero, laughing and holding its belly. In another person's house, you might think they don't care, but there's something in the way everything is folded or hung or displayed just so. She's picked and placed each of these objects with care.

And everything, from the kitty cat clock on the kitchen wall to the pink gone-with-the-wind lamp on the end table, is bright and happy and playful.

If you would have told me last week—hell, yesterday—that I'd be sitting in a rundown duplex in Petty's Mill, fixated on a woman's kitchen towels, I would have said you were crazy.

I spent the past twenty-four hours trying to get my shit straight, drowning myself in work, emailing *your father ryan Adam morrison* back. I told him I'd meet him, thinking that maybe settling that would cleanse me of this temporary insanity.

But hour after hour, I only got more pissed off that she left like it was nothing. I don't get treated like nothing anymore. Not for a long, long time.

I paid my dues. I did my school work, and Eric's. I fought and played hard and partied harder until everyone almost forgot I wasn't a Wade by birth. And all the while, I saved Eric from every fuck up and made sure we were the top of every class. Valedictorian and salutatorian. We finished first.

Eric took the cushy internship with venture capitalists. I went to work for the start up. And then we came home to Wade-Allyn and made it relevant in the new economy. I did that. I'm ambitious; I seize every opportunity. I don't have to tell people my name anymore. They know.

And some stripper's gonna sashay off with the contents of my wallet like she's got better shit to do? After I treat her like gold? After I say shit to her I've never said to any other woman before? Let her in when I let *no one* in. No one even close.

The worst of it is that the whole time, I *knew* I was being an asshole. I was one of those entitled pricks I used to make a sport of taking down, one after another, their privilege a huge blind spot that could never let them see Thomas Wade's *adopted* son overtaking them. I knew it, but I was out of my mind.

I'm still shaken, sitting at Jo-Beth's table, eating a sandwich. I didn't know I had it in me—Eric's degenerate delight in taking out his frustration on those weaker and smaller. Someone who has to take it.

In that room in the back of The White Van, I was almost high on it, the indignation, and Jo-Beth's bare tits and skin, all mine if I wanted it because nobody can tell me I can't have it anymore. Nobody *will* tell me I can't have what I want anymore. I hated her in that moment. Hated what she was, and hated that I wanted her anyway. I should be better than this.

And then she threw my words back in my face, stepped funny, and cried out in pain, and reality came crashing through the sleep deprivation and the booze and this jacked up, early mid-life crisis. I don't want to hurt this woman. Never.

And I don't want this woman to *be* hurt. Ever. I don't understand what she is to me, but I know she's not like anyone else in my life. She's not a piece on a chessboard; she's not a cog I need to function properly or discard. I don't care what she's done. She's...real.

And she's drumming her long, pink nails on the table.

"Yes?"

She has an eyebrow raised. "You've been sittin' there

quiet awhile."

"Does it make you nervous?"

"Makes me bored. You have to do the dishes."

"All right. Do you want me to help you back to the sofa or to your bed?"

She snorts. "You'd like to help me to my bed, wouldn't you?"

I grin and grab our plates. "All the same to me. I can eat your pussy on the sofa same as in a bed."

Jo-Beth rolls her eyes. "That ain't a golden ticket like a blow job is for a man, you know that, right?"

"It isn't?"

"A woman ain't gonna go immediately stupid 'cause you promise her head."

"Why do you think I want you stupid?"

"'Cause for some reason you don't look like you're fixin' to leave. And I'd have to be stupid to let you stay."

"Why's that?" She's hobbling back to the living room. I'd drop the dishes and help her, but she's a proud little thing, and she's managing.

"Everyone knows. You let a man in your house, he don't ever leave. Worse than mice."

"Is that so?" I'm trying not to smile.

"You don't believe me?"

"No, I believe you. No man you let in your house would ever want to leave."

"That don't make me feel better!" she hollers from the sofa. She has her leg propped up and a magazine in her lap. I follow her, lowering myself carefully beside her. I brought the ice pack, fresh from the freezer, a glass of water, and one of her pain pills.

"Here." I drop a pill in her palm, and then I bend to inspect her ankle. It's swollen and bruised, and frankly, I'm surprised she's not complaining about it more. "How badly does it hurt?"

She's studying me, eyes narrow, as if I'm going to steal her foot. I can't stop grinning. So help me, I think she's the hot female version of Grumpy Cat.

"Bad enough. Why you smiling?"

I gently tug up her yoga pants and arrange the ice pack. Then I kiss the tip of her scrunched-up nose. "Because you make me smile."

She says harrumph. Seriously. Harrumph. I laugh, and she swats me with her magazine, and then grumbles, "Turn on the TV, won't you."

I grab the remote from the end table. "What do you want to watch?"

"I don't care. I just like the background noise." She's got her nose in her magazine, and one of those grease pencils in her hand.

I turn on Bloomberg.

She flips back and forth in her magazine—it's a catalogue, actually—muttering to herself, hovering over pages with her pencil and gnawing on her lower lip. Her blond hair falls in her face, a delicate ear peeking out between strands. She's not paying attention to me, and I've never felt more like a god.

This skittish critter trusts me.

She doesn't want anything from me, nothing more complicated than cash. She doesn't expect anything from me. I don't need to be anyone in particular for her. She's tolerating me next to her, and I'm as relaxed as I've ever been in my life.

I let all the bullshit go, and I let myself enjoy this strange, magical moment.

I yawn.

She yawns.

She finally circles something with her grease pencil.

"What did you pick?" I glance down in her lap. She has one of those general store catalogues from New England. Before she passed, Thomas Wade's mother was a fan.

She half-shrugs and shows me.

"What is that?"

"It's a heart-shaped cake of birdfeed. For Valentine's day."

"You spent all that time deciding on birdseed?"

Jo-Beth huffs and slaps the catalogue down on her end table. "Yes. I'm choosy." She gives me a look, daring me to argue.

"Then I'm even luckier than I already thought I was."

"Don't get a big head. I didn't choose you."

"No?"

She's blushing like crazy, looking everywhere but in my eyes. I love flustering this woman.

"No. You kept comin' around like a stray."

"Uh-huh." I lean in, take her mouth. She stills, and then melts, whimpering. I cradle her jaw, and she clings to my forearm. It doesn't take long before she's panting. "That's an upgrade, I guess."

She blinks and frowns as I draw back and go to set the ice pack aside so I can carry her upstairs. "Huh?"

"I started as a mouse, and now I'm a dog. I'm going to take you to bed now, and I'm going to show you until there's no doubt that I am all man. How about that, Jo-Beth?"

"That's the cheesiest shit I've heard today, Adam." She's smiling as I carry her upstairs, only wincing once or twice, and when I rest her carefully on her bed and unbutton my shirt, her smile turns nervous.

I'm not on solid ground right now. I know the script, how

to please the general woman, but with Jo-Beth, it's different. I can push her, but that's not what I want. I want her to come to me.

I unbuckle my pants and let them drop. Her gaze darts down to the tent my cock has pitched in my boxer briefs.

I hesitate. Wait for a sign.

And then she unzips her purple hoodie, keeping her eyes glued on mine. Blood floods to my cock, and my heart hammers in my chest. She peels off her tank top, and there are those gorgeous, wonky tits, the skin of her nipples a supple light brown that has to be so fucking sensitive.

She scowls down at herself. "I don't know why this one's always lookin' to the right like it's seen a squirrel or something."

I laugh, drop my boxers, and carefully crawl next to her, cupping her right tit and dropping a kiss on the pebbling nipple. "I love this tit. It's one of my two favorites."

She snorts. "You've got the worst lines. I don't see how you ever got laid before."

"I'm rich and fit and insanely good looking."

"And humble."

I nibble a path down her belly, easing her pants and panties over her hips and gently pull them off, careful of her ankle. Then I rewrap her ice pack in a towel and replace it. When she seems comfortable, I kiss a line back up to her tits and rest my head on her warm, soft belly.

It takes a minute, but eventually, her fingers tentatively wind through my hair, and my breath catches. Here's my girl; here's the sweet, fierce woman hidden under the hard-ass exterior. I want to coax her out, make her forget to hide.

I nip at her belly pudge. It's nothing, the kind of natural padding that my mother and her circle have vacuumed off by plastic surgeons because there's no number of crunches that'll tone it away. Jo-Beth yips, sucks it in, and slaps at my head.

I chuckle. "Leave me alone. I'm loving on your chub."

"You want me to love on your chub, you'd best stop," she grumbles, wriggling, and fuck, her skin feels so good against me. I nuzzle my cheek against her bare belly, inhale the scent of her arousal. She stills, playing with my hair, stroking her fingers down my neck, across my shoulders.

"How come you're so in shape if you work at a desk all day?" She's tracing the muscles in my back, and I can't help but flex for her.

"Boxing. Crossfit. Crew."

"What's crew?"

"It's where you row. On the river. I'm the stroke."

"What's the stroke?"

"The guy who sits all the way in the back of the boat."

"You got any ambition to work your way up?"

I laugh, and she squirms, ticklish. "The stroke sets the pace. He's the best rower."

"You know when you're bragging, you got to do it in terms I understand, right?"

"Yes, ma'am." My cock is throbbing, and this is so sweet, but I want more. I rise over her, gaze down into her face, my knee nudging at her uninjured leg, gently urging her to open for me. "How's the ankle?"

"Aches." She runs her hands over my chest, testing those muscles. Her eyes are a hazy blue, and the corners of her lips are ever so slightly turned up. She's fucking beautiful.

"Do you think you can take my cock?" I sip at her lips, slip my fingers between her folds. She's wet. Soaking. I knew she had to be from the musky scent that's driving me wild. I play with her clit, spread her cream over her lips, stroke a finger into her hot hole.

"You got to be gentle." Her breath has picked up, and she's craning her neck to kiss me now. She's bent her knee, and part of me wants to take in that pretty, pink pussy, but her face is too enchanting. Her eyes are big, rounded, and every feeling she has is clear as day. She wants me. She's needy, impatient, but she feels good.

Her body rocks, her hips rise, seeking, demanding.

I feel like I've got the strength of a hundred men.

"Always, baby." I notch my cock at her entrance, and she mewls, digging into my back with her little claws. I ease in, inch by inch, holding myself still while she arches her back, trying to draw me deeper.

I don't know where the self-control is coming from. I circle her hard nub with my thumb, and she starts crying out, sweet, little grunts. Her eyes are closed, and she's biting her lower lip.

I ease out, slip free, glide my wet cock over her stiff clit. It's only then that I realize I haven't put on a rubber. Fuck.

I freeze. She makes a sound I can only describe as a pissed off cat, and her eyes fly open.

"Baby, just one minute." I rummage in my wallet, shoot a prayer of thanksgiving when I find the foil packet.

"What?" She blinks, confused.

"Condom."

"Oh, shit. Yeah." Her face drops, worry dulling those blue eyes again. I hate how worried she is all the time. It shouldn't be that way. It won't be.

I sheathe my dick and resettle between her thighs. "I'm clean. No worries."

"Aren't you? Worried?" Her chin's raised, and she's tensed, bracing herself.

"No. Not at all. There is nothing about you I can't handle. There is no part of you I don't want." The words spill out; I'm hardly thinking them before I'm murmuring them in her ear. I touch my forehead to hers and slide home again. Already, the base of my spine is tingling, and I'm fighting to last a little longer.

"I'm clean, too. And I'm always safe. I don't know what—"

I stop, draw back. There's a faint roar inside me, an ugly mess of jealousy and fury and impotence that I won't look at, even as my body stiffens and a wave of nausea roils my guts. I don't need to think about this now. Or ever.

I force myself to meet her eyes, and—she's still my Jo-Beth. Walls down. All her vulnerability, all her strength on full display.

"It's okay. It's me and you. We're in this together, okay?" I can tell she doesn't understand, and to be honest, I don't fully get it, either. But I want this. I want her. For now, all I need from her is an ounce of trust because if she can believe a little, I can believe the rest. An ounce of trust—that's all— but I know how much that's asking from her.

I don't breathe until she answers. "Okay." She keeps her gaze glued on mine while she hitches up her good leg, wraps it around my waist, welcoming me deeper in her hot, tight pussy. I almost forget my promise to be gentle.

I reach down, flick her clit while I thrust into her heat, glorying in the wet slaps and the gasps and moans ripped from her throat. I forget everything but her.

"Adam. Adam. I'm coming. I'm coming." She's breath-less, panicked almost.

"Okay, baby. Come for me. Come all over me." And she does, clenching, fisting my cock with her pussy. My balls contract and my cum spurts from me, the orgasm shaking my body, sending chills racing down my extremities. I shout; I can't control it, and I clutch her quilt and take her sweet mouth, plundering deep with my tongue, swallowing her soft cries.

It's so fucking good. Better than the last time, which was better than any sex I've had before. I'm tempted to pass out, let the blessed drowsiness overtake me. But I learn from my mistakes.

I kiss her cheeks, her forehead, her nose, her ear lobes.

"You're beautiful. You're so fucking perfect for me. Jo-Beth. My gorgeous girl." I mumble anything and everything that comes to mind as her eyes clear and the wariness returns.

"Are you going home now?" She's tensed. "Can you lock the door after you? The key's in a rock in the flower bed."

Fuck. I forgot about the key. I drop a kiss between her tits. "I'm not going home. I'm sleeping here. Tomorrow, my doctor is going to come and reassure me about your ankle. And then we're going to spend the day together."

"Don't you have work?"

"I'll probably go back to work the day after. And then Friday evening, I'll be back. I'll bring groceries. Make dinner."

She's quiet, her head turned toward the wall. I'm hoping she comes to terms with this soon because I need to handle this condom. Finally, she kind of grunts. "Just like mice. Can't get 'em out once you let 'em in."

I laugh all the way to the bathroom, and it's not until I'm bringing her a cold washcloth and a glass of water that I realize, I don't think I've laughed this much, this freely...ever.

It doesn't make sense—Jo-Beth and I don't make sense—but it feels perfectly, *finally* right. The past doesn't matter. The world doesn't matter. Only this. Only us.

8

JO-BETH

"Haven't seen you around in a hot minute."

"I could say the same."

Nevaeh Ellis and I are facing off in the personal care aisle of the Shop Right, both of us pushing loaded carts. I nudge a few boxes to cover the condoms I just picked up. Nevaeh grabs a pack of extra larges and tosses them onto the top of her stuff. Basically, that sums up our differences in a nutshell.

Nevaeh and I spent many a night drunk as shit together at the clubhouse. This was back when she was Forty's property, before she skipped town to make it big in Pyle. She's back now, stirrin' up shit. I like her.

"You're cooking for a man, aren't you?" Nevaeh eyes the steaks in my cart.

"Yup. He eats like he got a hollow leg. You back with Forty?" If she's not, I'm probably supposed to be freezing her out like everyone else.

"Shit, girl. I'm hardly back in town."

"Why'd you come back?" I turn my cart so we're heading in the same direction, and we roll off, side by side.

"Got tired of everyone lovin' me. Wanted to get the scarlet letter treatment, you know?"

"I probably ain't supposed to be talking to you."

"Probably not."

"Want to go for a beer?" I been really bored, not working and stuck at home.

"Fuck yeah, Jo-Beth Connolly." We grin at each other and head for the check out.

"Nice boot," she says while she throws things on the belt, no rhyme or reason.

"Fashionable, right?" I pull out my canned goods and stack them neat, bar code accessible.

"Broken?"

"Only a bad sprain."

I got cleared by Adam's fancy, home-visiting doctor to walk on it awhile back, but I'm still in the boot. Dr. Das comes and does PT with me three days a week, which is weird as fuck. He don't even wear doctor clothes. He comes in khakis and a button down. He's also young and hot and Adam fucking *hates* him.

Adam'll drive all the way from Pyle to be there for the session, and then he'll drive all the way back. He's putting crazy miles on his vehicles. These past two months, I've learned that in addition to the Maserati, he's got a Range Rover, a Mercedes G class, and a vintage Black Shadow, which ain't a Harley but is still sweet as hell.

I'm fucking a very rich man. Ain't gonna lie. It's hard to wrap my brain around.

"So where to? Want to go to some chain restaurant so no one will see you with me?"

We've checked out, Nevaeh's loaded up her car, and now she's helping me with my bags. It's cold enough out that the milk will keep for an hour or two.

"Girl, you know Grinder and Boots live at the Chili's."

Nevaeh laughs, and I can't help but smile. She's got the biggest laugh. It's out of control.

"You know, I got a better idea. Let's go to Finnegan's." We used to beg the brothers to ride us into town—Nevaeh, Annie Holt, and I—so we could make ourselves sick on sundaes.

"Ice cream!" Nevaeh squeals, then she seems to think about it. "It's too cold for ice cream."

"So there'll be no one there to start shit. And I can get a malted. Perfect."

"Perfect," she concedes. "Can you drive in that boot?"

"I got here, didn't I?"

"True." She hops in my passenger seat, brown curls bouncing, more energy than anyone has a right to. Yeah, I like her. Always have.

There's not a soul at Finnegan's Ice Cream Parlor when we get there. I get a vanilla malted, and she gets a banana split, shoves half down her face, and then collapses in the booth, groaning.

"Why'd you let me do that?"

"There's not a soul on earth who can tell you what to do, Nevaeh Ellis. And you fucking know it."

"I do, I do." She pops open the button on her jeans. "So, you gonna tell me all about how you're banging Adam *fucking* Wade? Damn girl. If I'd have known you had that level game, I would've taken you with me when I blew this pop stand."

"I do not have big city titties. You know that. I'd have been broke and back here in no time."

"Adam Wade begs to differ."

"Adam Wade's out of his damn mind."

"I don't know." Nevaeh's smile doesn't falter, but her

brown eyes grow a touch warmer. "I always thought you had more sense than any of us. Except maybe Harper Ruth."

I lift a shoulder. "Sense ain't one of those things that catches or keeps a man."

We share a moment of silent commiseration, the kind you can have with an old friend who knows where you come from. I had a junkie mom. Nevaeh had a creepy stepfather. We both escaped with the help of men too old and too fast for us, and turns out, neither of us got too far in the long run.

"How'd you catch him, anyway?" Nevaeh's attacking her banana split again with grim determination. It's almost painful to watch.

"Didn't you hear from whoever told you the gossip?"

"It was Fay-Lee Parsons, and she didn't know. She said you haven't been around the clubhouse."

"Because of the ankle."

"You been out of work?"

"Yeah. Cue put me out on short term disability, and Deb hooked me up with some side work. She showed me how to do the bills for businesses. I can do it from home."

"Deb trusts you with that?"

I shrug and smile. Nevaeh's been gone almost ten years now. She left right before the shit went down with Deb's daughter, and all the shit that happened after. She ain't savvy to all the ties that bind us anymore.

Deb's daughter Crista was attacked by some enemies of the club when she was walking home from school. It was real bad. The doctors didn't think she'd make it, and it was touch and go for months. Deb's nerves got shot, but she's the VP's wife, right? And even though nobody talks about it, she's the money man. For the club and the businesses. She can't be losing her shit.

So, I hook her up with some weed, a few Xanax here and there when Crista's got a surgery or things are especially rough. I keep my mouth shut, and now when I need a favor, Deb's got me. It's how it works in the club. Nobody in the real world knows loyalty, but we do. We hold ourselves to that. The men *and* the women.

As far as the club's concerned, Nevaeh Ellis ain't loyal. She fucked around on Forty, although I got questions about that. The rest of the club, though, they convicted her a decade ago. It's gonna be hard for her back here in Petty's Mill.

"So why did you really come back?" I ask.

Nevaeh sighs and licks the back of her spoon. "I got into some trouble in the big city. I need a place to lay low for a while. Lou's still living in Mom's house. He said I could have my bedroom back if I cook and clean."

"You're a house mouse for your brother?"

"Don't be gross. But yes." She wrinkles her nose. "So, tell me about your whirlwind romance with Adam Wade. Let me live vicariously. Does he take you on shopping sprees? Buy you furs? Has he flown you to Paris?"

I roll my eyes, but my stomach kind of lurches. Except for that first dinner, we haven't really gone anywhere. He comes over during the week when I have PT, and he always shows up Friday evening and stays until Monday morning. We cook, go for rides, fuck for hours. Do stupid shit like take baths together. He works a lot on his laptop, and then he gets restless and tries to fix things around my house. It sounds lame, but it's...nice. Just nice.

"We don't go anywhere. We stay in."

"At his place in Pyle? I bet he lives along the river in some kind of penthouse. He does, doesn't he?"

"No. We stay at my place."

Nevaeh raises her eyebrows, incredulous. "You bagged a millionaire, and you hang out here?"

I shrug.

"Is he hiding you?" Nevaeh scrapes the bowl with her spoon. Looks like she's found more room. "Oh, fuck that shit, Jo-Beth. You deserve fur coats and trips to Paris."

"This trouble in Pyle. He buy you a fur coat?"

"I'm vegetarian." Nevaeh drops her spoon with a clatter and a drawn-out sigh. "I know we haven't seen each other in a long time, but I'm gonna tell you what I'd tell any friend. Don't let a man treat you like his mistress if you aren't getting mistress benefits. Pearls, at least. Something you can hock, after."

My stomach lurches again and goes sour.

I want to say that it's me who doesn't want to go to his place. That he does pay. He buys the groceries, and he's paying for the PT out of his own pocket. I want to say it's not like that. We talk. About everything and anything, for hours. And we can sit without talking, too, and it's...nice.

The thing is...everything I want to say sounds like an excuse, and I know it. And you can't bullshit a bullshitter, you know?

Nevaeh Ellis and I stared down the same shit, and we made different choices. When Forty left on deployment, she did things I wouldn't have done, and the club crucified her for it. But the Lord knows, I've done some shit, too, that I ain't proud of. I don't know how she made it in Pyle, but I know she started with the same thing I did. Nothing.

Anyway, we both understand how the world works.

We both know that nice is nice for now. And nice does not last.

"I guess I should ask him for a diamond bracelet or something. He's got some fool idea about tearing up the floor in my living room to fix where it sags. He's been down in the basement, looking at the joists. That's gonna cost me if he bails with the job half done."

"You should ask for a matching set. Bracelet, necklace, and earrings."

I should. I will. I wince thinking about how he'll look at me, but he'll do it. He bought everything I circled in all my catalogues, and I didn't even ask.

It don't set easy, but I should start making plans. I can't get comfortable, let this strange, warm feeling I get when he's around burrow too deep. It's shifty, like a good buzz that can put you on your ass, puking in the bushes with no warning. A not-to-be-trusted high.

"Maybe I will." I want to change the subject. This is depressing the hell out of me. "Want another banana split?"

Nevaeh groans, unzips her pants, and tugs down her sweatshirt so you can't tell. "Hell, yeah. You go get it. We'll split it."

"Split the split?" I push my chair back.

"Only ever with you, Jo-Beth." Nevaeh grins, and I feel a little better. She was always a good time. When she left town, it was like a light went out. I don't care what everyone says. She had a reason for what she did to Forty. Probably a shitty one, but still.

We all have reasons.

Adam Wade is keeping me away from his real life for a reason. No doubt because I'm a stripper who whores on the side. Because I blew his stepbrother and got him beat up. Because I'm not the kind of woman you take home to the country club.

He's got a hundred reasons, I'm sure.

It's shitty. But still.

We all got reasons.

ADAM SHOWS up a little past nine in a brand-new truck. It's a Ford F-450 Platinum. It almost doesn't fit in my driveway.

He hops out, suit still on, black dress shoes all shiny, and my heart flips like always. He smiles as soon as he sees me on the porch.

I always come out as soon as I hear him pull up. He always texts as soon as he leaves work so I know when to expect him.

For all the money and the crazy work hours, he's an easy man. He takes the stairs in one leap, grabs me up, and takes my mouth, hungry, molding me to him, urging my legs around his waist. His glasses dig into my face, and he shoulders open the front door.

I laugh, and I nestle my nose in the crook of his neck, draw in the smell of him. He smells so damn good.

He carries me right up the stairs and plops me on the bed, gently but quickly. He peels off his jacket and goes to work on his shirt while I tug off my T-shirt and yoga pants. I love the moment we're skin-to-skin, and I can curl up into him or climb him. He's so big compared to me, and anything I do, he fucking loves.

"Oh, oh. Almost forgot." He's on the bed, and then he's not. He's rooting around in his jacket pocket. "Present."

He presses a small piece of cool glass into my palm, and I squeal. It's got to be the tomtit. I peek. It is! It's the size of my thumbnail, and the prettiest blue with the tiniest black beak.

"A tomtit!"

"A tomtit." He braces himself over me, smiling down as I roll the bird figurine in my fingers. I think I have almost every kind of bird now. He brings them to me one or two at a time. He gets them at a convenience store in Pyle run by a Russian. He says he stops in on his daily runs.

"How much was this one?"

"Now, this fellow set me back. He was two dollars and eighty cents."

"They're all two dollars and eighty cents. I don't see why the guy ain't marking them up. He's ordering them for you special, now, isn't he?"

Adam nods, and when I push at his shoulder, he lets me up so I can put the tomtit with the hummingbird and stork and the dozen others on my dresser. I rearrange them so they're in a perfect circle on the mirrored tray I found at Goodwill.

"I'll let him know my woman thinks he's missing an opportunity to fleece me."

He's teasing, but still, my stomach feels queasy, and my mind goes back to the conversation with Nevaeh. To tell the truth, it's been on repeat in my brain all day.

I saunter back to the bed, and try to change the subject. "So, you bought a truck?"

He's reclining on his side, his head propped up in his hand. His black hair is tousled from the rush to undress. He takes up two thirds of the bed. It's so hard to believe he's got this body under the suits. Every muscle is defined, even when he's totally relaxed.

It's so hard to believe a man this magnificent is in my creaky bed.

"I did. I need something to haul the lumber for fixing the floor joist."

I sit cross-legged at the foot of the bed. My pink panties are still on, but I still feel exposed when Adam's eyes linger on my pussy. I flush. We're not so desperate as we were at first. We can wait now and talk for a spell before we finish what we start each time he comes home.

Huh. Comes home. I force that aside. Don't look at it too closely.

"Are you sure you know what you're doing?"

"I have a contractor coming over in the morning. He's going to confirm that we can fix it with sistering, and then he and I will do the work together. I want to learn."

"Worse than mice. Let a man in your house, next thing you know, he's in the floorboards."

"You're prickly today. How's the ankle?" His look turns speculative, and I pull my knees to my chest and wrap my arms around them.

"It's fine. I went grocery shopping. Bought steaks."

"Yeah?" He waits, giving me space and time. I used to be able to keep my own counsel, no problem. With Adam, though, all he needs to do is get quiet and pin me with those bright blue eyes, and I spill.

"I saw an old friend. We went out for ice cream."

He smiles at that. "It's thirty degrees outside."

"She just moved back from Pyle. She's heard of you."

He nods, patient.

"She thinks I should ask you for jewelry." I feel my face harden.

"You don't wear jewelry." He's alert now. He hasn't moved, but he's watching me extra close now.

"She says if I'm being kept like a mistress, I should get the benefits a mistress gets." I say it, and it's ugly, and as soon as the words are out of my mouth, I want to shove them back in.

Adam sits up, swings his legs over the side of the bed. He's closer to me now. He's facing the wall, and I'm facing him, all huddled into myself. His hand rests on the quilt an inch from my feet.

"Do you feel like that's how I treat you?" His voice is measured, the way he talks on the phone for business.

I bite my lip. "I don't know. You always come here. I feel bad sometimes. Your whole life is in Pyle."

"My whole life?"

"Your family. Your place. Work. Crew. All your gyms. That's a lot of monthly fees going to waste." Adam signed up for Future Fitness last month so we could go together. When he found out how cheap it was, he could hardly believe it.

"My whole life." He exhales, and then he turns to me. The lamplight reflects off his glasses, but I can still see how deep blue his eyes have turned. "My whole life is right here."

I can't stop myself from arguing. "It's been two months."

"Do you know how hard it is not to—No. Do you know how it feels when I pull up in front of this house, and you're there, arms crossed, trying to look like you don't care, and then you melt on me?"

He waits. Oh, lord, he wants an answer. We don't do this. Talk about feelings. *I* don't do this. "Don't you miss your people? Your family?"

We've gone to Sawdust on the Floor a few times, and he holds his own with the locals. I know he isn't a homebody, per se.

"Shit, Jo-Beth. No. I don't." There's a realness in his voice. "You know what I am in Pyle?"

"Hot shit?"

"Sure." He's bitter, and again, I wish I could take my words back. I'm not used to being able to hurt someone with them. 'Specially not someone who's always so strong. "I'm everything to everyone. I'm the one with the plan that saved the company. I'm the one who keeps his brother from partying himself to death. The perfect son. Bachelor of the Year. I'm whatever someone else needs me to be."

I don't know what that's like, being the hero, but in another way, I understand what he's sayin'.

"I'm that. Whatever someone needs me to be."

The quiet after I say the words almost rings. It's the kind of silence you rush to fill with more words, and it's always a mistake. Still, I go on. "It's like I got a different face, worked by a whole different set of muscles. I catch my face in the mirror at work. It's me, and it's not me, you know?"

I duck my head, my cheeks burn, and wrap my arms tighter around my knees. I didn't mean to say so much.

"Your superhero mask," he says. "Come here now." He holds out a hand.

I shake my head. I'm too raw. He understands, dropping his hand and stretching his legs. After a minute or so, he says, "You know what? If my life all fell apart? I don't think I'd even care. It's that I've been doing it so long, I don't even know what I'd do if I were living for myself. Well, I didn't."

The corner of his lips curve, ever so slightly. "Turns out, I'd be into home improvements. Investments, home improvements, and Jo-Beth Connolly."

My eyes burn, so I blink real quick.

"My family is complicated, Jo-Beth. I told you about Ryan Morrison? How he emailed, and how we're meeting for a beer when he gets back to town?"

We've talked about that a lot. His biological father works construction, and he's been on a project in Florida. When he comes back, they're gonna meet. Adam replied to the guy's messages when he was in a weird headspace, but now, I think he's genuinely curious.

"I told my stepfather, and he told me I didn't need to

bother. Write the man a check, and he'd go away. My stepfather said he'd done it before. Several times."

"Fuck," I exhale.

"Yeah. He told me that the same way he told me how to negotiate at a car dealership when I was a kid."

Again, in some ways, this ain't anything like my life, but in others? Having family that don't care about you, holding shit together on your own? I get that.

I creep my feet forward, burrow them under Adam's thigh. He smiles and wraps a hand around my good ankle, stroking the indent of my heel with his thumb.

"You got cold feet?" he asks.

"Yeah."

"Better now?"

"Yeah." He reaches with his other hand to tuck my hair behind my ear. I scoot forward so I'm pressed close to his side. "I'm sorry your family sucks."

He cups my neck and angles my face up to his. "I'll buy you jewelry if you want it, but you're not my mistress. I'd buy you the moon, Jo-Beth. I love you."

A warm tingling swirls through my belly. I love him, too, I think, but I don't say it back. I can't. I get real nervous when he talks this way. I don't linger on it. I start asking myself questions like *why* and *for how long*, and I get uneasy.

"You can buy me a little bullfinch if you can find one," I say instead.

"You want a bullfinch?" Adam's sly smile breaks, and the tingles turn to a hot flush, creeping up my chest. His smile does things to me; it's not right. "I'll get you a bullfinch."

He scoops me up and lays me under him, already hard against my belly. I feel my panties go damp, and I spread for him, pull him down. I could never budge him, but he does what I want, his chest covering my tits, his nipples rasping against the tender flesh.

"Whatever you want, Jo-Beth." He hooks my panties in a finger, pulls them to the side, and then he slides home, to the hilt, filling me with his heat. We stopped using condoms a few weeks ago after Dr. Das ran some tests. I get the shot, so that's not a worry, but it still makes me nervous when he takes me bare. Old habits.

It feels so good, though, like he's touching me deep inside. When he cums, it's hot and sticky, and he loves to make a mess of me. He won't let me up to clean myself off until he's looked his fill and played in the mess we've made.

Remembering brings me back to my body, focuses me on the moment, his hands cupping my shoulders, holding me in place as he drives into me, harder and harder. I tilt my hips so my clit hits his pubic bone, and then I'm circling, getting closer and closer. I close my eyes. He kisses my eyelids.

"Are you ready, baby?"

"Almost there."

He drops a hand to lift my thigh, slams into me at a new angle, the perfect angle. "There! There! Don't stop!"

"Never, baby. Cum for me now. Show me how much you love this cock."

And I do. The coil erupts in my belly, and my channel pulses, squeezing him, and I go stiff and hot and then cold, and then go limp like a noodle as he groans and spurts into me.

I'm half-laughing, half-sighing, and he raises on an elbow to look at my pussy. He reaches down, swipes his cum with his first two fingers, and rubs it over my mound, into the triangle of curls I don't get waxed. He draws those fingers up my belly, and then paints them across my lower lip.

"You're mine, Jo-Beth. All mine."

I murmur in agreement, opening my mouth to suckle those fingers, greedy for the look of adoration he gives me in these moments.

"Say you belong to me."

"I belong to you."

I say it, and I almost, almost believe it, too.

9

ADAM

I hate leaving Jo-Beth on Monday mornings. I hate how her face goes hard, how she busies herself in the kitchen and offers me her cheek to kiss when I leave. Every damn time I have to take her chin and make her give me her mouth.

And I really fucking hate how I say, "I love you."

And she ducks her head and says, "Drive safe, okay?"

I spend the entire commute thinking about how I'm going to set things up so I fall asleep beside her every night. I've engineered hostile takeovers, and I've restructured a company from the foundation up, but I struggle with all the moving pieces in this situation.

Jo-Beth doesn't trust me. She doesn't trust *us*. She's not going to quit her job or sell her house. She's waiting for me to fuck up, and sometimes, I forget to be patient, and I get pissed. I've put a lot aside to give us a chance. My family. Her past. She's perpetually hedging her bets.

But then, how would moving her to Pyle go? It'd be the equivalent of packing her into an old Ford and driving her up to the mansion on the bluffs. She won't know anyone. She's too proud to let me take care of her, and I'll be damned if she goes back to dancing. As it is, I don't know how much longer Dr. Das and Cue from the White Van will go along with my suggestion —accompanied with generous gratuities for services rendered —that her ankle won't allow her to work quite yet.

And then there are the Wades. Jo-Beth is right; they won't welcome her with open arms. And my Jo-Beth's proud, but so fragile. This is a woman who has never taken a dive, who's never let the dirt she's had to eat define her. She's fought for her entire life, and she's lost battles. She doesn't talk about it, but the clues are there.

She startles—violently—when I open the bedroom door at night after the lights are out. She won't watch family sitcoms or Hallmark channel romances because "if I wanted to watch bullshit, I'd drive out Route 13." And sometimes, when we're making love, she drifts off, and I have to bring her back by stopping, saying her name, and cradling her to my chest.

She won't talk about it, won't even talk around it. Part of me knows she needs to, but a larger part—the coward in me —doesn't want to know. I put the clues in the box with what she had to do before, and I lock it away. That shit can only rip your heart out if you look at it too closely.

I think about quitting Wade-Allyn. I could work from Jo-Beth's house, do some consulting, some investing. I'd have to travel, but I could take Jo-Beth with me. I'd love to show her New York, London, Tokyo.

But then I pull up to the office, like I do this morning, and I stare up at the brick façade, the iron pilasters, and my last name in three-foot-tall letters above the revolving door. I pause for a minute on the sidewalk, crane my neck, count the stories.

I didn't build it, but sometimes, it feels like mine. Thomas Wade didn't build it either. His father bought it from a competitor when they went under during the recession of '81 and '82. It's funny, come to think of it. Thomas Wade Senior shamelessly built his legacy on the bones of his rival, and here I am, always half-convinced I'm nothing more than a lucky imposter, despite all I've done to keep the place afloat.

Of course, an hour gives the lie to that feeling that I don't belong. Eric needs me to resolve a fuck up with ArrowX-change. Thomas brings by a buddy, the C.F.O. of Western Coal Legacy, to troubleshoot a tax issue. A dozen people need a dozen things, and before I notice, I'm back in the grind. And it's gratifying; it's work that I love. Could I walk away?

I held this company together when it was three months from insolvency. What happens if I leave? I don't really need to ask. Thomas would reverse course in a second, and the company would go under. He's never understood the new economy. He doesn't *believe* in it.

If I left, Eric would follow, probably fund a start-up with nothing but a good story and money from his VC drinking buddies. He'd be bankrupt within a year.

I can't destroy what I've worked so hard to save. I've sold my soul for this place. For my position in this town. But how does Jo-Beth fit? She'd change in this life, and I don't want her to change.

So, I'm back to square one. Frustrated, missing Jo-Beth, snapping people's heads off. I'm staring at a spreadsheet, the numbers blurring, when an email notification catches my eye.

your father ryan Adam morrison

I scan it quickly. He's back from Florida. Wants to know when I can grab a beer.

Fuck it. *How about now? Are you in town?*

He writes back right away.

i can be there by dinner. where at?

My heart speeds up, all the garbage in my mind pushed aside by the adrenaline. I can't believe this is happening. I shoot off the name of a brew pub downtown, a casual place by the stadium. It's large. Crowded. Not my usual scene.

He says he'll be there at five o'clock.

I want to call Jo-Beth, and I'm reaching for my phone when it rings. It's Mom. She wants to talk about the Hearts and Diamonds Gala. It's this weekend. She wants to know who I'm bringing. What I'm wearing.

I haven't thought about any of it beyond vaguely resenting the time it'll take away from Jo-Beth. I hint that I might take a pass this year, and then Mom brings out the big guns. I can hear the tears in her voice.

"Just tell me you'll be there. Marjorie is coming. It's the only time all year that my three children are in the same place. I don't ask much, Adam. It's for the foundation."

"I'll be there," I promise. Another reason to call Jo-Beth, but as soon as I get off the phone, I'm called into a meeting with project development, and I hardly get out in time to drive across town to meet Ryan Morrison.

As I walk into the pub, tense as hell, I realize it was a good thing I didn't have the time to psyche myself out about the meeting. I don't know what I'm feeling, and I don't have the time to untangle the threads of resentment, bitterness, and curiosity. I'm also checking my phone, part of me convinced the guy is going to cancel.

But the hostess knows exactly who I'm talking about when I say I'm meeting someone. She leads me to a table by the bar, and there he is. He stands as I walk in. There's no mistaking it. He has my height, my black hair, although his is shoulder length and streaked with grey. He's got a paunch and a straggly beard. He's wearing a Harley T-shirt, and his arms are covered in full sleeves, the ink faded, mostly denim blue. He's wiping his palms on his worn jeans.

"Adam?" His voice cracks. He clears his throat.

I cross the rest of the way to the table, and stand, eye-to-eye with this stranger, his voice the same as mine, but gruff from smoking.

"Yeah." I offer my hand. What else do you do? He takes it. He's got a firm handshake, but his fingers are thin.

"Should we, ah—" He gestures to a chair. He already has a beer. "You look, ah—" He offers a wry grimace, and there's the gap in his teeth I remember. "You wanna order something?"

Yeah. I should. I need something to do with my hands. I wave over the waitress who clocked me the minute I walked in and order a stout. Then I take my phone out of my pocket and put it on the table, face up, make a show of checking it. For some reason, I need this man to know I'm not like him. I need to be accessible. People rely on me.

"So, you wanted something?" I keep my tone even, professional.

"Um. Yeah. Shit." He's nervous, taken aback. He's drumming tobacco-stained fingers on the table, his knuckles swollen and bent. Arthritis. He has the hands of a man twenty-five years his senior. "I—Uh."

He fumbles in his pocket and takes out his own phone. Then he fishes out a pair of thick-rimmed glasses from somewhere and slides them on, squinting. He taps, and when he finds what he's looking for, he seems to exhale.

"Here she is." He flips the phone to face me, and I don't

know what I'm expecting—a sibling I never knew about, maybe—but I'm faced with the photo of a bike. It's a road racer. Vintage. Maybe from the eighties. It's pristine, mint condition, and gorgeous.

"Is that what I think it is?"

"Yeah."

"Is it street legal?"

"Not at all."

He grins, flashing that gap again, as well as more than a few missing teeth, and there's a moment when we're just two men, admiring an exquisite piece of machinery.

"She's a V-twin, five speed. Won a lot of money off her back in the day, out at the speedway."

He flips through the phone, shows me other angles. He's a proud papa. The thought sours my stomach.

"You looking to sell? Is that what this is?"

Ryan Morrison's back straightens, and he sets the phone down. "No. Ain't like that." He's flustered. He shifts in his seat, leans forward and braces his elbows on the table.

"Listen. I know you don't want nothin' to do with me. I've always respected your wishes. But I just thought—" He's casting around for words. "I can't ride no more." He holds up his gnarled hands. "And I saw you in the paper. With the Black Shadow. And I thought maybe I could give you something."

I know the article he's talking about. Last year, the local paper did a puff piece on the "movers and shakers" in Pyle. My PR people sent them a picture of me on the bike.

I don't know what to say, and as I'm grasping, I get caught on his words. "What do you mean? Respected my wishes?"

"Mr. Wade, I mean, your stepfather. He made shit clear. You didn't wanna see me. I get it. I was fucked up, man, for a long time. Step nine, right? You don't get to make amends if it hurts someone else. You were happy, doin' well. I get it."

"I don't. When was this? When did you talk to my father?" I knew he'd called for money. Thomas made it seem like that's all it was.

Ryan Morrison tugs his beard and says, "Shit." It comes out long, almost like a whistle. "I don't know. A half dozen times over the years. I'd call your ma. He'd answer. I get it. Shit couldn't have been easy when I left. She didn't owe me nothin'."

"And my stepfather told you that I didn't want to speak to you?"

"Yeah. He'd offer me cash to fuck off. Ain't gonna lie. In those early days, before I got straight, I took him up on it. But I didn't come here for your money. This is a gift. No strings." He thinks for a minute. "Well, we'd need to figure out a trailer. I could borrow one from work, probably. I'll work it out."

That's the moment the waitress comes back with my beer.

I slump back in my chair, mind numb. "Did my mother know you wanted to see me?"

"Couldn't say." Ryan Morrison taps out another rhythm on the table with his thumb and the side of his palm. "She did all right for herself, for you. Considering how it was. She's a tough woman."

"When? When did you first call?"

He sighs, scratches his face. "I always called. Christmas. Birthdays, you know."

"You asked to see me?"

"Sure." He half-snorts. "This once, I had the half-baked plan to take you to Sturgis. Your stepfather said you'd just gone away to school."

I would have been eleven. My first year at Mountchassen. The year I didn't talk to anyone but Eric as I tried to learn how to speak like the other boys.

I don't know how to wrap my head around this, and I can't tear my eyes from this grizzled, old man who has my eyes and my jaw. This would have been my future if we'd stayed on Gilson Avenue. Old too soon. Tired. Falling apart at the seams.

A road trip to Sturgis.

Suddenly, it's too much. I need air. Space to think. "Okay. Yeah. I'll take the bike."

"Yeah? All right, all right." He rocks back in his seat, satisfied. "I'll need a few days to figure out the trailer, but it shouldn't be a problem."

We both take a minute, nurse our beers.

"So, where do you live?" I ask, more to make conversation than anything else.

"A little town, about two hours southeast. Petty's Mill. Heard of it?"

Yes. You could say that.

It's hard to believe in fate, but sometimes...it punches you in the face. Jo-Beth's not going to believe this when I tell her. Shit, I bet she knows this man. He's a biker.

And my gut roils. Yeah, she could know him. Really fucking well.

"Do you know a woman named Jo-Beth Connolly?"

"Jo-Beth? Sure."

"How? How do you know her?"

Bile is rising in my throat, and all the shit I don't think about swells up in a screaming chorus, pounding in my ears, almost drowning out his response.

"She's a sweetbutt. Hangs around my club. Steel Bones. Mean bitch. Like a Rottweiler. Won't give you the time of day unless you flash the cash. Whatever, you know? Plenty other gash. Steel Bones is doin' all right. Ain't hurtin' for pussy."

"So you and she have never—?"

"Nah. Not with that one. I mean, she's fucked most of the club, but I guess I never happened to get paid the day she needed to pay her bills. I seen her suck dick. Bitch deep throats like a doped-up porn star." He laughs. "How do you know Jo-Beth?"

"We're—" I don't know what to say. I want to puke. This is too real, too much. Fuck. It was easy, in her house in bumfuck, in her full-size bed that hardly fits two. So easy not to think about this. About what she is.

And suddenly, a door flies open. All the shit I hold back when I'm trying to sleep floods my brain. Pictures of Jo-Beth with my brother's cock in her mouth. Old fights, pummeling my fists into pasty boys who laughed when I didn't know how to take off my skis. Thomas Wade calling me into his office, a shoebox on his desk, filled with leftovers wrapped in linen napkins, rotten and reeking.

You're a Wade now. You don't have to do this anymore. Do you understand, son? This is disgusting.

I'm a Wade?

Absolutely.

Fuck. Is that all I do? See shit with other people's names on it and delude myself that it's mine? That because I want it, it belongs to me?

Nothing belongs to me. Not my past. Not my choices. Not Jo-Beth Connolly. She's not for owning. She's for rent. I can't be mad. She's never suggested otherwise.

Fuck. So many houses of cards blown over today with the breath of a few words.

I raise my hand for the check, and I ask to see the bike again. Ryan Morrison happily passes over his phone.

I MEAN to wait to confront Thomas Wade, but when I return to work, he's waiting in my office. He's sitting in one of the Eames lounge chairs in the glass alcove overlooking the river, sipping a bourbon. He gestures for me to take the other seat.

"I didn't know we had a meeting." I pour myself a drink before I sit. I see my stepfather's helped himself to my bar globe. It's gaudy as hell, a gift from Eric after our first quarter back in the black.

"We don't. I was here late, and I dropped by. Your girl said you'd be back."

"Any reason in particular for the visit?"

Thomas Wade eases back in his chair, and slightly raises his eyebrows. It's a look I recognize from all the times Eric and I were called into his office to account for some scrape or another. When I was younger, I respected how calm he always remained. No matter how Eric blubbered or raged, Thomas was unperturbed.

Now, the expression grates.

"You met with Ryan Morrison." He's not asking. I'm not surprised he knows. The secretaries, including "my girl," are all his hires, from his time. I'm not unaware that they'll check my inbox for him if he asks.

"I did."

"You've been keeping some other interesting company."

My jaw clenches. This is not a topic I'm ready to discuss.

At my silence, my stepfather sighs. "I suppose you know that your father made overtures. I declined them on your behalf."

"Why?" I think I should be angrier about this than I am, but I can't fathom it, really. How would that man with the warped hands and smoke ravaged voice have fit into my life? Back then, I was enthralled with being a Wade. Had I known Ryan Morrison had reached out, I probably would have refused to see him.

"To be frank?" He pauses. I nod, my gaze even. "It was difficult enough, ensuring that you were worthy of the Wade name. But you never quite accepted us—never accepted me as your father. Even after the adoption. I didn't think Ryan Morrison would help you embrace your new life. And I'll admit; my motivations weren't entirely selfless."

"What do you mean?"

There's a look, almost like chagrin, on my stepfather's face. "Well, God doesn't often gift you with a second chance." His lips turn up in a wry smile. "I didn't do my best by Eric. I can admit that. His mother was..." He sighs. "I thought indulgence was love, and by the time I was wiser, well, it was too late. And then I met your mother. And you. You were this tough, *brilliant* young man with a mind like nothing I'd seen before. And grit. You had such *grit*. Everything I gave you, you took as an opportunity, and you didn't just do well. You dominated."

I shift in my seat, uneasy. We don't talk like this. At least, he never has before.

"All I wanted was to share my legacy with you. My son." He raises his glass. "But you never saw yourself as a Wade. As my son."

"Thomas, that's—"

"It's true," he interrupts. "You think I don't know that you and Eric plot together about leaving Wade-Allyn?" His eyes go hard, the sentimentalism gone.

I won't deny it. "We want to build our own legacy."

"You already *have*. I gave you the keys to the kingdom, and you made this company your own. Do you think I actually understand what we do here now? But that's not enough for you." He sets his drink down with a thud. Rage fills his flinty gray eyes.

"I gave you all this, I gave you my name, and you drag it through the *mud*." He leans forward, his face growing red. "Playing house with a *whore*."

"Don't you—"

"Do you even know who she is?" He grabs a manila folder from an end table. "Public indecency. Prostitution. Shoplifting. Did you even look at her health records?" He flips through the papers in the file. "She's been passed around this biker club for *years*. How can you touch her without your skin crawling?"

I rise to my feet, fingers curling into a fist. "You need to leave."

He stands, dropping the file to his empty seat. "Do yourself a favor and read that. Think about how far you're really willing to go to reject this family. To turn your back on all I've done for you." A vein bulges in his forehead, and his hands shake.

"This isn't your business." My fury and disgust wars with old desires, old longings. The respect of this man was once everything to me. The imprint of that feeling is powerful, almost a muscle memory.

"*You* are my business." My stepfather smooths his hands on his slacks and squares his shoulders. "And if you spit in my eye one more time, so help me God, I am done with you. You're out. You won't have to quit Wade-Allyn; I will put you out on your ass. If what I've given you means so little, we are *done*. Your mother is with me on this. Make a decision, Adam. You can't go on with one foot in. It's not fair to anyone."

My stepfather exhales as if he's said his piece, and heads

for the door, and then he stops as if he remembered something. "And son? Your mother and I both read that." He nods at the file. "If you choose to force that woman into our lives, you do so with the full knowledge that we can never accept her. You cannot expect us to stand by and watch you debase yourself and shame this family." He nods firmly, as if to himself, and walks out the door.

I stand there a long time after he leaves, staring out the window at the wind rippling the river and the buildings rising beyond it. And then I sit at my desk, and I open the file.

There, in black and white, is everything I've been averting my eyes from. Justifying. Pretending it didn't matter.

This report is much more thorough than the one from the company's background service. Thomas hired a real investigator. This level of detail, they must have been working on this since I met Jo-Beth.

Public indecency. It was a plea. The original charge was prostitution.

Prostitution. There are two counts. She was eighteen both times. The first time, she got probation and court costs. The second time she paid a thousand dollar fine. Both times, she was arrested at a rest stop on Route 29.

Then there are her school records. Copies of letter after letter warning her mother that if her attendance didn't improve, action would be taken. The letters keep coming after her mother dies in hospice, but they stop when Jo-Beth drops out.

My gut is tied in a knot, acid scoring my throat.

There are screenshots of her health records. Definitely illegally obtained. It's mostly bronchitis and sinus infections, but there's a thick circle hand drawn around an antibi-otic prescription when she was nineteen. Chlamydia.

And then there are newspaper articles about a foster father, published long after she would have left the home. He was arrested in a vice sting, soliciting underage girls. His son showed the police a cache of videos. In most, the face of the girls weren't visible, but police do identify one victim as a former foster child. Not Jo-Beth. A woman a few years older.

A wave of powerlessness saps me of energy, and I slump in my chair. How does a person survive this? How do you live through this with your heart intact?

The answer, of course, is staring me in the face.

You don't.

In the part of the report for "associates," the only people listed are members of the Steel Bones MC and employees of The White Van. No family. No friends apart from the MC. No boyfriends or lovers. Not one.

And I feel like such a fucking fool. This whole time, I'm wondering if she feels this thing between us, this strange affinity. And I delude myself that she must. She lets me in her house. She cums so sweetly on my cock. And if she doesn't feel what I feel yet, it doesn't matter. She'll open up with time. Patience. Care. And if she doesn't, I can love her enough for both of us.

But can I?

I can walk away from Wade-Allyn. My family. I could give up everything for her.

And I could be left wondering every day for the rest of my life whether I gave up everything for a woman who could never feel the way I do.

I take out my phone and pull up her number. I crave her voice. I want to let the rush that I feel every time we speak reassure me that I'm not crazy. My finger hovers above the key. I can hear how the conversation would go. My muscles unknotting. Her salty teasing. At the end, I'd say I love you. And she'd say goodbye.

My email chirps. I reach for my mouse. Later. I'll call later. When I'm steady. When this sick roiling in my gut subsides. When I've figured this shit out, and when I can hear her voice without my heart bleeding in my chest.

10

JO-BETH

A dam hasn't called once this week. He texted one time that he's busy. Some merger, and there's a charity thing he has to do with his mother this weekend, so he won't be down. I called him. Twice. I didn't leave a message, but he didn't return the calls.

So I guess that's that. I can take a fucking hint.

You know what else? I learned something. The main reason not to let a man in your house? The way it feels when he's gone.

Last night—Friday night—I went down to the basement, and I took out the bottle of wine from behind the paint cans. I had a corkscrew in my hand, and I was about to open it, drink the whole damn thing. I almost did. But then I sat my ass down on the cold bottom stair and had a think.

I spent my entire childhood watching my mother beg one man after another to love her, tie herself in knots for them, reorder our whole lives, move in on a Monday, move out on a Sunday. I watched her poison herself after they left or put us out, and I thought how *stupid* she was to do their dirty work for them.

Now, I don't think she was trying to destroy herself. I think she was tryin' to get numb. Save herself. 'Cause this? This fucking *hurts*.

She believed their words. The gifts. Every time, she believed. I thought I was immune. Like I'd been vaccinated by her stupid. This hard, spiked, stabbing pain in my chest says I'm not. It's a raw, awful hurt. The kind of hurt that drags you down, drowns you.

I ain't going out like that.

This morning I dragged myself into the shower. I made myself blow dry my hair and put on mascara and eyeliner. Then I drove myself down to the clubhouse. I had some work to give Deb, but after, I stayed.

I haven't been around in a while, so I been gettin' my ear bent all day. Ernestine told me how she put Grinder out again. Grinder bitched about how Ernestine don't know how good she has it. Now, Creech is showing me some of his new work; he's almost done with the piece on his thigh.

Creech can talk for hours if you let him, in circles that'll make you dizzy. He's got ADHD, and generally, he can't keep on topic or stay in a seat for shit, which is why it's amazing he can work on a tattoo for most of a day without moving.

"See this, Jo-Beth? It's a Celtic knot, but look at it this way, yeah? Can you see it? Can you see it's a snake?"

"That's real cool."

"You see it?" Creech thrusts his thigh higher so I can get a real good look. I also get a peek at his hairy balls through the gap of his Dickies shorts. Ugh.

"I see it. It's like an ouroboros."

"A what?"

"A snake biting its own tail."

"What's that called again?"

"An ouroboros."

"You learn that word from Heavy?"

"Probably."

Creech is the one who hooked me up with Steel Bones. I was in foster care after Mama died. He was crashing in the basement of the house. He was friends with their real son. The dad had a habit of coming in my room after everyone was asleep. He said if I didn't say anything, I could have his son's car when they bought him a new one for graduation.

They lived way out on the flats. If I had a car, I could get work in town. I could move out. Get a place of my own. I wanted that car so fucking bad. The son totaled it on prom night. Creech was the one who pulled me off the dad that next night before I had the chance to do real damage. I couldn't stay there no more, so he gave me a ride to the Steel Bones clubhouse and told me to go talk to a guy named Heavy.

I think I can count on one hand the number of men who ever did anything for me without expecting something in return. Creech Nowicki is one of them, and the rest are all members of the Steel Bones MC.

I would have said Adam Wade last week, but I had my head up my ass. That man expected everything, and what did he give me? In the end? A lesson I shouldn't have had to fucking learn.

"So, when are you gonna let me give you a tattoo, Jo-Beth?" Creech tugs at the neckline of my tank top, baring a shoulder. "We could put one of them snakes here. It'd look fuckin' insane."

I swat his hand. "Maybe when I have the money."

Creech gives me the once-over, flashing his gold tooth. "I'd do it in trade."

I shake my head as a bitter taste fills my mouth. This is why Adam bailed, isn't it? We never talked about what I do.

What I've done. He said it didn't matter. I knew better, but it was a sweet lie, you know?

For a man like Creech or most of the brothers, I'd have believed it didn't matter. They have a simple view of women. If she don't put out, they don't have much time for her. Adam isn't like the brothers, though.

He's not like anyone. I thought he was like me, a little. Doing what he has to do. Making a space that's only his. Finding peace where he can.

The hurt pulses, knocks against my ribs, burning. I make myself stand up. I ain't letting this drag me under. I fucking refuse.

"Get you a beer?" I ask.

"All right, Jo-Beth. Thanks." Creech has already turned to a prospect, shoving his thigh in his face.

I pad over to the bar. Crista's working, but she's busy down the other end with Boots, so I belly up to wait. I'm playing with my phone when the smell of expensive hair product and a whiff of brimstone fills my nose. The stool next to me creaks.

Oh, just what I fucking need. Harper Ruth.

I wait for her to spit it out, but I see the game's afoot. She wants me to ask. I sigh.

"Whatcha doin', Harper?"

"Getting in your business," she singsongs, sipping from a martini glass. In this massive converted garage that still smells faintly of grease—and strongly of beer and cigarettes —Harper Ruth sticks out like a sore thumb. She's wearing a black tailored suit, pearls, and the kind of dangly watch that clinks and sounds like money.

"Now, there's no need for that." I always keep my distance from Heavy's sister. If it wasn't enough that she's a lawyer, she also makes sport of fucking with sweetbutts and generally causing misery. She's trouble I don't need.

"Well, don't you know we have something in common," she purrs. "Or should I say *someone*?"

I guess I'm slow because when it clicks, I want to slap myself. Harper's dating Des Wade. He has to be a relation of Adam's. It's a small world in these parts.

"Your boyfriend related to the guy I was banging?" With a woman like Harper, you got to be direct. Your best shot of minimizing the drama is keeping it as brief as you can.

"Des and Adam are cousins. Des' mother is Adam's stepfather's sister."

"Fascinating." I wave at Crista, but her head's turned. I don't think she sees.

"*Was* banging? Don't tell me you lost the goose that laid the golden egg so soon?" Harper drums her long, red nails on the bar. "Seriously, though. It beggars belief that you'd land that man in the first place. How did you do it?"

I shrug. "Blew his brother."

Harper laughs, and it's so rusty it might be real. "Eric Wade! Shut the fuck up!" She shoves my shoulder.

"There was a disagreement. I got clocked. Nickel ended up beating the shit out of Eric, Adam tapped in, Cue and Forty had to break it up. A real fuckin' meet cute."

Harper rounds her perfectly-applied smokey eyes. "Why you little agent of chaos. How'd you lose him?"

If it feels like a knife to the chest, I don't let on. "Maybe I didn't. Maybe he's really busy. But probably he's come to his senses."

"Yeah, yeah. The Wades would shit themselves if their adopted golden boy went off the rails and took up with a whore. No offense."

"None taken." I wave again, higher, but Crista's got her blinders on.

"That kind of scandal could really strain the fabric of a family. People would take sides. Lines in the sand would be drawn."

At this point, Harper's almost rubbing her hands together in glee. I guess she really don't like her future in-laws.

"Moot point." I haul myself up and bend over the bar, try to see if I can reach the cooler myself.

"Sit your ass back down." Harper grabs the back of my tank top and pulls me back into my seat. "How would you like to earn a thousand bucks for an hour's worth of work?"

"Doing what?"

"Just putting on a pretty dress and making an appearance at a charity ball."

"This have to do with Adam Wade?"

"Of course it does."

"No."

Harper stares me down, weighing me with her dead, gray eyes, like she's never seen me before. I hold her stare because it ain't my habit to back down, but there's a casual malevolence there that sends chills down my spine. I don't believe in evil outside of the things people do, but if I did? I'd say there's evil in Harper Ruth.

"You care about him." Her eyes pop wide as if she's just figured it out, and the corners of her red lips curl. "Do you love him?"

I don't answer. I draw myself behind my resting bitch face and wait.

"Of course you love him. He's filthy rich, crazy smart, and he looks like Superman. He's only missing the curl.

Shit. Maybe *I* love him." A cackle bubbles from her impeccably lined lips.

"Are you almost done? I promised Creech a beer."

"Crista Holt isn't going to get you a beer until I'm gone, and you know it. She hates me. She's been pretending not to see us this whole time."

Fuck. Harper's probably right. Why won't she leave?

"I'll go." Harper reads my mind. "If you'll tell me one thing. Have you always been this stupid?"

This *bitch*. My fists clench. I ain't above a throwdown, and I don't give a shit about fucking up her fancy-ass suit.

She smiles, gleeful. "I mean, I know you're tough. You've gotten this far in life sober and with all your teeth, and that's a fucking miracle. But how is it that you manage to hook a millionaire? *You.* Jo-Beth who rides the pole and will suck cock for a twenty. Jo-Beth with the junkie mother who never finished school. How is it that you manage that, and you don't even try to fight to keep him? I mean, are you stupid?"

I don't owe Harper Ruth anything. My hands are shaking, but it's not 'cause of what she said. It's from trying not to pop her in the face. I'm fairly sure the brothers would just gather around and place bets, but she is family, and I ain't. They won't let me win. It'd feel *so* good to break that perfect nose, though. I could do it quick.

"I mean, I'd at least be curious." She leans so close I can smell the gin on her breath. "If I had a whale that big and lost him, I'd want to know why. Do you know why he bailed on you?" Harper drains her glass, eyeing me over the rim, and fuck her, 'cause she knows she's got me.

I do want to know. *Need* to know, now that she says it. Somehow, getting angry at her has stoked a deeper fury, a burning, jagged thing that I don't think I can fit behind the hard, blank face I wear.

I want him to say it to my face. I'm a whore, and he's too good for me. I want it to hurt so bad that I get so filled with rage I don't ever have to feel this way again.

He fooled me twice. He said pretty, pretty things, and then he showed his ass.

That man is a liar. The worst kind, the kind that believes his own bullshit. And all week long, I've been playing right along. He gets to *come to his senses*. Fuck, even I was writing him an excuse note. *Of course*, he'll realize he's making a mistake, ghost on me, leave my basement all torn up. 'Cause I'm trash, right? And he's slumming it.

Fucking *bullshit*. *I* didn't bulldoze myself into his life, his house. That's the thing about rich people. They think they *deserve* to do whatever they want to do. Well, you know what? I deserve a decent *fuck off*. Look me in the eye and tell me how you woke up and remembered you're better than me.

"I see those wheels turning." Harper twists her stool so she's facing me. "I can set it up. You can find out why."

"Does this involve putting on a pretty dress and going to a charity thing?"

"Oh, yeah. The Wade-Allyn Foundation Hearts and Diamonds Gala. It's the social event of the year."

"He's gonna be there?"

"Oh, yeah."

"I'm in."

"You need a dress?"

"Can I wear Lycra?"

A peel of laughter rings out, and heads turn. It's a strange sound. Terrifying. Across the room, a cluster of sweetbutts shiver and flee out the back. "You need a dress. Lucky you, I've got you covered."

Harper slides from her stool, and lands lightly on her

black six-inch heels with the red bottoms. "We'll go to my place. I know exactly which dress you should wear. The Wades aren't gonna know what hit them."

The prospect of being beholden to Harper Ruth is almost enough to change my mind, but my Irish is up now. And the anger hurts so much less than the loss.

"You have beef against these people or are you just out for the drama?"

"A little from column A, a little from column B."

"I want the thousand in cash."

"It goes without saying." Harper eyes me critically. "Do you need to wear that brace?" She gestures to the soft wrap around my ankle.

"I don't think so. Why?"

"It'd kind of ruin the effect we're going for."

"And what effect is that?"

"Bombshell." Harper Ruth grins, shimmering her fingers. "*Kaboom.*"

I FEEL like a woman in a James Bond movie. I'm standing at a rusted back door of the art museum in Riverfront Park. Harper had a prospect, Washington, drop me off on the street, and I had to traipse through the park in Harper Ruth's sneakers, carrying my shoes and the skirt of my gown clutched to my chest.

It's dark and freezing cold. It snowed a few days ago, and then it rained, so Harper's Keds are caked in mud. When I reach the door, I toe them off and wedge my feet into the purple platform heels with peep toes and buckles around the ankle. They look like stripper heels to me, but Harper says they cost her two thousand bucks in New York, so I guess they're not.

I'm supposed to wait here until Harper can shake Des Wade and let me in. It's all really cloak and dagger. She's being dropped off in a limo out front, and then she gets her picture taken. I caught a glimpse of the museum entrance as I hiked through the brush to the back. There are floodlights, a slow procession of limos, and a cluster of photographers at the end of a red carpet.

This must have been on Adam's calendar the whole time we've been together. He didn't mention it once. All the *I love you's*. All the sweet talk. He was so sincere. But when it came time to be seen in public with me? Seems he couldn't bring himself to do it.

I'm not surprised. In the end, to him, I was the same as I am to every other man. Disposable.

I knew this is exactly how it'd go down, and that makes it so much fucking worse. I grit my teeth and stamp my feet to keep warm.

Thank goodness this shindig ain't fancy enough for outside security 'cause Lord knows I ain't stealthy in this dress. It's sleeveless and painted on from right above my nips to the bottom of my ass, and then it flares out like a tree skirt. A big, puffy one. I've got it gathered in my arms like a triple load of laundry.

This might be a shitty idea. Strike that—it's *definitely* a shitty idea, but at least I'm distracted. My eyes aren't burning like they have been all week.

While I wait, I think about what I'll say. All I can come up with is "How dare you?" and a Scarlett O'Hara slap, which is not my style and not what I want to say either.

I don't know what I want to say.

I love you. Come home. I'll be different. I'll be whatever you want.

Cold slices down my middle, and my nose prickles. No. Fuck that. I ain't cried yet, and I'm not gonna.

I should punch him in the face. I'm more of a punch than a slap girl. He's so tall, it'd be a stretch, but he wouldn't see it coming. I picture it a few ways, and it keeps me from thinking about how fucking cold it's getting, waiting in the dark.

After what feels like forever, the door flies open, and there's Harper Ruth, perfect in a red sheath, diamond earrings, and a diamond choker, her eyes sparkling. She's tipsy.

"Come on," she stage whispers, dragging me in by the elbow. We're in a sub-basement of some kind, but she seems to know her way. She leads me through narrow linoleum corridors to some stairs. It smells like equal parts bleach and mold.

"These open by the bathrooms. Just follow people back to the main hall. The Wades are all up front, at the table on the dais. You can't miss them."

"Aren't you coming?" My stomach's flipping, and way too late, I wonder if you can get arrested for crashing a charity gala.

"I'll wait here a few minutes. Plausible deniability." She winks at me, real big, and then shoves my ass up the last step. "Go on! Get your man."

I'm opening my mouth to answer her, but Harper's push has made me unsteady, so I can't help but step forward through the door. I instantly realize two very fucked-up things.

From the women in line at the bathroom, I figure out there's a dress code. Red and white with piles and piles of diamonds. I'm in purple. Not maroon or anything close to red. The color purple you find on a Hawaiian shirt. No jewelry.

I turn to duck back down the stairs, and that's when I realize the door locked automatically. That, or Harper has wedged it shut somehow. I face the guests by the bathroom and knock furiously behind my back. Nothing.

The other women are very politely ignoring me while whispering to each other—about me.

I need to get out of here before one of them calls security. There's definitely inside security at an event like this. I hustle down a thickly carpeted hall, so different than below stairs, and then I skid to a halt as the hall opens into a grand ballroom. I gasp.

It's...it's so *pretty.*

The ceilings are high, maybe three stories, and giant crystal chandeliers throw off sparkles. Nets filled with perfectly round red and white balloons are hanging in the corners of the room. There's a grand, curving staircase leading up to the second level, and on the mezzanine, there's what looks like a swing band. A man in a tuxedo with long tails swings a pointy stick while horns echo through the hall.

There are naked statues and huge paintings almost as high as the walls, and on every surface, there are massive bouquets of red roses and white calla lilies in glass vases as big as trash cans.

It's like the movies.

Everyone is beautiful, laughing, and dancing. Everyone fits in their red, white, and black.

I don't match.

My skin gets clammy, and I try real hard to ignore the stares and look for the exit. I'd like to say I'm the kind of woman who doesn't give a shit that she stands out like a sore thumb, but the half an hour in the freezing cold went a long way to extinguishing my righteous anger. Maybe retreat's the better part of valor, as Heavy says.

It's really hard to tell where I am with all the people. I suck in a breath and aim for the opposite side of the hall. Bathrooms are usually in the back, so the front doors should be straight ahead. I take a step, and my ankle wobbles. Oh, hell, no. I firm my stance. I ain't going out like that.

I walk, real calm and careful, picking through the clumps of people, skirting the dance floor. I make it almost to the other side when I realize that I'm not heading toward the doors. I'm heading to the dais. I know this 'cause the crowd parts spontaneously, and there, above me, Adam Wade is staring down from a long table, surrounded by perfect people, a gob smacked expression on his impossibly perfect face.

I stop in my tracks and wrap my arms around my middle. I can't seem to meet his eyes straight on.

He stands, his chair screeching back. His family have noticed me now. The blond man with the flushed face next to him is his stepbrother Eric. There's an older woman with perfectly styled black hair, the same color as Adam's. She's staring down her nose like I'm a walking piece of shit, and she just caught a whiff.

This is the worst idea I've ever had in my entire life.

A handsome man with grey hair and Adam's confident bearing stands, too, and puts a hand on Adam's forearm. He whispers something in his ear. Adam shakes his head.

I need to get out of here, but I can't seem to move. Adam's blue eyes are drilling into me. Broken. Hurt.

What business does he have to be hurt?

I lift my chin and narrow my eyes. That seems to break

the spell. Adam frees himself from the older man and comes down to me, his long legs covering the distance in no time. There are more eyes on us now. Everyone's eyes. Sweat breaks out behind my knees.

"Jo-Beth. What are you doing here?" He grabs me by the upper arm. Like how a bouncer does. I jerk my arm away.

He glances around, his jaw tightening. He's embarrassed. He's embarrassed of me.

"You owe me." It flies out of my mouth, too loud, the idea half-formed. It must have been the wrong thing to say. His face goes stone cold.

Adam grabs my arm again, pulling me toward the dais steps. "What are you doing, Jo-Beth?" he hisses under his breath. "You're making a scene."

As we approach the table, the woman who must be his mother hustles away a girl, a young woman in a pearly white gown. That must be his sister, Marjorie. He's mentioned her. She's in college. She's straining over her shoulder to get a gander at me.

"Sit," Adam orders, urging me toward the seat his mother vacated. "What are you doing here?"

"Holy shit." Eric, his bow tie crooked and his jacket unbuttoned, leans forward until he can see me. "I know you." He leers.

"Shut up." Adam points his finger at his brother.

"Both of you. Collect yourselves." The older man, I'm assuming Adam's stepfather, Thomas Wade, has lowered himself to sit on my other side. "Young woman. You know my sons?"

Eric chortles, almost spits the champagne he's swigging. Next to Eric, there's an older couple, the man gaping, the woman politely staring at the dance floor. Past them, there's another man, a handsome, older version of Eric, and next to him is Harper Ruth, a shit-eating grin barely hidden by a glass of red wine.

"Young lady." A rough hand presses on my bare shoulder. "I asked if you know my sons."

My gaze flies to Adam, search those blue eyes, and I realize that I don't want to say anything. I want—I *need*—him to speak. He needs to stand up and take my hand and tell all these people that I belong to him, only him, and he belongs to me.

He's said it a dozen times, under the covers, in the car as we ride home at night, while we walk together on the trail that runs beside the Luckahannock.

He can say it now. I'm here. I came. It can be real. I made it real.

I keep my back ramrod straight, and I meet his eyes and hold my breath. I came here. I came to him. It has to mean something. He can't just give up and throw it—me—away.

My bottom lip trembles, so I bite down on it.

And Adam sits there, frozen, his hands fisted on his thighs. Saying nothing. As if he's waiting. For what?

"Ain't you gonna say anything?" I ask.

"You came here, Jo-Beth. What is it you want to say?"

It's a dare, but I don't know the rules to this game. He's furious and cold, and I'm supposed to have the magic words, I guess, but I'm lost. "I don't know what I'm doing here." I kind of startle when I realize I said it aloud.

Adam just stares at me, his jaw clenched, his eyes unreadable.

"Young lady, let me call you a ride." Thomas Wade's voice is not unkind. He wraps his hand gently around my upper arm and guides me to stand.

I wobble on my feet, a hot dizziness filling my head. I very respectfully remove Thomas Wade's hand from my arm. "Thank you, sir, but I can see myself out. I ain't gonna cause any trouble."

I force myself to smile, and then I walk as calm as can be past Adam and Eric and the old couple and Des Wade and Harper Ruth, my nose in the air. I can't feel my body, and it's not the worst feeling in the world. It's kind of like floating.

As soon as I'm off the dais, everyone very politely stops looking at me. I assume Adam's still pretending he's never seen me before. I don't look back to check. I did catch Harper's disappointment when I passed. She was hoping for a scene.

Maybe I was, too.

I head for the front, the crowd closing behind me, and I'm almost there when I see the hall to another gallery. There's a bar at the far end.

You know what? Fuck it. I bet it's an open bar.

There're more black tuxedoes than red and white dresses in this space, and the ceiling's lower. If I remember from that one field trip, I think it's the museum café. There are high top tables lining two walls and stools.

I order a gin and tonic from the bar, and I was right. Open bar. I take myself to a seat in the corner, perch half on the chair 'cause of the huge-ass skirt of my dress, and get down to business. Maybe I'm hoping Adam comes after me. Maybe that explains the sinking feeling in my gut as minute after minute passes.

While I wait, I check out the company. Less hair, fewer tattoos, and better smelling overall than my kind of people, but the men still laugh louder than the women, and the women still weigh each other up with their eyes. They seem less likely to end up brawling out back, but the night's young, and I don't know these people after all.

My heart gives a kick, so I chug the rest of my drink. He ain't coming. I need to go.

"Looks like I'm just in time." A beefy hand slides a fresh drink in front of me, and then a sturdy man in a black tux eases himself into the seat next to me. He's a big guy, maybe forty. He's got the beginnings of gin blossoms, a lot of product in his thinning hair, and a chunky watch.

That's one difference between rich and poor people. Apparently, rich people still wear watches.

"Dan Gershund." The man offers me a hand. I shake it, dig deep, and summon up my stripper smile. This guy looks like a *great* idea. Adam Wade is done with me? I'm so beneath him he doesn't even need to say why? Fine. I'm done being a fool. I'm getting back to work.

"It's nice to meet you, Dan." I arch my back and wiggle in my seat. His gaze dips down to my tits.

"Somebody forget to give you the memo about the red and white? You should thank them. You look fantastic in purple."

I flash my teeth and hope it looks like a smile. "I thought I'd go for something different. What about you, Dan? Would you be interested in something a little different tonight?"

I rest my hand on his thigh. He licks his fat lips.

"Is this my lucky night?" He leans in, grinning.

"It could be. For five hundred." That's one thing I should thank Adam Wade for. Teaching me to value myself.

Dan Gershund backs up a hair, bristles almost imperceptibly. Aw. He really thought he was getting lucky. I can tell the instant when he sees this another way, forgets to be mad that he ain't hot shit after all.

There's a glint in his close-set eyes when he realizes that I'm not a woman after all. I'm merchandise. Oh, the possibilities when you don't have to care about what other people feel.

"Plus two hundred gratuity." I thrust my tits up until you see a shadow of nipple.

"Yeah. Okay. Ah. How do we do this?" He's looking around like a bed's miraculously going to appear. He's got me by the hand, and his grip is sweaty and tight.

"Wherever you want," I say. "However you want."

"For seven hundred, you're going to let me put it in your ass, aren't you," he slurs in my ear as he pinches the nape of my neck with one hand to steer me toward the door. I hate the feeling, but I'm kind of above it all.

"Whatever you want, baby. I'm yours."

I'm already floating away, up with the red and white balloons, losing myself between the notes of the music. The numbness is so familiar it feels like home.

I breathe in the flowers as we pass them, attach my mind to the colors, the glittering crystal vases. I like the combination of roses and calla lilies. Come spring, I'll buy some. Plant them out back by the fence line.

I let my thoughts fly, and it's spring already, and I'm not here. Whatever is about to happen doesn't matter. Nothing matters. Not Adam Wade. Not me.

"What the fuck are you doing?" I'm dragged back to earth so suddenly, I stumble. I'm in the great hall, a yard from the red and white balloon arch marking the entrance, and Adam has stepped into my path. He's looming in front of me, blue eyes spitting fire, glaring at the man at my back.

I blink. Try to focus. "Why do you care?"

Eric's standing at Adam's elbow, as if he's trying to drag him back where he came from.

"What the *hell*, Jo-Beth?" The way he says *Jo-Beth*, it

makes me hate him, makes the fury flail in my chest like it's gonna break my ribs.

"I'm gonna go fuck this guy for money." I jerk my head.

Adam breathes through clenched teeth. "Jo-Beth. Can you not speak straight to me? For once? You come all the way here, and all you have to say is I owe you? For what, Jo-Beth? What do I owe you?"

"I take it back. I don't need anything from you."

"You make that crystal clear. So why come? Why, Jo-Beth?" He plunges his hand in his hair, and his blue eyes blaze. "Just tell me. For once. *Let me in.* I can ignore it all, if it's real. If you feel it, too."

A lump nearly swells my throat shut. "You can ignore it all?"

"I can."

Me. He can ignore me. What I am. Fuck. That's a hell of a kind of love. When you love so much, you can pretend a person isn't who they are.

"No worries, Adam. I'm gone. You don't need to ignore anything." I reach out and grab Dan's hand. He's been hanging close, watching this go down.

Dan circles his hand back around my neck, tightening his grip. Adam's eyes catch fire.

"I think she said what she's gonna say, buddy." Dan kind of urges me forward.

"Get your fucking hands off her."

"Listen, buddy. This is not your—"

I think he was going to say "business," but before he can, Adam pulls back and sails his fist into the guy's mouth, lunging forward as he does so they both end up on the floor, several feet behind me. There's scuffing, grappling, and Dan lands a blow, bloodying Adam's nose.

The band plays on while everyone backs up, shocked

gasps and startled screams rippling through the crowd away from the scene. Adam swings Dan into a table, and it tips. A vase crashes to the ground, and by some miracle it doesn't break, but the flowers go everywhere, getting kicked and crushed as the fight rages on.

Adam's winning, but Dan has stamina. He's got to be ex-military, a boxer, something. I can't pull my eyes away. I'm rooting for the fight to come my way so I can kick Adam Wade in the balls.

Before security can show, Thomas Wade elbows through the crowd, Des Wade and Harper Ruth at his heels. Harper is trying to swallow a gleeful laugh, her lips sealed together, her eyes bugging out. It's the first time I've seen her ugly.

Thomas Wade barks at Eric to help him break it up, and then he flashes me a look of pure poison. This man hates me.

Ain't gonna lie. I don't think I've ever felt so powerful in my life. It's kind of heady shit.

I sketch a salute to Harper, and then I flip Mr. Thomas Wade the bird as I gather my skirts to my chest. These are rotating doors, and the end of this story is not me getting stuck in them and waiting for somebody to find a pair of scissors.

"Jo-Beth," Adam pants, staggering to his feet, his crisp white shirt bloodied and hanging open. His tie's gone. His blue eyes burn into me, raising goosebumps on every inch of exposed skin. A shiver shoots down my spine. "Jo-Beth. Say it, then. What did you come here to say?"

I love you. Don't leave me. I'm sorry all the times you said I love you, and I was too much of a coward to say it back. I miss you. I can't breathe without you. Come back.

That's what I meant to say. Before I got it shoved in my face that Adam is like every other man who's ever paid me.

He holds all the cards, but I'm the one that's got to show mine. 'Cause having all the power ain't enough. He needs my pride, too. Fuck that. Fuck him.

Dan Gershund finds his feet, and Adam's attention is drawn away. His lips curl back in a grimace.

"What were you doing, Jo-Beth? Goddamn. Here? You had to do that shit here?"

There's betrayal in his voice, and it sends a wave of rage cresting through me.

He's gonna ghost me? Act like I don't exist? Then act like I owe *him*? I take in the scandalized crowd, the knocked-over table, water pooling, flowers stomped to soggy mush. That's what you get from me. Ignore *that*, motherfucker.

I hoist my skirts again, flip my middle finger at his perfect, stupid face, and I keep it raised until I'm through the door and out in the cold, damp air.

As I stalk off down the drive, I recall Dan Gershund's shiny black shoes cracking Adam's glasses as they slammed each other into the marble floor. I knew those glasses would break easy.

This night did not turn out as planned. I don't know what I wanted, not exactly, but maybe it doesn't matter. Whatever fool shit was in the back of my head, I see now I was never gonna get swept into his arms at first sight and twirled around that ballroom. It was clear that I don't belong with those people. I don't belong with *him*. He's too good for me, but he'll ignore the fact, the stand-up guy.

But I got a home. I only need to make a call, and I got a ride there. And unlike other people, I don't break easy.

If my heart don't agree, that's all right. I can live without it. I have this long.

11

ADAM

After Thomas smoothed things over with security, he took Mom and Marjorie home. I was still drunk, worse due to not having slept more than a few hours all week. The blows to the head probably didn't help either. I wandered outside, found the stone stairs that led to the sculpture garden, and collapsed. It was cold and wet. My knuckles throbbed.

I hadn't been in a fistfight since a parking lot brawl after a football game in college, and in the three months since I met Jo-Beth, I've been in two. Clear evidence I'm on the wrong path, right?

But God, she was so fucking beautiful tonight. Her skin was a little splotchy like it gets when exposed to cold air. It would be tacky to the touch. I remember that man's hand circling the back of her neck, and my fists clench, sending shooting pains radiating from my busted knuckles. I force myself to shake out my hands.

I love her skin. It's soft, warm. I love her skin because it's *hers*. Because maybe I do have some kind of kink. I know she doesn't care who touches that skin, but I still want her to crave my hands on her. Is that masochism? Probably.

Fuck, I wish I had a drink. And then a voice calls out, "He's over here." And it's like God answers my prayers.

Or the devil. Two stumbling figures lurch toward me, one wrapped in the other's jacket. I can't tell who it is until they're sprawled on the steps with me. It's Eric and...Des' girlfriend? Harper Ruth.

They both have bottles of champagne. Eric presses his into my palm. "Here, bro. An olive branch. I seriously didn't think you were going to punch that guy out. I thought maybe you'd have some words with the girl. A little drama. You can't blame me, man. These things are boring as shit."

He's babbling like he tends to do when drunk. He was the one who came and told me Jo-Beth hadn't left, that she was talking to a man by the bar. I knew he was stirring shit at the time, but I didn't think. I never have when it comes to Jo-Beth. I'd already been standing, ready to go after her.

On my other side, Harper Ruth hiccups, very delicately and ladylike. "You really fucked that up, didn't you?" She crosses her legs and takes a swig from her own bottle.

"Where's cousin Des?" I ask.

"The men's room? Wandering around, looking for me, after using the men's room? Whatever." She gesticulates by swinging the bottle wide, and I duck.

"Did you have anything to do with Jo-Beth coming here tonight?" It didn't make sense, the dress, how she got in. Not until this moment.

"Yeah. Did you like that? Surprise!" Harper chuckles to herself. I haven't had many conversations with her, but I'm struck again by the sense that she's the female equivalent of a fast car whose brakes have failed.

"Was it your idea?"

"Hard to say, in retrospect. And drunk. I'm drunk."

"So I gathered."

"She wanted *closure*." Harper overenunciates the word. "She wanted to know why you dropped her like a hot potato. Well, she knew. 'Cause she's Jo-Beth Connolly, club pussy, that's why. But she wanted to *know* know. You know?"

I pry the bottle from her hand and return Eric's. "Thanks, man."

I polish off Harper's bottle in two gulps. There wasn't much left. "You don't know anything."

"Oh, I know some things. I'm a fly on the Wade family wall. I know you've been cleaning up after this fuck up your entire life." She reaches behind me to slap Eric upside the head. He grumbles and jerks away. "I know all the Wades are shitting themselves about what happens to the family fortune when the goose who lays the golden egg decides to take his chances in New York or Silicon Valley."

She giggles and shoves her hands in the pockets of Eric's jacket. "You know what I know that you don't?"

I grit my teeth, wishing this fucking night was over. "What, Harper?"

"I know what it's like to be a whore. But what am I saying? You know what that's like, too, don't you? They own you," she croons. "Do you even know what you actually want?"

Jo-Beth. In a purple dress. In a purple sweat suit. Curled up on a saggy sofa. Sorting through apples at the grocery store with the seriousness of Job.

Peeking at me from the corner of her eye. Making me feel big and certain and worth something without having to do a damn thing but tease her and hold her and sit by her side.

I want Jo-Beth with the look on her face when she first saw me across the ballroom. Vulnerable, scared, defiant.

Oh, fuck. She came to me. In all this, it's the first time it registers. *She came to me.* Hands shaking, goosebumps down her arms, hands fisting the skirt of her gown. And I wanted words? Reassurance?

The bottom drops from my chest. Oh, God. I fucked up.

Harper pats my arm. "They own me, too," she confides in a whisper. "You want to know something else? About Jo-Beth Connolly?"

Yes. I want to know everything about her. She's it for me, and I've been so hung up on all the complications, I forgot the big picture. I want her more than anything I ever have before. *And she came for me.* I exhale, leaning my elbows on my knees, and I hang my head.

Harper goes on, oblivious to my agitation. "This guy Creech dropped her off on our doorstep when she was sixteen. She was twenty pounds underweight, and she had, like, a pair of jeans and a T-shirt to her name. Her foster father had been diddling her, and that'd gone south."

My gut churns, and my brain connects the pieces. The startling in the middle of the night. The fading out. I didn't want to know. I never asked. Guilt stabs at my chest, constricts my throat. I need to do something, fight someone, but there's nothing coming at me but words. I want to rip my own skin off, but I force myself to focus on Harper's words.

"Heavy, that's my brother, put her under his protection. He kept the brothers away from her until she was legal. She'd been tricking on the side all along, but it didn't matter. Heavy's got principles, you know? Very inconvenient sometimes."

"Why are you telling me this?"

"I'm getting to it. Patience, friend." She pats my thigh.

"Anyway. Heavy has a soft spot for Jo-Beth. She's smart. She'd play his games with him for hours. Fucking board games. I'd blow my brains out."

A warmth seeps through the ugliness in my chest. It's a picture. Teenage Jo-Beth playing board games with the grizzled president of the Steel Bones MC. I know the man by sight. He's a giant—long, wild black hair and beard. Like a creature from a fantasy novel.

"She's smart as hell."

"She is. She won't 'waste' money on books, but Heavy still buys her these fancy coffee table books when he goes to the book store. The most random subjects. She reads them. Cover-to-cover. Who the fuck reads coffee table books?"

"No one."

"Jo-Beth Connolly. Lot lizard." Harper snickers, and a mix of fury and disgust rises again to burn my throat. "You know, when Heavy found out about the tricking—she got busted a few times—he sent her to work at The White Van. You know what she was doing with the money?"

I can guess.

Harper continues, "She handed it all over to Deb, our bookkeeper, to put in a savings account. Cum-crusted twenties from truckers. Tens. Fives. She handed 'em over in an envelope, all the bills facing the same way. Deb told me about it. Cracked her up."

"Jesus, Harper. Fuck. I feel bad enough." I drive my hands into my hair.

"She bought herself a house with that money. The other club pussy is in the bathroom putting powder up their noses, and there's Jo-Beth, offering to wash brothers' clothes and then hassling them to tip her once she's done." Harper laughs.

We're both silent a moment. Harper seems to have lost

her point, and I'm trying to breathe through the vice squeezing my chest.

"Why are you telling me this?"

She turns to me, her cold eyes glinting in the lamplight. "Because take a woman like that. Take her away from her shitty life when she's nine or ten. Send her to the best schools. Introduce her to the right people. Give her a company to run. You know what she becomes?"

I wait. There's silence except for the whoosh of cars along the riverfront.

"You."

The word slams into me with the force of a punch. It's true. Something in my soul recognized her the moment I first saw her. We are made from the same stuff.

Harper leans back, resting her elbows on a stair. "The only thing I can't figure out is how you did it."

"Did what?"

"Dragged yourself halfway out of the cesspool of greed and evil that is the Wade family. No offense," she calls to Eric over my shoulder, but he's distracted by his phone.

I bark a laugh. Until recently, I would have protested. Now, the question makes me think. I welcome it.

"I don't know." I sit up. Think back. Just let the words come. "I guess a long time ago, I took a dive. I compromised. I did whatever I was asked, and I got what I wanted."

Harper's gaze is trained on me, inscrutable and unwavering. "Don't beat yourself up about it too much. We all do it."

"Yeah. Maybe. Then somewhere along the line, I'd compromised so much, I'd gotten so used to doing what I was asked, I didn't even know what I wanted anymore."

"And then you met Jo-Beth." You'd expect Harper to sound jaded or caustic, but there's a strange wistfulness to her voice, utterly out of character.

I nod. "Then I met Jo-Beth. She's compromised more than I ever have, but she never lost herself. She's fucking gorgeous, and strong, and proud. And I wanted her. I haven't wanted anything in years, but I want that woman."

"It feels good." Harper's lips curve, and there's sympathy in the softening.

"It does." I draw in a deep breath of brisk winter air. "What the fuck do I do?"

Harper leans her head against the metal rail and shrugs. "I don't know. Big grovel. She likes birds. Something with that. You probably want to get your head all the way out of your ass first."

"Marry her," Eric pipes up, and I startle, the moment broken. I'd almost forgotten he was there. "I call best man."

"That would be awkward as fuck." I shouldn't have to point that out.

"I bet her friends are freaks in the sheets." He smirks.

"I will beat your ass."

Eric laughs and slings an arm around my shoulder. "We quit, right? Allyn-Wade is in the rearview. Wade Brothers is in the house. Yeah?"

I think a minute. My stepfather's voice echoes in my ear. *Make a decision, Adam.*

"You need to stop the partying. Clean up."

"Yeah. Probably." Eric wobbles drunkenly.

"And stop being such an asshole."

Eric grunts, his eyelids drooping so he doesn't see the elbow I drive into his belly. "Fuck!"

"Day-um!" Harper whistles.

Eric folds over, wildly throwing out his arm to fend me off. I dodge it easily.

"What was that for?"

"You hit my future wife in the face."

"It was an accident! And, like, months ago."

I shake out my arm.

"That all?" Eric eyes me warily.

"I think we need a new name."

"Whatever you say, brother. You're the brains."

No, I'm not. I'm a fool. I let Jo-Beth Connolly walk away. I smile, remembering her stomping off, finger in the air.

She's at peace with herself in a way I envy, truth be told. The world had its way with her, but it didn't warp her. It made her hard. She's never going to give me another chance.

I don't deserve one.

I am a Wade, though, in this, if nothing else. I'm not going to stop until I get her back. All of her. Her forgiveness. Her real smiles. Her respect. Whatever it takes. I know what I want.

I want my soul back. I want my pride.

I want Jo-Beth.

12

JO-BETH

I slept at the clubhouse for the first time in years last night. I couldn't bear being alone in the house. I dropped by to change and grab a bag, and then I headed over. Creech let me crash in his room. He never sleeps, and when he does, he passes out where he falls.

I've missed the clubhouse in the morning. It reeks of stale beer with a hint of motor oil and tires, and the sunlight's hazy, filtered through the cigarette smoke still lingering in the air. There are always a few people passed out around the place, and some diehards playing cards or shooting the shit.

Gus and Boots are still at the bar, regaling a half-passed-out prospect with old war stories. Forty's playing pool by himself, a line of empties edging the table.

I pop into the kitchen for a trash bag. There's comfort in old habits. Eases the ache in my chest a little.

I start with the tables, leaving the really gross shit for the younger sweetbutts still sleeping it off somewhere. I try so hard not to think about Adam, but I do. *What did you come here to say?* I hear it over and over again, and I have to force down the panic. It's like a nightmare where you want to scream but no sound comes out. Why didn't I say anything?

"Rough night?" There's a crack of balls. I blink, drawn from my thoughts. Forty compresses his lips, the closest he comes to a smile, as he lines up another shot.

I meander over and start dropping his empties in the trash bag. "Maybe as bad as yours."

"Mine was fine. Still going strong."

"Looks like you're having a blast."

"I'm winning every game, doll." Forty draws the cue back and takes his shot. Table scratch. "Ignore the evidence of your eyes."

I snort. "Want to talk about it?"

"Nope. You?"

"Nope."

"Get me a beer?"

"Comin' right up." I drag the bag out to the dumpster and snag two bottles and a broom on my way back. When I return, Forty's sitting at a table, chalking his cue. I hand him a beer.

"I've missed you, Jo-Beth." He nudges a seat back from the table with his foot. I sit.

"You see me all the time at The White Van."

"It isn't the same. We're working."

"What's this look like?" I jerk my chin at the broom that I rested on a chair beside me.

"Don't recognize it. Can't say I've seen one before in my life." Forty raises an eyebrow, and I can't help but grin. I guess I do miss him.

We never did fuck. He was either with Nevaeh or deployed. When he came back, he was never interested in what I was offering. He keeps tryin' to date uptight bitches from town. Never works out, but it's funny as shit watchin' their faces when he brings them around.

"You see Nevaeh's back in town?" His gaze is purposefully fixed somewhere across the room, unfocused, the cue forgotten, leaning against his knee.

"Yeah. I ran into her a little while ago. At the Shop Right." That gets his attention.

The cords in his throat bob like he's trying not to ask, but I know he will. "She say what she's doing back here?"

"Something about laying low. She wasn't specific."

He tenses, his muscles flexing, the burns on his right arm blanching. It takes him a minute, but he breathes, sucks down a swallow of beer, fixes the cold face that says he doesn't care. "That woman makes trouble like she was born to it."

"You should talk to her."

"Oh, yeah?" He lifts his lip in a sneer. "Now why would I do that?"

I shrug. "So you don't regret anything."

"I think maybe we're talking about you now."

I sniff. "I got no regrets. I got a ton of shit I wish turned out different, but no regrets."

"I don't see a difference."

"I'll give you an example. Nevaeh. You wish she were here now?"

His jaw tightens and his fingers clench around his bottle. He don't answer, but I don't expect him to.

"You sorry for anything you did?"

"No." He doesn't hesitate, biting the word out.

Forty's a solid guy, no bullshit, no hassle. I've always liked him, but I never saw that I had anything in common with him before. I see it in his eyes now, though. We're both miserable as fuck, clinging to our pride like it'll make anything better.

Damn my chest hurts. It's like I got kicked by a mule.

I guess how I'm feelin' shows on my face, 'cause Forty drains his beer, sets it down, and asks, "You need me to beat anyone's ass?"

"Danielle owes me twenty bucks."

"I ain't steppin' to that woman. I like full use of my arms." We both try to smile, and if mine is as sorry as his, we're a sad-looking pair.

"You done?" I grab his empty and stand. "I'll get you another."

"Get two." Forty goes to rack up the balls and the moment's over.

"Look forward to talkin' to you again next year."

Forty snorts, already lining up a shot, and I wander off toward the kitchen. Maybe I'll make some eggs for the brothers who're now stumbling out of their bunks, scratching their junk and tryin' to find their cigarettes.

As the day goes on, my feet get heavy. I keep myself busy, first making breakfast and then cleaning out the kitchen fridge. I help Crista stock the bar, and I volunteer to take her dog, Frances, out to take a piss. The boys go out for a run and come back hungry, so I pick up sandwiches. It's a normal Sunday, except for how I can't seem to suck down a whole breath. It's like my hurting heart is crowding out my lungs.

Around three, I collapse on a couch and watch Wall and Heavy play darts. It's like two giants throwing tiny, feathered pins. Like something out of that movie, *Gulliver's Travels*.

I'm curled up, my fist clutched to my stomach 'cause for some reason the pressure eases the ache, and I'm kind of out of it, so I don't notice at first when the mood in the place changes.

Then I hear my name, and it registers. The scraping of chairs. The raised voices.

I sit up. The ruckus is coming from the front.

"I want to see Jo-Beth. Jo-Beth!"

My heart leaps, and I rise to my feet. It's Adam, and Creech has him by one arm and a prospect, Boom, has him by the other. Adam's struggling, and Creech ain't exactly built, so Adam's making headway. Every time Adam shakes loose, though, Creech comes back. The other brothers ain't making a move, happy to hoot and holler. Probably makin' bets.

He's gonna get his fool self killed.

"You lose something?" Heavy's eyes glitter under thick, black eyebrows.

I grimace.

"Best get your boy."

My cheeks flush hot, and I pick my way through a bunch of drunk idiots toward what's become a full-blown fight. Creech must have thrown a punch 'cause Adam's got his hands up in front of his face. Adam's only blocking, though, occasionally throwing a jab to ward Creech off. The prospect seems content to let Creech make a fool of himself.

Creech ain't exactly feared for his fists. More for the STDs.

I come to a halt behind the ring of onlookers. My brain's all numb, and I can't do what my body wants—run to him, which is stupid, stupid—so I watch him, and the half of the club that isn't watching the fight watches me.

It's a pretty sorry fight, and it's abundantly clear that if Adam took a real shot, it'd be over, but then Creech wheels back to throw a haymaker, and he plants a fist in Pig Iron's face instead. I swear, Pig Iron's whole cheek swings like the jowls of a bulldog. Everyone holds their breath.

"*Mother. Fucker.*" Pig Iron pulls back, and he probably hasn't gone a round in years, but I guess it's like riding a bike. Creech kind of runs into Pig Iron's punch, his neck snaps back, and he sprawls into a cluster of sweetbutts.

At this point, Boom must figure he needs to tap in 'cause he goes after Adam, and at the same time, Hobs and Bucky, who're Creech's boys from way back, jump into the fray. Both are dumbasses, so they can't seem to figure out if they need to go after Adam or Pig Iron, so they kind of throw punches at whatever target opens up. The old timers don't like this none. Grinder elbows in, and Big George grabs a chair and starts swinging.

There is so much hollering and hooting and cussing, the rafters shake. Bullet shouts that he'll take ten-to-one bets on the "dumb fuck who got lost," which is Adam.

And then from the corner of my eye, I see Gus leap over the bar and come out with Pig Iron's shot gun. I duck a good few seconds before he racks the slide and fires a shot into the ceiling, blowing a hole the size of a golf ball into the metal roof and letting the sunlight in. As soon as the boom echoes through the clubhouse, everyone except Heavy, Forty, Gus, and Adam are on the floor with me.

"That's my kid. Leave him the fuck alone." Gus racks another one. Heavy and Forty throw their heads back and bawl, shoulders shaking.

"You gonna plug that hole, Gus?" Heavy manages to wheeze out. People are getting to their feet, me included, and Adam is shaking out his arms. His jacket's been yanked down, and his blue sweater, tight across his chest, is torn at the neck. It looks like cashmere.

"Yeah. Ima plug those holes in Creech's ears while I'm at

it, he don't lay off my son."

Holy shit. *Gus* is Ryan Morrison. Now I see it, and I can't unsee it. Gus is a guy who's rode his body hard, and he's got the yellowed skin, paunch, and missing teeth to show for it, but if you squint, you can tell. He's got Adam's dark hair, his height, and his square jaw.

My stomach coils in a knot. Gus has known me since I showed up at the clubhouse, desperate with a ratty backpack filled with a few shirts, a pair of jeans, and nothing else. Adam must have met him. Heard stories. I guess that's what happened, why Adam changed his mind about me.

Something akin to grief rolls over me in a wave, and my face heats. Not with shame. I've never been able to afford that. Humiliation, though. I'm not too hard for that.

I hug myself and edge backwards. I've almost turned to duck out the back when piercing blue eyes find me and nail me in place.

"Jo-Beth." Adam steps forward. A handful of brothers move to grab him.

Heavy raises his hand. "Stand down. He's Gus' kid. Somebody get him a beer."

Heavy's rumbling voice breaks the spell. Everyone talks at once, the old timers slapping the young brothers on the back, cackling and chortling and rehashing the whole shitshow like it was some epic battle. Deb emerges from her back office to call Pig Iron an old fool and bark at Angel and Starla to pick up the mess. Everyone but Gus wanders off, but they're watching us. We're primetime TV right now.

We stand there, the three of us, staring at each other.

"Gus?" Adam speaks first. He's still in fighting stance, his chest heaving from the melee. His hair's mussed, and he's never looked so much like a movie star from a superhero flick. My heart surges with longing.

"Oh. Yeah. That's, uh, my road name." Gus shoves his hands in his pockets and shifts on his feet.

"How come?" Adam seems to be playing for time as he collects himself.

"Uh, Heavy's dad. Slip. He was the president when I prospected. He forgot my name once. Called me Gus. That was it." I've heard the story, but I never knew his real name.

"Thank you. For that." Adam raises his eyes to the hole in the roof.

Gus chuckles uneasily. "Don't guess you came for the bike, did you?"

Adam looks past Gus and sears me with those electric eyes. "No. I came for her."

"Yeah? Guess she's a beauty, too." Gus sniffs and offers me a wry, gap-toothed grin. I curve my lips into as much of a smile as I can manage. Gus and I run in different circles, but he's good people.

"She is." Adam takes a step toward me.

I tighten my arms around my belly. He's making me twitchy. There's too much swirling inside of me. I'm pissed and hurt and confused, and I can't tell if I have to pee, or if I'm nervous as hell.

I open my mouth to tell him to fuck off, but nothing comes out. Only tears. I start leaking, and I'm too freaked out to raise my hands to wipe them away. It's like I need my arms to hold myself together.

Adam covers the distance between us in one step. Every woman in the place inhales sharply at the same time.

"I'm so fucking sorry."

"You bailed on me." Tears are tickling my nose and dripping into the corner of my lips. I can't show weakness, but I don't cry, so I don't know how to stop.

"I got my head twisted, and I hurt you, and I'm so sorry."

"You acted like you hardly knew me."

"I was fucked up. I couldn't handle...I couldn't handle what you've had to handle for most of your life. I'm a weak man, Jo-Beth, and I can't make a decision for shit, and as of today, I guess I'm unemployed and disinherited, but if you give me another chance—" His voice breaks. His eyes glitter with unshed tears, the blue sparkling, and he seems lost for words.

"Oh, take him back, honey. He's hot as fuck!" That was Ernestine from over at the bar.

"Jewelry! Hold out for diamonds!" I think that was Danielle.

"You need to shut up brother, and give her the dick. Just haul her ass upstairs." This is advice from Grinder, which may go towards explaining why his wife put him out.

"Well?" I prompt. "You gonna finish what you're sayin?"

I want to know what he's gonna promise. Mama's men promised the world when they'd done wrong. They swore they'd never do it again, go back to meetings, delete their social media, marry her. What kind of bullshit does a rich man peddle when he's sorry?

Adam flashes me a sad smile, like he knows whatever he's got ain't gonna be enough. "Jo-Beth, if you give me another chance, I will finish fixing the living room floor."

Shirl and Deb hoot from the doorway to the kitchen. "Home improvements for the win! Give 'em another chance, Jo-Beth!"

He keeps going, and I can hear how he's serious, and how he knows it's useless, too. "I'll take you to London and Paris and Venice and Athens."

"Finish that living room floor, first!" Deb shouts.

"We'll make a home together, and I am never going to leave, and you're never going to regret it."

That promise is a punch to the gut, so painfully sweet. It's all I've ever wanted. The words burn inside me. He's dangling my heart's desire, and he's a liar. Fool me once, shame on you. Fool me twice...well, I ain't ever been in that situation.

Adam stands and holds out his hand. "I've decided on you, Jo-Beth Connolly. You're going to have to get used to it."

The whole place holds its breath.

"No." I force myself to shake my head. "No. I don't believe you." I don't have the strength for any more, so I duck past him and run out the front. The club explodes, their excited chatter following me as I bowl out the door and slide to a halt.

There's a flatbed truck parked right in front of the building, and it's stacked with cages and cages of birds. A bald man with a thick, gray mustache is leaning against it, chewing a piece of brown grass.

Cooing fills the crisp air.

I hear the door open behind me, and then heavy footsteps crunch on the gravel. It's Adam. I don't have to look to know it's him. I've memorized all his sounds and smells. He comes to a halt beside me.

"What is this?"

"I wanted to get you a hundred doves, but there were logistical issues. And some ethical concerns."

I catch a glimpse of gray and white between the slats. "You got me pigeons?"

"American Racing Pigeons." Adam speaks in a measured way, as if he's afraid I'm gonna bolt. That was my plan, but my car is blocked in by a truck full of birds. "My new friend John agreed to release them here on a little training run."

"You ready?" the man with the mustache asks.

Adam looks down at me, but I stare straight ahead. "Jo-Beth?"

"You do what you want."

"Not any more. We decide together. I'm for you, and you're for me, and we aren't from different sides anymore. We're one side."

My lips wobble, but fuck that. I ain't cryin' out in the cold. Mama always said the tears will freeze to your face.

"Talk to me, Jo-Beth. Please."

It's like 'cause I won't cry, my mouth opens instead and words fall out.

"You know why I like birds so much?"

"Tell me." Adam shuffles closer to my side, but he don't touch me.

I sniffle and swipe at my nose. "I guess most people like birds 'cause they make them think of freedom, you know? Flying away from your troubles. Not me."

I shiver. Adam peels off his sweater and drapes it around my shoulder. Part of me wants to shrug it onto the ground for spite, but it's cold as balls out here.

"Go on," Adam says.

"Mama and I moved around a lot coming up. I don't think we were ever in the same place for more than a year. You lose a lot of stuff moving around. Especially if it's a rush."

My heart twinges, remembering a stuffed elephant, but it's an old, faint loss. "One spring, we were camping out on a friend of Mama's screened-in porch. There was a maple tree nearby, and a robin red breast made a nest in it. I watched her build it from scratch. The next year, we were livin' in a motel off Gracy Avenue. I was sittin' out on the balcony, and I saw one. A robin red breast."

I watch the man with the mustache pull on his gloves and hoist himself up onto the truck.

"You folks ready?" he calls. Adam must nod because he starts pulling slats from cages. The birds bolt, flapping furiously until they're dark specks against the gray sky. They fly away so quickly, so certain of where they're going. They're out of sight in less than a minute.

"How much did this cost you?"

"Ten thousand dollars." Adam shifts.

"And you're unemployed now?"

"Yup." He glances down. "You don't need to worry. Money's not a concern. And I have a plan. I'll take care of you."

I want that so fucking bad. I want to lean into him, let him wrap his strong arms around me. It's knit into our souls, I think, the desire to rely on someone. To not be alone in the world. And it also feels inevitable, the moment when you're standing in the middle of a crowd, alone, reaching for someone who should rescue you, and they turn their back.

I stiffen my spine. "I was tellin' you about the birds. Why I love them? It's 'cause they come back. Year after year. Mamas get sick and die. Men who say they love you, and they'll take care of you—they change their minds. But every spring, robins come back."

I drag in a deep breath. "Maybe you think 'cause I've had the kind of life I've had that I don't want more for myself. That I don't know how it should be. But I know. The people who love you shouldn't leave you alone. And I ain't settling for anything I don't have to. Go home, Adam. There ain't nothin' here for you."

And I force myself to turn around and walk back to the clubhouse, my body as cold and brittle as ice, and my heart grasping for the man silent and still behind me.

13

ADAM

I'm standing in the Steel Bones clubhouse parking lot, staring after a flatbed truck as it pulls away, feathers fluttering in its wake, feeling every bruise and ache, wondering how I'm going to take yet another beat down when I go inside after Jo-Beth again, when my father emerges from the building.

He makes his way over to me, the arthritis obvious in his slow, shuffling gait. We both stare as the truck disappears down the road.

When it's gone from view, my father slaps me on the back, and says, "Whelp, since you're here, wanna check out the bike?"

"Sure."

My father leads me toward a six-bay garage. Its sleek, modern construction is an interesting contrast to the vintage beauty of the 1920s garage the MC has repurposed for its clubhouse. The analogy isn't lost on me. Jo-Beth doesn't see how we fit together, but the evidence is right here. Things don't need to be the same to belong together.

My father unlocks a side door and flips a switch. Fluorescent light floods the room, revealing rows of covered vehicles. There's a fully outfitted mechanic bay with a pit, and a massive truck is suspended, mid-job.

"This way." My father leads me to a far corner, and pulls back the cover of a relatively small machine. The shine hits you first, and then the shape which inspires a wave of nostalgia for a time I wasn't even alive to see.

Shit. Even with my mind on Jo-Beth, I have to acknowledge it's a beautiful machine. Sleek lines. All engine. Built to defy physics.

"She's gorgeous."

"Truth." My father grabs a chamois from a workbench and strokes the rag down her body lovingly. "She's a helluva ride. Nothin' to that woman back there, I'm guessin'. But a great time."

Suddenly, it's all too much. Too strange. There's a stool, and I sink down, watch my father—the man I haven't seen in over twenty years—fuss over his bike, dusting off imaginary specks of dust. The whole time, he's itemizing its specs. V-twin engine. Four speed transmission.

I grunt, and he doesn't seem to require more of me. When he switches topics, I'm caught off guard.

"I know it ain't my place to give you no fatherly advice or nothin', but maybe wait 'til she's alone next time. The brothers know who you are now, but still...that could've gone south. You got a piece? I can get you a piece if you need one."

"I'm good." I watch him with the bike, the care, the gentleness, and something ugly swells inside me. It mixes with Jo-Beth's words—*the people who love you shouldn't leave you alone*—still echoing in my head.

"Why did you leave? Back when I was a kid?"

My father exhales long, puffing his cheeks, and his

shoulders drop. He finds his own stool and lowers himself with the help of a hand braced on a workbench.

"Guess I had that question comin'." He digs in a pocket and pulls out a crumpled pack of cigarettes, lights one, and blows the smoke toward the ceiling to avoid the bike.

"Drugs, I guess." He takes another drag. "I was high a lot. Couldn't hold a job. Your ma told me to get sober or get gone. So I left. Figured I could get my shit straight without her voice in my ear all the time, you know? Do what she wanted. Get my G.E.D. Some kind of office job. She was always after me to sell cars. She thought there was money in that."

"So you just never got clean?"

My father's eyes dim, like he's taken back, and his gap-toothed smile is sad as hell. "Nah. I sobered up. I'd have done anything for your ma. She was—It don't matter." The smile's gone. "When I came back, she was already with that guy. The one before Thomas Wade."

I don't remember another man. My father must see my confusion. "Bill? Or Brian? He owned a few gas stations. Your ma said he was gonna move you guys in with him. A safe neighborhood with a gate. She said he didn't want no baby daddy drama. She asked could I provide what he could? Back then, I didn't need an excuse to fall off the wagon, but I took that as one."

The weight of all this adds to what just happened with Jo-Beth, bears down, an oppressive mix of regret and rage.

"I don't remember this."

My father grinds his cigarette out in a hubcap ashtray. "I guess it didn't pan out."

"You don't seem angry."

"At myself. Plenty. I couldn't give you or your ma what you needed. That eats at me. Always has. I guess seein' you in the papers, winnin' the science fair and buyin' this company or that. I tell myself it ended up for the best. I know it's a cop out, but still."

"What do you mean the science fair?" I was in the paper when I was in the eighth grade. I'd been on a robotics team that went to finals in China.

"You made a robot or something. It sorted shit."

"You saw that in the paper?"

"I think Grinder came across it. Or his old lady Ernestine."

"They knew about me?"

"Shit. Everyone knows about you. They'll be talkin' even more now they know you can throw down like your old man." He coughs and clams up as he realizes what he called himself.

I don't have the bandwidth to think about what this man is to me. I'm trying to wrap my brain around this alternate history I never suspected was happening, a timeline when my father wasn't shooting up in a heroin den, lost to the world, but bragging about me to his friends and following me in the papers.

The loss rolls over me in a wave, and blame follows in its wake.

"You don't blame my mother?"

My father shakes his head. "She needed me to be a man, and I failed. I kept tryin' to explain to her, but words ain't shit. I didn't get that back then. I needed to do somethin', but I kept tryin' to talk, and for your ma, that was all hot air."

That brings my mind back to Jo-Beth, the woman I've let down. Maybe that's why I'm not raging at this man. My own failure's too fresh.

"There's nothing I can say to Jo-Beth."

"Maybe not."

It's so strange, talking about women in a garage with a virtual stranger who has my face and voice, the smell of oil and smoke in the cold air, the silence punctuated by clanging from the mechanic bay.

"What can I do?" I don't know why I'm asking him. Maybe because he's got the tragic, worn air of a wise man. Or because he seems to have made peace with his own mistakes. "I'm not walking away. What do I do?"

"What does she need?"

Care. Gentleness. Patience. She needs me to be a better man than I am.

"Shit. I don't know. She needs her living room floor fixed."

"Floor boards coming up?"

"No. It's sagging."

"Someone fuck with the joist?"

"Not that I can tell. I think at some point, there was insect damage."

"You got a plan?"

"I was gonna do some sistering."

"Depending on the damage, might be better to shore it up." My father draws himself up, wipes at his greasy jeans. "I got jacks. Let's go over there in the morning. See what should be done."

"She's not going to welcome us."

"You give up easy?" There's an unspoken part to his question. You give up easy *like me*?

I'm nothing like this man. Or the man who raised me. If I'm like anyone in this world, it's going to be the woman who strode toward me across a crowded ballroom, terror and hope in her eyes, alone and brave, coming back to me.

"I have a truck, but it's back in Pyle."

"We can use mine," my father says. "I'll call some brothers who work construction with me. We can get it started in a few hours if she lets us in to the house." He snorts and leans back, admiring the bike from tailpipe to front wheel the way some men take in a woman.

After a minute or two, he raises his eyes to me. "Wanna take her for a ride?"

I don't have to think. "Hell, yeah."

He throws me an old plastic key chain, and shuffles off to find me a helmet and raise the bay door. I take the chamois and run it along her body. You can tell she's been maintained, protected from the elements, and rode with care.

I'm not surprised when I get her up to two hundred on a straight away outside of town.

I won't tell my father, but I didn't fall in love.

I like a rougher ride. I want to work for it; I want to *earn* the ride. And that's what it all comes down to. Why it's taken me this long in life to figure it out, I don't know, but that's what Jo-Beth's taught me. I need to trust myself to know the value of what's in front of me. And I need to earn my ride.

I'm starting with Jo-Beth. She's worth everything, and I'm not giving up until I earn her back.

14

JO-BETH

I came home last night. After the brawl and the pigeons, everyone wanted to talk to me about the rich boy. Everyone had opinions, most of them slurred, and none of them helpful.

I didn't sleep well. I felt feverish, cold and clammy. The wind picked up around midnight, and branches scraped the siding. I woke up with a start, heart pounding. I reached for Adam. And then I remembered he was gone; I'd sent him away. And I wanted him so badly. His warmth at my back. Soothing murmurs in my ear.

'Cause I was groggy and weak, I grabbed my phone and swiped, entering my passcode. My finger was hovering over the phone icon before I remembered Mama. How many times she'd locked herself in the bathroom, sobbing into the phone, bargaining with some man to come back. I'd shoved my phone under the pillow, rolled myself in my Amish quilt, and I tried to drift off again, but it took hours.

When I'm woken from a dead sleep at eight in the morning by trucks roaring down my street, I'm not in the mood. My eyes are crusted shut, and my stomach is sour.

For some reason, the trucks park in my drive, and doors slam. A man shouts.

I fight free of the sheet that's gotten twisted around my legs, and I stumble for the stairs. I'm wearin' a T-shirt that says "Pick Me Up In The White Van" and a pair of white sweat socks. I fling open the door, ready to tell whoever it is that they're lost, and my heart slams against my chest and stops.

It's Adam.

He's standing at the bottom of my porch steps in thigh-hugging jeans and a red flannel shirt. His hair's still wet from a shower, and he's carrying a tool box. His shoulders are squared, his chest straining the buttons, and his scuffed work boots make him look like the construction worker from a charity calendar. The shiner from yesterday's scuffle only makes him look rougher, hotter.

He's starin' up at me, stubborn determination in the set of his jaw, eyes burnin' as if I'm everything he's ever wanted. My stomach clenches, and heat rushes to my pussy. I press my knees together and cross my arms to hide my pebbling nipples.

A raggedy crew is assembling behind him. Gus and Grinder haul up what looks like a jack. Charge is unloading an armful of lumber. His kid, little Jimmy, is wearing a tool-belt so small it wouldn't fit around my leg, but he's got a real wrench, a screwdriver, and a hammer hangin' from it. The belt's so heavy it's tuggin' down his drawers. He's got that pissed off, serious look that cracks me up. He's as mean as his daddy is sweet.

It's hard to be unfriendly with Jimmy here, but it's early, and I ain't as strong as I was yesterday. If I give an inch, I'm gonna throw myself at that man lookin' at me like I'm air, and he's drowning.

"What are you doin' here?"

"I came back."

I know what he's tryin' to do. The conversation about the birds. I hadn't meant it as encouragement. Or had I? My brain's fuzzy. It ain't workin' right.

"You can turn around and go back where you came from."

"I'm here to fix the floor. I said I would. Are you going to let us in?"

"I don't need your help."

"I'm told fixing a sagging floor is a slow job. Takes a long time. I'm going to have to screw the jacks up a turn or two every month or so."

"I said my piece yesterday."

"I'm going to keep coming back, Jo-Beth. You're my home. You are where I belong."

The wind kicks up, and I have to hold my T-shirt down so I don't flash the whole crew. Truth be told, I'm happy to have something to do with my hands. I don't know what to do or say.

I can't give in. My heart can't take it.

But oh, hell. My heart can't take turning him away, either.

I sink down on the top step, tug my shirt down over my knees. Adam's closer now. He's maybe three feet away, and we're face to face.

"How am I supposed to believe you?" I ask quietly, and Gus and the rest have the good graces to take a few steps back and start chatting among themselves.

"You don't have to. Just let me in. I'll take you where you are, Jo-Beth. I'll take whatever you'll give. Let me in."

God, it sounds so perfect, so impossible to be true. "Bull-shit. You stood there in that ballroom and said you could

ignore what I was. Like you were doin' me a favor." Echoes
of that hurt unfurl, tearing up my insides. "That ain't takin'
me as I am. That's conditional. As long as you can pretend I
ain't who I am, everything's fine. But what happens next
time you can't ignore who I am?"

"Are you planning on throwing it in my face again?"

I bristle, about to get pissed, but something in his look
dissuades me. There's torment in his blue eyes. I cut him
deep when I rubbed Dan in his face.

I swipe my palms down my shirt, uneasy with the power
I have to hurt him. "No. And I am sorry I did that. But you
didn't answer my question."

He sighs, low and long. "Shit, Jo-Beth. I don't know how
to accept it." His face darkens, and he shifts. "I don't know
how to be okay with the fact you were alone so long, and
you could have been hurt—shit, you *were* hurt—and what
pointless shit was I doing?" There's real distress in his voice,
and even though I'm still mad and wary and heartbroken, I
want to soothe him.

I ease over so there's room for him to sit. "You didn't
know me then. It's not on you."

He waits a second, as if to make sure I mean it, then he
lowers himself to the step beside me. "It still makes me
crazy. And that's not helping me or you, and I know it."

"I ain't gonna feel bad about who I am. Not for you or
anyone."

He grabs my hand, drags it to his mouth, pressing kisses
on my knuckles. "You got me wrong. I don't want you to ever
feel bad. God, Jo-Beth, I love you."

"Why? Why me then?"

He gazes down, burning me with those blue eyes.
"Because you're tough. You're a fighter, and you've been a
fighter your whole life, and you're still standing. I want to be

that strong. You make me want to be my own man. You make me believe I can be. You're real, Jo-Beth. I want to be real, too."

I want to ask him to say those words again. And then again. Slowly so I can remember them. My skin heats until the brisk wind feels good on my bare legs.

He's wrong about being strong. I'm weak for this man. Maybe it ain't a bad kind of weak, though. Maybe soft's a better word.

I am soft for this man.

I rise to my feet, still holding his hand, and jerk my chin at the men congregating under my acorn tree. "You runnin' with Steel Bones now?"

The flood of relief, the pure joy on Adam's face is almost enough to turn me to jelly, but my pride won't let me leap into his arms.

"Seems so. Are you letting us in?"

"I guess."

I'm reaching for the door knob when Adam swings me over his shoulder, pinning me with a huge palm on my ass. "You all can find your way to the basement. Jo-Beth and I'll be upstairs."

Then he carries me up to bed, tosses me down, tugs my panties to the side, and slicks his cock down my slit before I can do much more than shriek and tell him to be careful not to knock my ass into the pictures on the walls.

"Are you taking me back, Jo-Beth?"

He's easing into me, and I couldn't tell this man "no" one more time if someone paid me a million dollars. He's mine. That's the end of it. He came back, and I'm keeping him.

"Yes," I breathe out, and it's an answer to everything.

EPILOGUE
JO-BETH

For the launch party, Adam's rented out the restaurant where we had our first date. We argue about that. He says Altimeter was our first date. I say it didn't count 'cause I was on the clock, so our first date was Sawdust on the Floor. He winces when I say "on the clock," but it bothers him less and less each time. I figure he's got to come to terms with what I am. Was. Whatever.

I don't dance at The White Van no more. Adam wasn't chill with that at all. We had a few knock-down-drag-out fights at first. It all worked out, though. Deb kept me on doing bills for her, and when Adam and Eric got their first round of financing for their new venture, they put me to work finding office space and buying cubicles and getting the phones set up. Turns out I'm good at office management. That was almost a year ago.

Tonight, we celebrate our first profitable month. I'm good at numbers, too. I know that after this shindig, we're gonna be back in the red next month.

The place is done up in purple in honor of the company's name: Plum Financial Services. Adam's idea. There's purple and silver silk streamers swooping above the room and lavender roses and lilies on every table. The vibe is fancy but not overboard. Formal attire is not required, but I'm wearing a puffy, white gown like Cinderella with a purple crystal waterfall dripping from the waist.

When Adam saw it, he said, "I want to ruin that dress." I told him if he did, he'd be ruining his evening, too.

Good thing there's no dress code. Heavy, Gus, Charge and the other brothers from Steel Bones showed up in their jeans and cuts. The old ladies dressed how they feel. Fay-Lee's in skin tight leopard print. Ernestine's got on the mother-of-the-bride dress from her oldest's wedding back in the nineties. Kayla's in a classy, pale purple sheath dress.

Steel Bones was one of the first to trust their money to Adam, but they weren't the last. Apparently, a lot of clients had been staying with Wade-Allyn because of Adam, and they followed him when he struck out on his own. These guys are the ones in expensive suits with wives in styled updos. It was awkward at first, but the liquor's been flowing a few hours now, and the band's playing everybody's favorites. People are dancing, and Story's letting some old dude in a jacket twirl her around.

Nickel's watching, the corner of his mouth quirked up. He's a different man these days. Less haunted.

"You checking out other men?" Adam eases up next to me, handing me a glass of champagne. I eye him, black hair to shiny, black shoes, admiring my handiwork.

I picked out a shirt for him the exact white of my dress, and his tie is the same shade as my purple crystals. His dark gray suit shows off the muscular breadth of his shoulders perfectly.

Pride swells in my chest. This brilliant man is mine. He's here with me. He has eyes only for me. Which reminds me.

"I'm just watchin' Nickel. Still don't trust him around breakables."

"Probably wise." Adam drops a kiss on the top of my head. "Did you talk to Eric?"

I nod. Adam's on a campaign to get me and Eric to bond. We like each other fine, but Adam wants us to be tight. Same as he's always having me hang out with Gus and him. I get that he wants me to feel like I have a family. He wants to give me everything, even things he can't. It melts my heart, but all Gus does is talk bikes, and I had enough of that in my younger years.

Thomas Wade has cut Adam out of his life, and his mother only calls to piss and moan about how I've ruined the family, so Eric and Gus have become Adam's hope to give me people. Adam don't quite understand yet that Steel Bones are my people. Always will be.

Plus, with Eric, none of us have forgotten that I've sucked his dick. That's actually kind of our thing when Adam's not around. No matter what we're doing, one of us ends up starting it, usually me. Tonight, it was Eric.

"Tell the truth, Jo-Beth. My dick is way bigger than Adam's, isn't it?"

"Couldn't say. You've got a totally unmemorable cock. Sorry."

"Bullshit. You dream about it."

"I do. And then I wake up wondering why I got a hankering for those little cocktail weenies."

"Ooo. Reminds me. They've got the best carpaccio here. Want some?"

"What's carpaccio?"

"Raw, pounded meat."

"Are you comin' on to me?"

Eric laughs. "Nah. It's a real thing."

"Pass."

"More for me then."

That was the extent of our conversation tonight. Adam would be pissed—he always insists I get treated with the utmost respect. Anyone tries to do me like they did Julia Roberts in that snooty boutique, Adam'll swing on 'em. His fists, his money. Whatever.

Eric don't mean no harm, though. He's a fuck up, but I understand him. He's always standing next to the most brilliant, perfect, confident man in the room, and that ain't easy.

That's where I am, now, standing beside my man. It'd be hard if he wasn't lookin' down at me like I'm the most beautiful, perfect, fascinating woman he's ever seen.

Swells my head, every time.

"Are you ready for the speeches?" Adam tucks a loose strand of hair behind my ear, sending shivers down my neck. I can't wait 'til later. He's been driving me crazy with these little touches all night. A brush across my knee. A kiss on my bare shoulder. I'm gonna jump his ass and ride him like a cowgirl as soon as we're alone.

"Yeah. We can ditch after this, right?"

"Of course." Adam chuckles as he clinks a fork to his champagne flute.

The crowd grows quiet. It takes Steel Bones a little longer than the rest—especially Creech who's drunk and tryin' to get lucky with a lady in a pantsuit and pearls—but then Heavy shouts, "Shut the fuck up." Everyone more or less gets silent, giving us their full attention.

I'm used to being watched from all those years dancing, but this is somehow different. I feel shy. I sidle closer to Adam. He wraps an arm around me.

"Thanks, Heavy." Adam tips his glass at the club president, and there's a ripple of drunken laughter. "On behalf of

Eric and I, we want to thank you all for trusting Plum
Financial to manage your money. The people in this room
have backed us from the beginning, and we're not going to
let you down. This is the first of many celebrations to
come." There's applause and a few hollers from the
brothers.

Then Adam clears his throat, and his voice loses some of
that supernatural confidence. "But now's the time to admit
—as almost all of you know—I had ulterior motives inviting
you here tonight."

He takes two steps away, so he can face me. Oh, fuck.
What is he doing?

"None of this would be possible without the woman
beside me. A little over a year ago, she dressed up and came
to me with her heart on her sleeve. I screwed up. Got into a
fistfight. Decided to quit my job and follow my dreams. You
know. Your average Saturday night."

The crowd laughs then gets quieter, hanging onto his
words almost as close as I am. You can't help it. Adam Wade
commands a room.

"Every day since then, this woman has challenged me.
Surprised me. Inspired me. And tonight, I've got my heart
on my sleeve." He kneels, and my hands fly to my mouth. Is
this happening? We've talked about it, but jokingly. Weren't
we joking?

He slips a ring from his pocket. It glitters in the soft light
of the chandeliers.

"You look scared as shit, Jo-Beth," he murmurs. "You're
not going to run, are you?"

"I might." Hot tears dribble down my cheeks. "But I'd
right come back."

He holds up a gold ring with a diamond the size of a
raisin and a dozen, smaller purple stones—amethysts—

around it. It's too much, and it sparkles, and it's perfect. Everyone gasps. I swear, even Nickel and Heavy.

"Jo-Beth Connolly, will you marry me?"

I fall to my knees, throw my arms around his neck, and arch my back as I draw him down to kiss me. Then I climb onto his lap, skirts billowing, and I take that ring and slip it on.

"Yes," I say, laughing, my eyes torn between his smiling face and my beautiful ring. Under all the layers of poofy dress, I feel him harden against my belly. "Can we go home now?"

Later, at the hotel room we booked for the night, I peel myself away from him, naked, sweat cooling, my pussy throbbing. I mince to the closet where the bell hop stowed my bags.

"You get cold feet so soon?" Adam's voice is drowsy and satisfied. It sends a zip of awareness through my used, sore body. I should grab an Aspirin on my way back to bed.

"Nope," I call. "Just remembered I brought us a treat."

"Yeah?" Adam props himself up to half-sitting on the pillows.

I pause in the doorway, pose with a hip cocked, my hand with the ring positioned just so on my waist. In my other hand, I have an $18,000 bottle of champagne.

"Want some?"

Adam laughs, and he beckons me back over, arms wide, carved biceps flexing. "I want you, Jo-Beth Connolly. Get back here and give me what I want."

And I do.

~

THE STEEL BONES saga continues in *Wall*.

A NOTE FROM THE AUTHOR

Will Ernestine ever take Grinder back?
Will Creech ever find someone who can love him?
What exactly happened with Boots and his California girl?

I have no idea!

But you will be the first to know if you sign up for my newsletter at www.catecwells.com.

You'll get a FREE novella, too!

ABOUT THE AUTHOR

Cate C. Wells writes everything from motorcycle club to small town to mafia to paranormal romance. Whatever the subgenre, readers can expect character-driven stories that are raw, real, and emotionally satisfying. She's into messy love, flaws, long roads to redemption, grace, and happily ever after, in books and in life.

Along with stories, she's collected a husband and children along the way. She lives in Baltimore when she's not exploring the world with the family.

I love to connect with readers! Meet me in The Cate C. Wells Reader Group on Facebook.

Facebook: @catecwells
Twitter: @CateCWells1
Bookbub: @catecwells

Printed in Great Britain
by Amazon

21532404R10142